I0831615

Dragon Chameleon: Episodes 1-4

Sarah K. L. Wilson

Published by Sarah K. L. Wilson, 2019.

This is a work of fiction. Similarities to real people, places, or events are entirely coincidental.

DRAGON CHAMELEON: EPISODES 1-4

First edition. May 16, 2019.

Written by Sarah K. L. Wilson.

For all the heroes who think they aren't heroes ... this one is for you.

Dragon Chameleon: Rogue's Quest

"Time, the ever-rolling river, takes memory to a place she's never been and warps even the truest tales to ghosts of themselves. Thus, it is with stories and legends. They ever grow and branch, even as their true origins fade, lost in the minds of the dead and from the tongues of the living. Who knows today who will be the hero of tomorrow or what strange event, small to us now will be the splinter in the heel of Fate."

- Ibrenicus

Chapter One

DRAGONS.

They haunted my dreams and brought their magic to my thoughts. I'd watch the sun come up and wonder what it would look like from up there in the sky, smell a fire and think of their burnt breath, hear their roar in the howl of the wind. I'd do anything to ride one again – even if it meant running over rooftops, dressing up as a foreign assassin, or even stealing magical artifacts that might come to life and steal my soul.

If that old man hadn't promised me the chance ... if he hadn't made that absurd agreement ...

I was angry just thinking about it. I don't like liars. But that's only because I am one.

A boy's got to make a living somehow and in a world like this one, sometimes a lie is worth more than the truth. I hate it when I lie – but I hate other people's lies even more.

The old man lied to me. That was becoming more obvious every day. If he hadn't lied to me, I wouldn't be stuck in the decomposing city that I used to think of as home.

I trudged through the hardening mud as snow swirled around me and I tried not to think of the night when it had been magic, ashes, and flames filling the air instead of snow. Those memories were still too fresh. If I thought about them the wrong way, they drew blood.

I didn't even bother to clutch my cloak close around me to keep the wind out. It was threadbare and had been for months. There wasn't cloth to make better clothes. There hadn't been any in the months since the armies had swept across our sky city, first toppling it to the ground and then burning it to cinders.

A man in a once-rich tattered cloak shied away from me as we passed, clutching the pommel of his sword. As if he had anything left to steal! That cloak was as worthless now as mine was. War made all men equal in suffering and despair. And what was left when it was over? Was death by armies worse or death by the slow grinding starvation of ruined stores and winter here?

"Tor! What does Ephretti say about supply trains? Will they return soon?" a voice called to me. It was old Badge. He'd been a hawker before the city fell and still was – though he mostly hawked crow pies now or stew that he assured me contained no rat. I knew better. He'd need to be a Magika to have any real meat here.

I glanced around at the burnt-out buildings around us. Someone had set up a pair of shanties and a washing line across the street. A strong wind could knock the whole establishment into wreckage. Why did anyone bother washing clothes? We all smelled the same. No one could get the smell of fire out of our clothes or consciences.

I sidled up to Badge's hand-cart. I should be hurrying. I could almost hear Castelan Ephretti chastising me in my mind.

"Cities don't run themselves, Tor," she'd say. "Not even ruined ones."

But the smell of the stew made my mouth water even when I knew what was in it. Badge had carefully carved the sign of the Lightbringers into the side of the cart – a sign to potential customers that he was trustworthy, or at least smart enough to pretend to be trustworthy.

"Any rat in the stew today?" I asked.

"Shhh!" His wrinkled brow furrowed, and he scanned the people hustling past – mostly remnants of the city of Vanika's population before the war, but with some strangers bearing the marks of the conflict on their bodies or in their scattered minds. Badge leaned into the cold wind to avoid being blown over. "No lies about my food! I serve only the best!"

It was amazing we had anything to eat – even rat. Winter is a bad time when you have no stores, goods, or coin. Worse when shelter has all been burnt up and wood is scarce.

I had a feeling someone was watching me and I turned to follow Badge's scanning gaze but nothing looked amiss in the hurrying shoals of gaunt people. We were all the same these days – drab, mud-covered, cold, and hungry. No single person stood out in the crowd. Everyone could be watching us – or no one. Why couldn't I shake that feeling, though? I could almost feel the gaze of a hidden watcher burning a hole through my back.

"Ephretti doesn't know, old friend," I said. "She sent a request to the Dominar for help. Who knows if it will even be read."

"They can't leave us here to starve – even *you* don't get enough to eat and you work for the great lady," Badge objected. "We used to be one of the great cities of the Dominion. Castelan Ephretti will find a way to save us, just you watch!"

I always felt nervous when the city folk talked about Ephretti like she was a great glowing savior. I hunched my shoulders uncomfortably. There was a time when I thought the same way. Ephretti and her great Green dragon had filled me with the same awe she inspired everywhere. Our savior. The magical, death-defeating, Ephretti Oakborn who had saved us all. Char was still in the air from the night she'd saved us.

It didn't take long in a place like the crumbling ruins of Vanika to realize she was mortal, too. I wouldn't usually care. Wouldn't usually concern myself with false promises, but I was still stinging with the lie I'd believed.

I wish I'd never believed it. If I'd never hoped, then I wouldn't need to despair. But more than a month had gone by since the old man promised to return for me. How much longer should I wait before I gave up?

"There are rumors," Badge said leaning in. "Rumors of spies. I think I saw one today."

"Only rumors," I said, but I felt the creeping sensation move up my spine.

"Word is that the nations banded together against us in the war. Word is that some of them still have it in for us."

Maybe it wasn't too late to head south. Find my way to Leedris City or another Sky City. There had to be food somewhere. And shelter, too. I was sick of crowding into a room three to a bed – if I made it indoors in time to get a place at all.

Maybe I'd go all the way to Dominion City and see the Dominar with the shining Dragon Crown. They said he rode a purple dragon. They said he destroyed the dust demons that razed our city. They said he commanded dragons and brought up magical ghosts from the ground to do his bidding. They said he was the son of the Skies and Stars.

Badge leaned further in, frowning when a passerby turned to look at us. "Ko'Torenth, boy. Rumor says they're out of magic and turning an eye to us to take ours."

"Do you see any magic around here?" I asked, stepping back. "All I see is ashes and ruins."

"Sometimes the best magic is hiding in plain sight."

I ran a hand over my face. No point in thinking about leaving. Better to be hopeful. I'd heard some of the boys say they were going on a treasure hunt tonight, looting the burnt-out husks that had once been shops and homes. That could be fun. If we were really lucky, we might even find something worth trading for. Maybe even something magical. I must be hungrier than I knew if I was daydreaming like that!

Or we might find what we found last time. I shivered at that thought. A lot of people had died in the flames. People I knew. Best not to remember.

"Can you spare a bowl of stew?" I asked Badge, shivering and forcing my thoughts back to the here and now.

"Not for a boy who can't pay."

I grimaced as my belly rumbled, pulling out a set of cups and a small wooden bowl from my pockets.

"How about a game of Find the Weevil? You guess where it's hiding and no stew for me. Fail, and I get the stew without paying?"

Badge shrugged and looked bored, but I knew he'd say yes. He liked my antics. Most people did. If you could keep a man watching and entertained, you could convince him to give you almost anything. The key was to get his attention in the first place. The cups helped with that.

I set out the cups on his cart with as much drama as I could muster in the cold. My hands felt slower than usual in the icy wind, but the smell of the meaty stew cut through the cold and my mouth began to water. Don't think about rats, Tor. Concentrate on the game.

I produced the wooden ball with a flourish, placing it under one cup and then began the dance of shuffling cups, fast and furious. I was already raising an eyebrow and getting ready for the mind game that would lead Badge to the wrong cup.

"Which cup?" I smiled charmingly, my hand hovering ever so slightly closer to a cup I knew was empty.

"The left."

I pulled it up to reveal the empty space. "One more try?"

"I don't know why I let you do this to me."

I did. There was little to entertain in a despair farm like this ruin. A man would give up real coin for a few moments of forgetfulness – never mind a bowl of rat soup.

I shuffled the cups again. Quick and dramatic, so he would lose track of the actual cups in the motion of my hands.

"Guess again."

"Middle."

I looked up with a grin, lifting the cup to show the space beneath was empty. Badge's mouth was open and eyes wide.

"I know, it's shocking how good I am at this."

His mouth worked like he was trying to talk, and I turned curiously to look over my shoulder. Panicking wasn't my style. Neither was breaking a sweat.

Behind me, a man was standing stock still in the courtyard, his mouth open, hands held before him with fingers spread wide, as if he had been holding ice that had melted suddenly through his fingers. There was something strange about his eyes. I squinted to look closer.

Who was this guy? I didn't recognize him but considering the size of the city and the constant influx of refugees, that wasn't saying much. I would recognize him if I'd met him before, though. You had to be good with faces if you wanted to pull cons. Otherwise, you couldn't keep your marks straight and you'd end up putting your foot in it.

So, who was this guy stealing my show?

He stared directly at me, like he knew me. Abruptly, he howled, and a swirling silver light filled his eyes and then with a sound like a *pop* it burst down his cheeks and flowed out like water. It trickled down his body, down his legs, down to the muddy ash of the street.

The silence in the road was so thick, I could have eaten it to fill my rumbling belly. No one moved. No one spoke. I sure didn't. If I spoke, that might make it real.

Skies and stars, it had better not be real!

Where the light puddled around his feet, tiny dust devils swirled like localized storms. I shivered, gripping the cups in my hands. My memories of the dust demons that once filled this land were still too fresh. But whatever this was, it wasn't an Ifrit. The ash swirled up, building in height and strength until it formed a branching figure like a mockery of a man. The ash kept bulging and swirling until three figures surrounded the man. He was frozen in place with his mouth open – whether from fear or awe – just like the rest of us.

I swallowed. I had no weapon – but then again, these swirling figures had shown no aggression. The man in the center of them moved, breaking the stillness, but his gaze was still locked on mine. With a single cry, he lunged toward me. I jumped, but I didn't need to. He didn't take a single step. The swirling ash creatures pounced, covering him in their dark, fluttering forms and then – as if the wind had stopped – they fell to the ground and the man under them was gone, leaving nothing but a heap of black ashes where once they all had been.

There was a clatter behind me and I turned to see Badge leaning on his cart, his face white. The stew was strewn across the street as the pot rolled away. As if by magic, life returned around us. People shook themselves and began to move again, asking questions, cursing under their breaths.

"I think I'm seeing things," Badge said, tracing the sign of the Lightbringers over his chest. A lot of people were doing that these days, as if a sign could ward off evil. I'd never seen a sign do anything. I'd only seen people doing or not doing.

That old man had better hurry up and keep his promises or I wouldn't be here when he returned. This place was getting too creepy for me. I could have sworn that man was after me ...

I hurried to gather my ball and cups, but a second clatter startled me. Badge's ladle rolled across the street, his eyes wide as saucers.

"Skies and stars, man! Get a hold of yourself!" I said, rolling my eyes to turn a second time and look at the square behind me.

I turned just in time to see a purple dragon skidding through the pile of ashes in the center of the street as he landed. His claws bit into the stone-mud-ash of the street and he sneezed violently, filling the air with an acidic smell. People scattered, screaming and running or standing like frozen nightmares like old Badge.

It was easy to forget how big dragons were. This one was large and gnarled, bulges and knobs on his forehead and down his legs reminded me of the hoary eyebrows and wrinkles of an old man. But old or not, the towering height, glaring eyes, and fiery breath of the great beast was enough to make anyone freeze in fear.

At least his breath was warm – the kind of warm that suggested he'd flamed something recently. I tried not to squirm at the thought. Free warmth was hard to come by, no matter where it came from.

I swallowed instead, keeping my hands where he could see them, but offering my most charming grin at the same time. Rule of thumb: never let them see you sweat.

Around the hulking purple dragon, the last remnants of the crowd scattered like dry leaves in the wind, but I stayed steady, looking past the dragon's beady eyes to the grizzled rider on his back. His purple scarves flapped in the wind, but his old back was straight and his gaze level.

"There's no time for staring, boy. Are you ready for what I promised you or should I leave you here in the dust and ashes?"

Chapter Two

"YOU'RE LATE, OLD MAN," I said with my cheekiest grin.

"I've been busy, boy. The war might be over, but the trouble hasn't stopped," Hubric said. He looked just as I remembered him. Old and weathered like a rock in the rain - but just as unyielding. His gnarled hands were sure and capable. His Dragon Rider leathers creased and worn with words inscribed on the belts. He was too bright against the dark silhouette of the broken city.

I'd been waiting for him for so long that it was hard to disguise my excitement. I tried to stay smooth and unaffected, but I could tell my excitement was leaking out in the tone of my voice.

"Trouble?" I arched an eyebrow.

"Trouble. Trouble everywhere." He ran a hand over his face. The rest of the city was back to business as usual, fleeing the cold with cloaks and hoods pulled in tight around their faces. Nearby, Badge blew on his fingers to warm them as he collected his ladle and pot. I moved in closer to Hubric. Everyone was listening. Everyone was always listening, and his look told me these words were for me only.

"When the war ended ... I thought. Well, it matters not what I thought. It only matters what is. And what is ... is trouble. A lot of trouble." He looked up, startled as if he hadn't realized he'd been rambling and then shook himself. Tiny flecks of snow and ash flew off of him like a dog shaking itself in the rain. "I've been on my own so long I've forgotten what it's like to be near people. Forgive me. Let's find Ephretti – I have a message for her – and then you and I best be off. You have much to gather?"

I looked a question at him. After all the build-up of the weeks of waiting, this felt too simple, too abrupt.

"You are coming, aren't you?" His brows knit together.

"Are you still offering to teach me to ride dragons?"

He scoffed. "What do you think we've been talking about, boy?"

I laughed. All this talk of trouble had me more shaken than I'd like. But I'd give just about anything to ride a dragon again – and this time, I'd be sure the dragon was mine.

"Follow me, old man."

I strode through the city, smiling and waving to anyone who looked our direction – and everyone looked our direction. There were only three dragons in all of Vanika – Dax the healer's white dragon and Ephretti and Lenora's green dragons. And those three dragon riders were like legends come alive to us. A fourth dragon caught everyone's attention. I glanced behind me to see Hubric strolling along looking indifferent, his dragon ambling behind him, almost knocking over street-side carts and booths with his whipping tail, but Hubric's sharp gaze took in everything.

If I were the Castelan of this city, I'd be blushing. But the old Castelan was dead and Ephretti had nothing to blush about. She'd dragged us out of the mud – figuratively, if not literally – and given us a new future.

"Not how I remember the place," Hubric said.

"Last time you were here it was on fire," I reminded him. "We saved who we could."

"We, is it?" He chuckled.

"Well, I showed you where to go."

"That's not the visit I was thinking of." He caught up to me, so we could walk side by side. I was leading him through the New City – an area where people were trying to construct new buildings from the wreckage. It was as dingy as the rest, but a little more hopeful. If we lived through the winter, it was possible we could rebuild.

"You were here before that night?"

"I was here when it was a sky city, boy, towering up into the air so high only dragons would think to fly there. A glorious place, Vanika. Rich as a ripe plum, busy as a beehive, dripping with wealth."

"I remember." My mouth watered at the memory of the sticky buns I used to steal on the streets. Even being an orphan in Vanika had been a good life when the city still rose above the land, held in place by magic. All that was past now. "Best to forget, though. We'll never see that again."

"Not here. But you aren't staying here."

We were almost at Ephretti's Hall – that's what they called the half-ruined granary she'd taken over for her work. I could see the people lined up to be heard and the guards stationed outside the Hall. She'd be hard at work at this hour, trying to shore up weaknesses in the city and resettle people into shelters where she could. Not really the job for someone like me. I preferred the fresh air and freedom of the outdoors, but she kept me working for her. Street Eyes, she called my work. Someone to tell her what was happening in her city.

"Are you taking me to Dragon School?" It was hard not to hold my breath. He'd promised. I'd been waiting all these weeks for him to return and take me there. But I'd proven I'd be a good fit, hadn't I? I'd proven I was brave when I dove through those fires with him to rescue people from the flames. I'd proven I was loyal when I stood with him and the girl on the other dragon to fight against our oppressors. I'd shown I was a great choice. Of course, he would take me!

"Not quite."

I clenched my jaw.

"So, you're here to tell me you aren't keeping your promise?" I kept my words bold, but inside my heart was sinking – a lead weight thrown into a pond.

"Not quite."

It was all I could do not to retort. I bit back my words and then smiled – a false, manipulative smile. "Maybe you could try to slip a little more information into those responses."

But we were already at the Hall and he ignored me as he turned and met his dragon's eyes. No words were spoken, but the dragon turned his back on the Hall and settled into a resting position as if he was just going to take a nap beside the line of gaping people.

"Go collect your things and meet me back here. We leave within the hour."

Was he kidding? No explanation, no respect at all and he thought I'd just be happy to jump up and follow him?

"Stop looking so angry, boy. I'm the best thing to ever happen to you." He looked wry, like he really believed those words.

He turned and strode away so quickly that I couldn't even curse under my breath before he was out of earshot.

Great.

Decision time.

Risk everything on an old man who may or may not keep his promises or stay in this ash heap? I looked around at the tumble-down streets and burned out buildings. This ash heap was home. It had been when it was great, and it was when it was ruined.

I took a few steps forward, looking up into the sky. That one night when I flew with Hubric on Kyrowat's back, helping to save people from burning buildings ... well, it got under my skin. The feel of the air rushing around me and of nothing but dragon under me – the feeling of freedom and limitless potential – I wanted that again. I wanted it so badly that I could taste it. But he wasn't really promising that, and he wasn't at all clear on what he *was* promising. I felt torn.

In the crowd, I thought I caught sight of a man looking at me. Was that a swirl of light in his pupil? I froze, but a moment later he was drawn away in the flow of foot traffic and I lost sight of him. My mouth felt suddenly dry. There was something about that man today with his ash creatures and swirling eyes. Something wrong, like the smell of rotting meat. I'd be a fool to stay where men like that roamed. And was it my imagination, or were they all looking at *me?*

You're driving me crazy.

I jumped at the voice. It was so loud and clear, it was like it was right in my brain. Wha-?

I spun around in a circle, looking for who might be talking to me.

Up here.

Up where? My head tilted up and I moved again in a slow circle. There were no more buildings in Vanika that towered above a man, though once there had been many. The only things above me were birds. I turned a little more and confronted Kyrowat – the purple dragon. He'd stretched toward me so that my vision was filled by one massive eyeball and a grinning line of teeth.

Me.

Skies and stars! He was talking in my mind! Impossible. He hadn't done that before!

I only talk to people I like.

He liked me! Maybe I didn't need to wait to see what Hubric would do with me. My eyes narrowed. Maybe I could just climb aboard this one and we could leave together.

Flame burst from Kyrowat's mouth and I leapt sideways, stumbling to the ground and leaping back to my feet amid screams and shouts. The ground where I had been standing was blackened and hot. Steam rose up from the patch of black earth. Behind me, the line of people scattered, and the crowd drew back, cursing and muttering.

Kyrowat grinned.

I don't like you that much. Stop being a big baby and go get your things – if you have any.

Chapter Three

I COULD TURN AROUND at any time. That was the thing to remember, I told myself as I hurried to the tumble-down ruin where I'd stashed my gunny sack of things that morning - a ragged blanket, a long dagger and a tiny handful of things that were too inconvenient to carry around all day. I always kept the essentials on my person – fire starter, belt knife, a waterskin, a pot, and the only two coins I still possessed.

If I held on to that, it wouldn't matter what trick the old man was pulling. I could just turn around and come home, no harm done. I grabbed the sack and hurried out of the alleyway and back toward the Hall. No one tricked the trickster and no one was going to trick Tor Winespring.

Not even that old musty dragon

I heard that.

I kicked a rock in my surprise and hopped on one foot, cursing. That old devil had better get out of my head. I turned the corner out of the alley and ran smack into a man in a dark cloak. The set of eyes that turned to look at me swirled silver. I blinked and the swirl was gone. The man hurried away, leaving me gaping.

I was losing my mind. I was jumping at shadows. I needed to leave here before I went crazy.

I arrived back at the Hall breathless, but I managed a grin and a saunter when I caught sight of Hubric mounting Kyrowat. Castelan Ephretti stood in the street beside him, her guards gathered in a knot around her, peering in every direction at once.

"Here he is!" Hubric said with a smile. "Is that all boy?"

He pointed at my gunnysack and I dodged under the arm of a guard, slipping into the inner circle with the Castelan. All the guards frowned at me in unison. Did they practice that together? I could just imagine it. 'On three ... one ... two ... three ... frown!' Ha!

I handed Hubric the gunnysack.

"It's all I trust in your care."

Hubric raised an eyebrow. "We won't be coming back."

"Ever?"

"For a while at least."

Ephretti spoke, finally. "Which is why I've come to see you off, Tor. I have a present for you."

She handed me a cloth packet tied in string.

"Thanks, I guess. I don't really need a tablecloth, though."

Her wry smile told me the joke wasn't very funny. What did she expect me to do? Break down and cry? Tell her that I looked up to her? Admit I was nervous about leaving? Skies and Stars ... she didn't expect a ... thank you ... did she?

"I'll miss you, too," she said, hugging me suddenly. I patted her back awkwardly until her outburst was over. "Don't sleep in the rain. Stay out of trouble. And for the love of the skies and stars don't try your tricks on foreigners."

"I'm not going to war," I objected.

She sniffed like she was holding back tears. Skies and stars! If I stayed around her like this I might even cry. I coughed abruptly, frowning to prevent any emotions from leaking onto my face.

"Just be careful," she said, pulling me in close so she could whisper in my ear. "That man who was eaten by ashes on the street today ... I heard a rumor he was looking for a boy with a wicked grin. Don't come back here for a long time. Not until I find out what's going on here."

"Try to fix this dump while I'm gone," I said, pulling back from her hug and trying to manage a cheeky grin instead of the terrified rictus my mouth was trying to form. I grabbed one of Kyrowat's stirrups and pulled myself up onto his back.

"Are we done with the touching goodbyes?" Hubric asked as Ephretti gave me one last firm nod of encouragement. Was that a tear I saw her brush away as she turned back to the Hall? Of course not. She had work to do. Obviously. But couldn't she have spared one more minute for a goodbye?

You don't even know your own mind.

Great. And now I was being criticized by a dust-rug of a dragon.

Kyrowat launched into the air at the moment I thought that, leaving me scrambling to hold on. I wasn't quite settled and definitely not strapped in yet.

"Skies and stars!"

When I chose a dragon, I'd choose one who wasn't so bad tempered. One who was respectful and wanted to do things my way.

Was that laughter I heard in my head?

"Hang on!" Hubric called to me. "We won't be there until just before dark. Make sure you buckle in. Kyrowat says a storm is coming and you don't want to fall off."

Like I couldn't stay on the back of a dragon.

Kyrowat dropped suddenly and my belly dropped, too. He stabilized in the air and I hurriedly strapped in. I could feel a scowl forming on my face. So, he liked to play dirty, did he?

There was more laughter in my mind.

I didn't think it was funny at all.

Chapter Four

KYROWAT, DESPITE HIS age, flew like a fire was nipping his tail. We roared out of Vanika and rose into the sky, higher and higher until my home was nothing but a speck on a rolling horizon of grey and brown. I'd never been so high before. The giddiness of it filled me and I found my attention flickering between the landscape and trying to identify the mountains and rivers I knew and then conscientiously watching Hubric fly. He hardly seemed to guide his dragon. The old Purple just flew as if he required no guidance.

The day was grey and overcast, making it impossible to see where the sun was and the wind was so fierce that it whipped my scrap of a cloak around me like a flag. I must be turned around because it felt like we were headed toward the Oakbrim Forest. No one went there. Or at least, no one went past the wood cutting camps on the edge of the forest.

Wait. This had to be Oakbrim. I could pick out a tiny wood camp beneath us. I remembered Ephretti giving orders to double the cutters there. Wood was desperately needed to rebuild and warm Vanika over the winter.

I leaned forward and tugged on Hubric's sleeve. Skies and stars, it was cold up here! He was busy trying to light a pipe. How did he expect the pipe to light in this wind? He should get the dragon to light it for him.

I'm a dragon, not a flint. Forget that and I'll scorch your boots while you sleep.

Friendly fellow.

Hubric turned around.

"Any tips for lighting pipes in a high wind?" he asked.

"We're going the wrong way!" I shouted over the wind.

"Headed west and north, boy. Exactly as planned." He tried the flint again, nearly dropping it. He passed me the pipe. "Here hold this."

"But Dragon School is South-East. Even I know that! Ephretti told me about it. She says that on your first day you get to choose your dragon and I've already made a choice. I want a big Green like Ephretti's. Ephretti says that the Greens are explorers and adventurers – like me!"

"Ephretti says a lot." He struck his knife on the flint, trying to angle it to a handful of dry grass in his other hand. "You shouldn't be too hasty. You've only ever seen a few colors of dragon. Purples like Kyrowat, Ephretti's Green, and that sleek White thing Dax used to fly with before he set up the hospital for you all. What does he do now?"

"Relaxes. Sometimes Dax pays me to polish his scales if I catch him in the right mood. He pays well. The dragon sleeps through the whole thing."

"Well, there you go. That's not many colors of dragon."

"I also saw a Gold."

"Hmm?"

"I saw the Prince of Baojang arrive on a Gold dragon that night I helped you. What do Golds do?"

"Diplomacy. Negotiations. Boring stuff like that. Not a good fit for a lively fellow like you. I can just imagine sending you into a negotiation. You'd probably try to play Find the Weevil, only while you thought you had them distracted, they'd be fleecing you."

"I doubt that." No one pulled tricks on me. I had fast eyes and faster hands. When it came to marks – I knew a few, but I wasn't ever one of them.

"Keep an open mind, boy." The dry grass flared to life and Hubric snatched the pipe back from my hand, lighting it deftly with the dry grass before tossing it away into the wind.

"Ephretti told me other things about Dragon School. There was a lot about hot savory meals and learning to fly a dragon."

"You're flying on one now."

"But I'm not holding the reins!"

"Neither am I."

I sighed. "Hubric?"

"Yes?" He puffed out a stream of smoke but the wind snatched it away as quickly as it formed. I could hardly tell where the smoke ended and the light snow began.

"Be straight with me. We aren't going to Dragon School, are we?"

"Nope. We're headed in the wrong direction."

I gritted my teeth, trying to keep from losing my temper. "Then do you think that you might want to tell me what the plan is?"

"The Dominar has commissioned me with the task of setting up a spy network for the Dominion. And it occurred to me that I knew someone who'd lived his whole life hiding, being chased, and taking things that didn't quite belong to him."

"You lied to me." My voice sounded tighter than I would have liked. I didn't want him to know how close I was to throwing him off this dragon.

Don't even try it.

He snorted. "How's that?"

"You said I would ride dragons!"

"What would you call the thing you're riding right now?"

"Agh!"

I was silent after that as the hours stretched out. I should tell him to turn around and go back to Vanika. This wasn't what he promised me. I'd never signed up to be a spy. Spies had bad things happen to them – daggers in the back, torture in dark rooms, beautiful women trying to steal their secrets ...

Well, maybe I would stick around just a little bit longer. I didn't have my own dragon yet, but I was flying. And it felt good. It felt like what I was made for. And while Hubric didn't seem to have much with him, he probably had food. And I was hungry. And up here in the air there weren't men with swirling silver eyes following me – which was a pretty big consideration now that I thought of it. So, maybe I'd wait until nightfall and see what happened. Maybe, if things looked grim, I could still talk Hubric into turning around and heading straight to Dragon School.

I let my mind wander as I studied the landscape below. There seemed to be a trail in the forest. It was a narrow thing. I wouldn't have even noticed except for the people walking along it. At first, there was just one or two, but now that we'd gone further, there were more. Dozens of people with packs and horses walking through the Oakbrim Forest – a place that no one ever went. I felt a chill at the thought. What could they be up to in this place? Not that it was any of my business.

"Do you see the people on that trail?" Hubric said at last.

"Sure."

"That's trouble right there. Pray – if that's something that you do – that they haven't found my stash."

His *stash?* What would he be stashing up here? Gold? Weapons? My eyes widened suddenly. Maybe being patient and waiting to see what happened next had been a good idea. Especially if –

"Skies and Stars! Hold on!" Hubric yelled.

I barely had time to grip the saddle before we were diving toward the ground.

Chapter Five

IT WAS ALL I COULD do to hold down my bile. We were falling like a stone from the sky, my stomach in my throat. I held tightly to the saddle, but images of Kyrowat, Hubric and I splatting on the stone like overripe berries made me ill.

The wind whipped my cloak up, so that it flapped above my head, leaving my body exposed to the harrowing cold. I clenched my jaw and squinted my eyes against the rushing air. The trees punched into my vision like a bad memory, suddenly filling every empty space with swinging evergreen branches and *thwack* sounds as we hit one branch after another. No wonder Kyrowat was so gnarled if this was how he landed!

And then he was rolling in the air like a fish in water, so that I went from falling to spinning to the side. I ducked as a branch nearly took my head off. I couldn't tell if I was more terrified or exhilarated.

Kyrowat completed the roll. Oof! The air was knocked out of me as we spun back upright. Something must have hit me on the way. I couldn't even be sure what it was. My head was spinning. Were we slowing?

Bright lights flared in front of me, and for a moment I thought they were in my pounding head. But wait! Was that -?

Magic!

A ball of fuchsia fire arched across the sky, smacking into one of the trees and lighting it ablaze. Sparks rained down with pops and crackles. I wouldn't mind standing near that right about now. My fingers were losing their grip on the saddle they were so cold. I flexed them, trying to get them limber again. What if I had to grab something? I needed my fingers!

Yells and calls filled the air along with the continued *thwack thwack* of branches hitting dragon.

"You had a knife with you, didn't you, boy?" Hubric called back to me.

I barely managed to answer, "Yes!"

"Unbuckle from the harness."

Was he crazy?

"Do it now!"

He *was* crazy! What was I thinking getting involved with this? I gulped a mouthful of air and fumbled at the buckle, my cold fingers dull and thick.

"When we get close to her, jump off and cut her free! Kyrowat and I will do the rest!"

Her? I had a sudden mental image of a pretty girl in a red dress half-fainting against a tree, wrapped in ropes as thick as my wrist. I'd save her and she'd be so grateful ...

I strained to look, but I couldn't see anything past Hubric's blowing white hair. He should cut it.

"Ready?"

A fireball whizzed past us, inches away, and smacked the tree right beside me. It lit up like a torch. I yelped – a distinctively unmanly yelp and felt my face heat. Who were these guys? What kind of people flung fireballs around like stones?

"Three ... two ... one .. go!"

Go!

I leapt. Why? I couldn't have said, but there was something about Kyrowat's voice in my head that made him difficult to disobey. I landed lightly on my feet, gasping in gratitude that the drop hadn't been very far. Kyrowat must have been flying with his belly skimming the ground.

Now, to find the girl ...

A second fireball splashed across the frozen ground in front of me, lighting dead grass and sticks up in eerie half-normal, half-magical flames. I dodged to the side, trying to get my bearings. Men with arms raised surrounded me. Some in colorful ornate robes. Some dressed like normal townsfolk. Normal townsfolk didn't throw arcs of green flames the way that man was, though. The arc barely missed Kyrowat as he spun through the trees, circling to come back to where we were.

Where was the girl? I scanned the trees, my eyes skipping across them so quickly in my haste and fear that I barely seemed to digest what I was seeing.

There was a tumbledown cabin – in flames now. Men and women in Magika robes were pawing through the brush around the cabin and standing in a ring nearby throwing fireballs at Kyrowat. They had packs and packhorses with them like they were travelers and the one nearest me had a frown that furrowed his brow worse than a farmer's field. What were they worried about? They were the ones desperate to share the gift of fire with the world, not us!

Behind you!

I spun. Stumbling over a root as I turned. The world was swimming in my view and the sounds disoriented me even worse. Was that my heart thudding so hard that it seemed to be knocking me off my feet?

I caught my balance and looked up to see a dragon tied around the neck between four trees with wrist-thick ropes. How would you tie up a dragon like that? They must have caught him while he was sleeping! His hide was blackened and sooty, so I could barely tell what color he was underneath. One eye was swollen and there was a nasty rip in the corner of his mouth. He hadn't let them take him without a fight. Good on him!

Cut her free!

Her who? What was the old man's dragon talking about?

Saboraak!

I don't speak dragon, you musty old rug! And I don't see a girl. And you fools put me down in the middle of a hornet's nest!

One of the Magikas rushed toward me and I fumbled to find my knife. The hurt dragon's mouth was bound with rope – a thinner rope than he was tied with. He wouldn't be any use. He might make good cover, though. Kyrowat had better hope they didn't tie him up like this.

I won't be surprised in my sleep.

I stumbled to the dragon's side. Actually, if I cut that rope, maybe he could add a little flame. On an impulse, I pulled out my belt knife, grabbed the dragon's snout forcefully with one hand, ignoring his widening eye, and then tucked my knife in behind the rope and sawed at it. This had better work! I never signed up for heroics.

My back was exposed. If I didn't hurry, one of those magical creeps would plant a knife in it. There! The rope came apart in my hands like wet parchment and I flung it to the ground, diving for cover under the dragon's belly.

He roared, flaming wildly.

Overall, it was one of my smarter choices. Under a dragon beats being in front of him when he was flaming. Maybe I should free him the rest of the way before I looked for this girl. Yeah. After all, I couldn't save her if I was dead.

I rushed to the ropes holding the dragon's head in place and began to saw at the first one. I tried not to look too hard at the blackened corpse smoking in front of the dragon. The snow was melting around him.

That guy really had been about to plant a knife in my back – or a fireball – or whatever magic creeps used to kill. But the smell of him brought back memories of my ruined city.

One rope down. I rushed to the next one, sawing at it, too.

"Hang in there, guy," I said aloud. "I'll get you free and you can roast the rest of them."

I could hear him flaming again, but I didn't turn to look. I didn't need to see the carnage. The heat was nice, though. I was sick to death of being cold. Maybe this dragon would be grateful and light a fire for me to warm up next to. It was really the least he could do.

I cut through the third and fourth ropes as fast as I could with numb hands and a racing heart. I was going to have to sharpen this knife when I was done. I'd taken the edge off.

Another scream told me the dragon was doing his part.

When the last cord was cut, I finally looked up.

"Go get 'em, fella!" I called.

Now, where was this girl?

Who, exactly, are you calling 'fella'?

The voice speaking into my head was distinctively feminine and I froze in place, looking around. Wha-?

The dragon fixed me with a single-eyed glare like a shard of ice.

Well?

Skies and stars! The dragon was a girl.

Chapter Six

KYROWAT LANDED BESIDE us, skidding to a stop.

"They burned my cabin!" Hubric said with a curse under his breath.

He was worried about his cabin when enemies lurked in the trees? I spun around in place, looking for any sign of our attackers. Blackened trails from fireballs and dragon flames spread out in every direction from our epicenter. The only sight I had of living enemies were flashes of color as figures slipped through the trees.

They've fled. For now.

The feminine voice in my head still surprised me. I thought dragons only spoke to people they liked. Kyrowat had only ever shared a few thoughts with me and Ephretti's dragon never had.

Males don't like talking to humans – most of them can't even do it except for Purples – and they are only supposed to talk to the people they are bonded to. They say your minds are too strange for constant contact.

My mind wasn't strange. It was quick and clever. Maybe that was the problem. I was smarter than most dragons.

There was a hiss of steam beside me.

Hubric glanced over at us from where he was dismounting.

"Don't irritate her. She's been through a lot. They took her by surprise when she was in a deep sleep."

"I didn't do anything!" I protested. "She's mad at my thoughts."

"Then stop thinking stupid things! Here, come and look for the root cellar with me. I stashed some things in there. This place was supposed to stay hidden, but who could have predicted a mass migration through this forest?"

I backed up from the dragon, trying to keep some distance between us and nearly stumbled over one of the fallen Magikas. It was all I could do not to heave. What had I gotten myself into?

I gathered myself and followed Hubric over the frozen ground. This was too much. I needed to get out of this situation right now before it was too late. I didn't owe Hubric anything. I didn't have to stay. If I left now, I could get back to Vanika in a week or so and go back to my normal life. Why were my hands shaking like that? Stupid hands!

I dodged a small grass fire and looked over my back at the girl dragon. She was puffing flame across her own hide. Weird. I never would have suspected she was a girl. She didn't look at all feminine. She paused to hiss at me and I jumped. Just nerves. I wasn't afraid of her. I'd just been in a battle and I was standing in a forest that was partly on fire. Anyone would be nervous.

"She's cleaning her scales," Hubric said, following my gaze. "Heat helps. The Magika fire leaves an irritating residue." Hubric kicked a pile of moss and leaves aside to reveal a wooden square in the dirt. A rope loop stuck up from it and he pulled up the trap door with ease. "They took what was in the cabin – which will be a problem for us. Either that, or they burned it, but at least there are supplies in here – or should be. Water. Food. A spare saddle and hopefully a cloak. You're going to freeze to death in that one."

"Well, excuse me for not being wealthy."

"Come on. We don't have all day. They'll be regrouping and planning a counterattack. Two dragons are formidable, but a big enough group of Magikas can overwhelm them."

He tossed me a thick wool cloak and I caught it, quickly ripping off my old threadbare cloak and replacing it. That was nice. Warmth and coziness. I could get used to this. I glanced up at Hubric stuffing gunny sacks into what looked like leather saddlebags.

"Why did they attack Saboraak ... that's her name, right? Saboraak?"

"They want all dragons and the power they represent. Their power is dwindling and they're panicking. Have you ever seen people fight over the last drop of water, over the last scrap of bread?"

"Yes."

He looked up, startled, and then cleared his throat. "Well. Yes. It's like that. A lot of people will throw moral compunctions aside if it's a matter of survival – which is why we need to hurry."

"Thank you for the cloak." I felt awkward saying the words, but I was in his debt now. I didn't like being in debt to anyone. It wasn't a big debt though, was it? A nice gray cloak wasn't enough debt to bind me to him forever. After all, I was still leaving as soon as I could figure out a good way to go. I couldn't exactly leave when we were surrounded by hostile Magikas.

"Don't thank me yet." He threw a leather dragon saddle at me and I caught it awkwardly.

"Why not?"

"Because your next job is saddling Saboraak and she won't like that."

"Why would I saddle her?" I asked.

"Remember when I promised you I would push you off a cliff and let you fly a dragon?"

"Sure."

"This will be worse. I'm gonna ask you to go up to that dragon and request a ride ... nicely."

I laughed. How could that be worse? I was a charming guy. No one said no to me. Besides, this wasn't the worst idea. I'd ride with them until tonight and then bail once the threat was gone.

"Watch and be amazed, old man."

I left him to finish packing and climbed back up out of the root cellar. The burnt cabin and leafless trees were eerie and the scattered bodies even more so. I tried not to look at them. I tried not to think about how I'd helped put them there. Best not to think about it. There were things that were your problem and things that weren't. People who tied up dragons and thought there wouldn't be consequences definitely fell into the 'not my problem' category.

Aren't you planning to tie me up, too?

The girl dragon was looking at me. I didn't like how those golden eyes seemed to be able to see what I was thinking.

"It's your lucky day," I said with a smile. "You get the best rider in the Dominion – me."

Were her golden eyes rolling?

I haven't agreed to that.

Well, this wasn't going the way I'd imagined. I'd imagined going to Dragon School and just picking the dragon of my choice. Green – obviously. I'd show him I was a good rider, strong, brave and not to be messed with and then we'd fly off into the sunset. Now, I just wanted a ride for a single afternoon until I could bail and this dragon was getting all snooty about it.

You have got *to be joking.*

Her soot-darkened skin changed suddenly from a soft grey color to a vibrant green and then she morphed into something larger with flashing yellow eyes and a wide frill.

I felt my jaw drop open.

That ... that ... that ... what? I was seeing things. Obviously. Dragons didn't just change shapes and colors.

Female dragons do.

Hubric trotted up to stand beside me, looking up at the dragon with a smile on his face.

"Neat trick, hey? It's a secret. Don't tell anyone."

"What's a secret?" My mouth felt dry. "That she's a ... a ... shapeshifter?"

"I like to think of it as being a Chameleon. She hides in plain sight. She can be any color or any shape. As long as it's still dragon."

The dragon smiled. Oh great. She knew she was better than me. That was going to be a problem. In my experience with girls – limited as it was – you really had to work to make sure they didn't think they were better than you. If they did they'd order you around and try to dress you and feed you.

"Saboraak," Hubric said, "Meet Tor. He shares your talent. He's more than he seems." Hubric turned to me. "Tor, stop gaping like a fresh-caught trout and ask Saboraak nicely if she will accept you as a rider."

"Accept me?"

Hubric smacked me on the back of the head and I stumbled forward rubbing my skull irritably. How did he expect people to react to dragons just shifting color and shape? You couldn't trust a creature that wasn't the same from one minute to the next.

Saboraak's eyes narrowed.

Can't trust me? You're not making much of an impression.

Was she kidding? *I* wasn't making much of an impression? She was arrogantly demanding that Ibeg to ride her! That's not how it was supposed to work! I was supposed to be the one choosing my dragon, not begging a dragon to take me. I saw a blur of color racing through the trees. I swallowed. There was no way to run off right now. Not unless I fancied dying in a burst of green or fuchsia. I could either ride away on her or die magically.

That's right, trout. It's me or a painful death. Which do you prefer?

Oh, she'd picked up on that, had she.

"Boy!" Hubric's word was almost like a dog's bark. I startled.

"Will you let me ride you, Saboraak?" I asked with one of my patented false smiles. That saddle came with reins. She might think she had all the cards, but all I needed to do was get that saddle on her and she would have to do this my way.

This is why only males have ever gone to Dragon School! They're the only ones fool enough to deal with you humans. I promised the Prince of Dragons I would do this but ... gah! I didn't expect you.

Me? She was lucky to have me!

I turned to Hubric.

"I think we're a poor match. We should go to Dragon School. I'm sure there will be a suitable dragon for me there. For now, I can just ride Kyrowat with you."

Are you serious? The opportunity to ride me is an honor you are not worthy of! You should be so lucky.

Hubric's expression was wry. A second flurry of color in the trees told me our time was limited. I bounced nervously from foot to foot. We needed to get into the air!

"I've decided to take you on as an apprentice, Tor. You aren't going to Dragon School. Not now, not ever. Ashana Willowspring runs Dragon School now, and she's given me full authority to take any trainee I want under my wing outside the training of the school. Last time I was there, I told her I was taking you. Do you know what that means?"

"What?" This was starting to feel like a trap. Why was he pushing this when we were surrounded by enemies and running out of time?

"It means that if you say no to me, you won't be welcome there, either. This is your *only* chance to ride a dragon. And this is the only dragon who might be willing to take you. Do you see any other dragons around here? Kyrowat doesn't count. He's mine. You have a choice right here and right now. Choose me and Saboraak and a life of adventure or choose to go back to your dirt-city and scrabble for scraps."

My stomach rumbled and Hubric rolled his eyes, reaching into his pocket and pulling out a thumb-thick piece of jerky. He offered it to me and I took it before he could change his mind, barely chewing it before I swallowed. Oh boy, that was good. How long had it been since I'd last eaten? I glanced at the treeline.

"Well?" he asked.

"We're surrounded. We need to get out of here!"

"First we do this. Then we handle that."

I swallowed. So. That's how it was. This haughty dragon, or nothing at all. And I was on the clock. Decide now or die by fireballs while I dithered about it.

It figured. Tor Winespring always got the short end of the stick. But he also always found a way to turn that stick around. I wasn't going back to Vanika. There was no way through these Magikas and no way to change Hubric's mind and if I was honest there was nothing for me there – not really. But a life riding a dragon – that would be something, alright. And I was no stranger to risk. Plus, those guys in the trees were getting closer. I swallowed.

"Fine. Yes. I'll be your apprentice." I was trapped by my own promise. I clenched my jaw at it. Responsibility wasn't really my thing.

"Then I want your vow right now. A vow of fealty to me. Apprentice to master. You know how it's done?"

"No." I wasn't the vow swearing type. Commitment made my skin itch.

"Repeat after me. I, say your name."

"I, Tor Winespring." This felt ridiculous. Was I really going to go through with it? Was that a green glow I saw? The fireballs were about to start flying again.

"You should put your fist over your heart for this part." He nodded when I did. "Swear fealty and full allegiance to Hubric Duneshifter, Dragon Rider of the Purple, until death takes one of us."

Seriously? That was a bit dramatic. I repeated his words, stumbling in my haste to get them out before we were attacked but at least that kept me from rolling my eyes at how serious they were.

"And I swear this by my honor and the Truth which is all I have to give."

His knife flicked out of the sheath again as I repeated his words and then he slit the end of his thumb and pressed the blood to my forehead. I stumbled back.

"Hey! No creepy blood stuff!"

"I, Hubric Duneshifter, accept your pledge, Tor Winespring, and I swear to protect and guide you, shelter and provide for you, as my liege-sworn until death takes one of us. I swear this by my honor and the Truth which is all I have to give." His smile widened. "It is done. Now, go give Saboraak your oath, too, or you can be my living footstool for the rest of your life."

I frowned. I felt a little warm inside – not that I'd let him know! No one had ever promised to take care of me. It was weird. Like I was too old for it. So why did it make me feel like tearing up?

"And then can we get out of here? They're about to attack!"

"There's always time to do the right thing, apprentice."

"So wait, I have to commit to her, too? This feels – a bit much. Can I take some time to decide? Maybe after we fly for the afternoon?"

Hubric frowned. "Swear to her, or I leave you here."

Behind us, as if on cue, I heard twigs breaking. Our enemies were about to start throwing those fireballs they'd been preparing. I could almost imagine Hubric and Saboraak flying away and leaving me here to be consumed by magenta fire. Tension filled me. I didn't like being forced into things, but what choice did I have?

I strode over to where the dragon stood stiffly, her shoulders back and her head extended as high as it could on her long neck so that it towered far above me. Ridiculous. She was nearly as tall as the trees when she did that. Those Magikas were definitely going to notice her.

"Saboraak?" I said. "That's your name?"

You know it is.

I felt strangely vulnerable as I pulled out my belt knife. I licked my lips. I probably should know what to say. Maybe Castelans and other dragon riders did. I was going to look like a poor street kid if I didn't think of something but I was going to look a lot worse if I died because I didn't do this fast enough. Maybe a modified version of what Hubric had said.

I swallowed. The words were a bit hard to get out. But if I didn't say them, then it would be too late to run. Besides, I was good at getting around promises ...

I had meant to have a ringing, loud voice, but it came out as more of a stutter.

"I, Tor Winespring, swear to protect you and provide what I can for as long as I can as your rider, that is if you'll be my dragon."

Her huge eyes narrowed. Had I missed some part of it? Seriously, we were going to be attacked and she was worried about the details?

"Ummm ... and I swear it by the Truth?"

I nicked my thumb with the knife and offered it to her. My eyes went wide when her huge head ducked down but I didn't back up or tremble even when that flame-hole of a snout leaned in and pressed against my thumb. Had I just promised to take care of a massive furnace with wings?

She seemed hesitant, like she was as nervous and reluctant as I was. Which was ridiculous. I was the one being asked to gamble my future here with a knife basically to my throat.

After a moment she spoke in my mind – her words heavy, like they meant as much to her as they suddenly did to me.

By the Skies and Stars, I pledge my loyalty and life to you, Tor Winespring. I give you truth and the bond of dragon to man. With your death, I will die, with your life, I will live.

That seemed intense. I shivered.

I'm taking a huge risk here. Don't disappoint me.

Harsh! She should talk about disappointment. I'd expected an exciting school and classes and being able to choose a dragon from among a dozen options, not forced to swear what was basically a marriage vow in the middle of a smoky forest.

I didn't even know that there were female dragons.

How do you think we make more dragons?

I'd never heard about one in the Dominion.

I'm the first one to leave the lands of Haz'drazen.

That must be lonely. Was that a pang of pity I was feeling?

A little less lonely now.

Chapter Seven

HUBRIC BOUNCED FROM foot to foot impatiently. "Take the saddle and go put it on Saboraak. These saddlebags tie in behind it. Hurry! Those Magikas are about to attack!"

Like I didn't know that! I'd been the one telling them to hurry!

There was a crash in the woods and a yell.

I rushed to Saboraak and nervously tried to place the saddle on her back.

"Just get the job done," Hubric called, mounting his own dragon. "While you two were doing your ooey gooey thing I threw your sack of things into the saddlebags. Hopefully, we won't get separated, but if we do, you'll have what you need in there."

There were more yells coming from the trees around us and I hurried to cinch the belly strap of the saddle.

"If we get separated, I don't even know where I'm going," I muttered.

"Saboraak does. You can trust her."

I fumbled with the buckles that held the saddle in place. A second crash sound made me jump.

Not like that!

I hurriedly tried it a different way. How did she know? Had she ever been saddled before?

I know what will hurt me. Have a little respect, human.

How much more respect did she need? I already was nervous of her palm-long teeth! A blaze of magenta soared overhead and I ducked.

"Will those Magikas try to steal Saboraak again?" I called to Hubric.

I can't be stolen. I'm not property!

Boy, she was touchy!

"Are you kidding me?" Hubric asked. Kyrowat ambled up to beside Saboraak and Hubric leaned out of the saddle to help me finish fitting the straps in place for Saboraak. "She's an invaluable asset and a magical creature. They'd be fools not to try. Here, this is where you put your foot to mount up. There you go. Now, strap in so you don't fall out if she does a barrel roll."

The saddle itches.

Yep, touchy.

And you squirm too much!

I was just trying to find a good place to sit. She could ease off with the criticism any time now!

"What about reins?" I asked, but before Hubric could answer a fireball splashed across the ground beside us, so close that my skin felt singed. I smelled burnt hair and then Saboraak crouched down, muscles bunching, as she launched into the air. Pine branches scraped and scathed me as we gained height. With every powerful flap, I was buffeted by them.

Great. Of all the dragons in all the world, I got the one who didn't know how to fly with a rider. I'd have to watch out for my own well being, she certainly wasn't going to. And the reins were still in the saddlebags, so I was at her mercy when it came to direction.

Stop complaining.

Whoever said girls were more nurturing was full of dragon-

My thought cut off at Saboraak's sudden barrel roll. I would have screamed, but the breath was ripped from my throat. Blood rushed to my head with my stomach following quickly. Just as I thought I was going to lose that nice beef jerky, we spun around and I was upright again. I swallowed. Well, she'd proven one thing. She could make both of us green.

I felt her laughing in my mind as we continued to climb.

Hubric says to stop goofing around. He says to look down at the Magikas.

I wasn't the one goofing around. That was this dragon I'd been fool enough to pledge to.

Are you going to sit and sulk or obey orders?

I leaned over in my stirrup to look down below us. Fuchsia and green fireballs arched up, losing speed and height before they could reach us, only to crash harmlessly in the forest below.

Not harmlessly. Those could start a forest fire. Do you see how many trees are burning? We'll be lucky if the fires stay localized. We dragons are much more careful with our flames.

I pushed back memories that tried to bubble up. Memories of snatching little children from buildings just before the licking flames consumed them. Memories of helping Hubric pull an old man out of the flames. Memories –

Now is not the time for bad dreams. Concentrate.

Well, there wasn't anything we could do about Magikas except to fly away, which suited me just fine. It seemed strange, though, that they were traveling north so poorly supplied and in such numbers.

Haven't you heard about the great battle around Dominion City?

Sure. Everyone heard of that. The Dominar destroyed the Ifrits and freed us all.

That's a real garbling of the story! But you should know – the Magikas fought against your current Dominar. She had a –

She?

You need to get over whatever prejudice you have against girls.

I didn't have a prejudice. I liked girls – a lot, in fact. Girls with long golden hair and girls with raven curls, tall girls, short girls, girls with curvy-

Agh! Stop it. Why did I swear my life to a simpleton? Back to world events. I will teach you to think or die trying! Your Dominar – a girl, now – made an alliance with the ancient elders of dragonkind and with our Queen. Together with the Chosen One, they fought the pretender, the Magikas who allied with her, and the Ifrits. They destroyed the pretender and the Ifrits, but the Magikas were scattered. Some are dead. Some are fleeing.

The ones below weren't dead.

They're fleeing north, to Ko'Torenth, which is also where we are headed.

Because they lost the war?

Partially. They also have a big problem – and so do we. The magic they have always tapped – in seams beneath the ground – is running out. There are only so many more colorful fireballs they can throw.

Well, that didn't seem to be stopping them. What did I care if their magic was fading?

They're hurrying to our enemies because together they are trying to find another source of power. They think they can get it from dragons.

Still, not my problem.

Ahem.

What?

You swore an oath to me just now. I'm afraid, Tor Winespring, that from now on, dragons are very much your problem.

Skies and Stars! The freer I tried to get the more I got tangled up. I never volunteered to join a war. I never volunteered for more trouble.

In life, you are only guaranteed one thing: adventure.

Chapter Eight

WE FLEW ALL DAY UNTIL I thought my inner thighs were so chapped that they would never recover. Maybe this was why real Dragon Riders wore leathers. I'd have to ask Hubric about leathers when we got where we were going.

My stomach rumbled viciously. There had been no food – except that mouthful of jerky – and no stops all day. We flew above the trees, still keeping an eye on the knots of Magikas working their way north through the forest. How were there so many little trails and paths in a forest no one ever entered?

That's probably a myth. There are no truly untouched places in the world. If you set down there, I bet you'd find someone who has been living in that forest all their life.

How would you know? This is your first time around here, too. It's not like you traveled the world. You were just in Haz'drazen's lands all your life.

I studied. How do you think I can speak human? Besides, you were just *in Vanika.*

Oh, so she was going to throw that in my face, was she? I was going to have to travel a lot. I didn't like having a haughty dragon rubbing my nose in my own inexperience.

Everywhere you go, I'll go too.

I made an annoyed noise in my throat, but I wasn't really upset. I was starting to get used to her voice in my mind. It was like a steady stream of entertainment. I could probably get her pretty riled up if I wanted to.

Don't even think about it.

We caught our first glimpse of the mountains when the clouds finally lifted an hour before dark. I squinted at the frosty peaks. Cold as I was, it looked colder there.

I hate the cold.

Something we could agree on. But we were headed north and by all accounts that should mean warmer weather.

Not in Ko'Torenth. Oh, they have deserts on the plains, but they don't live there. They live in the great mountains and those are cold and frosty.

Wait. What?

It's cold in the mountains of Ko'Torenth.

But why would we be going there? Wait, she had mentioned that, hadn't she?

Didn't Hubric tell you that he wants us to be spies? I did mention Ko'Torenth before and you didn't seem surprised.

I just hadn't realized what she was saying before. It made sense for her to be a spy. She could easily disguise herself. She could hide in plain sight. I wasn't interested in risking my neck to steal secrets.

I can only disguise myself if we go somewhere with other dragons.

But what if the place we went to was full of Magikas? A dragon was an impressive thing, but she was hardly magical.

Sometimes the best magic is hiding in plain sight.

I'd always been good at hiding. I'd been good at pulling fast cons. But that was just for fun. Or for food. Or for something to do. The worst I could expect was to have my stuff – what little there was – stolen, or to be turned out of wherever I was holed up, or to be taken by the city guards – back when there were city guards. Somehow, spying on a foreign country seemed a lot more intense. Like the kind of intense that I definitely wasn't going to agree to.

I stole a last look at the Magikas forging through the woods towards Ko'Torenth. I could barely make them out in the fading light. What would happen to a man who tried to pull a con on a Magika? Was it true that they could turn people into toads?

No.

That they could send you into a deep sleep for a thousand years?

Your body would starve and rot long before that. You'd have geraniums growing through your ribcage.

Pleasant thought. Could they ... torture me?

Undoubtedly.

With magic?!

Does that make it worse?

Yes! My breath stuttered like my lungs wanted to force me to panic. I frowned and forced myself to breathe normally.

I don't know what you want me to say.

What had I gotten myself into?

I felt something that seemed like a mental sigh.

You made all those promises to me with no idea whatsoever of what it would mean for you, didn't you?

Ummmm ... well, there had been a bit of urgency to save all of our skins from fireballs.

Here's some advice: think before you leap.

Great. I'd accidentally committed to a suicide mission with a dragon playing the role of my conscience. Worse, now she was dispensing advice that should be obvious.

It's called common sense. You should try it.

As darkness fell, thick as a blanket, lights blossomed on the edge of the mountains.

They were always there. Your eyes just couldn't see them until it got dark enough.

We were headed straight for those lights. Did that mean shelter and warmth?

Hubric says yes.

Did that mean a warm meal?

Hubric says yes again.

Then speed up, old girl! Let's get there fast! I'd figure out how to say no to the suicide mission once I had a full belly and a night of sleep.

Fine by me. And I'm not old. I'm barely forty.

Saboraak sped up, and I didn't even mind that the icy wind bit harder because very, very soon I could warm up these frozen dead weights I used to call feet and these poor clumsy stones I used to call fingers. My mouth was already watering at the thought of food.

The lights grew bigger and closer and after a moment Hubric and Kyrowat passed us, leading the way toward the light.

Eventually, we drew close enough for me to see a massive wooden structure nestled into the side of the mountain. A wide platform ringed with lit lanterns was waiting for the dragons to land and a large house with wood beam walls and well-lit windows waited beside it.

Excitement mixed with longing inside me. There might even be a bed there! I hadn't slept in a soft bed in ... years.

Hubric and Kyrowat landed neatly on the platform and he was already dismounting as Saboraak descended. Her landing was just as minimalist and tidy. At least she could fly, even if she was bad at being ridden.

I heard that. I've been flying all my life, you know. Kyrowat says there are dragon cotes here. I'm looking forward to seeing them.

Me, too. It will be a first for both of us.

A greeting party was already assembling, three men carrying lanterns and displaying wide grins strode toward the platform over a long wooden walkway from the large house. The leader carried his lantern on a pole and a dark cloak swirled around him. I had a sudden memory of a crow I'd seen picking through the ashes of Vanika, but that was probably only because his nose looked exactly like a beak.

I'd better go be polite.

I leapt off Saboraak's back, hurrying to join Hubric. Out of the corner of my eye, I saw something flash, but when I looked up there was nothing there, only the welcoming smile of the leader.

I was seeing things.

Wait.

Was that a silver swirl in his eye?

Chapter Nine

"HO! GRANTON!" HUBRIC called, as if he knew who these people were, but though the men approaching us waved, none of them spoke.

I reached for my belt knife, wishing I had the dagger with me. It was still stuffed in my saddlebags, of course. There was something strange about these men. Hubric shifted from foot to foot and in the gleam of the lanterns, I saw a knife appear in his hand.

When they were still two paces away their leader addressed us.

"Hubric I know, but who is this?" His eyes glittered in the lamplight, but I didn't see a silver swirl in them this time. Was I just seeing things? I was still nervous about Ephretti's warning – that these men with silver in their eyes were looking for me.

"Where is Granton?" Hubric asked.

He adjusted his stance to put his weight on his back foot. I'd seen that in men before. They shifted like that when they expected a fight. My gaze shifted back to the three men holding lantern poles. Those could be used as weapons easily enough.

"The old man that kept this place? Gone. He left it to us." The leader tilted his head slightly.

"And the girl with him?"

"A pretty thing and so set on adventure ... " He let his voice trail off as if the answer was in the words he didn't say. I shivered. I wouldn't want a man like that near anyone I cared about. Who was this girl to Hubric?

"What did you do to her?" Hubric asked, his tone low, almost a growl.

The leader grinned. "Nothing. She decided to travel."

Hubric's body tensed.

"Come in and eat with us. It's too cold to stay out here. We can share all the news inside," the leader said.

I took a step backward. Inside, we'd be separated from our dragons. Saboraak and Kyrowat could toast these three where they stood, but I doubted Hubric and I would be as capable. Hubric looked torn. Clearly, he was worried about his friend. Was he trying to find a way to get more information about her? It was too bad that the dragons couldn't read these men's minds.

We can, but we can only read what they are thinking.

And do they know where Hubric's friend is?

I don't know.

Are they enemies?

Certainly.

Hubric took a step forward and I cursed inside. Better to fly away and figure out our next move. We could sneak in here later if we needed to. If we followed them into the house now, we'd be outnumbered, and they could easily overwhelm us away from the dragons. How many more men could be hiding in that house?

"Where did Granton go?" Hubric asked, head cocked to the side.

Ah. A testing question. Even I could tell that his next move would depend on the answer. The glitter in the leader's eye told me he knew, too. He smiled easily, but was that a flash of nervousness in his eye?

"North. He needed supplies and said-"

Surrounded! We're surrounded.

I spun at Saboraak's panicked thoughts, only to see dark shapes rushing in. One of them held a rod high over his head. Silver light spun out from it, crackling into lightning bolts. The first one struck Saboraak's tail and she shrieked. The shriek turned to a roar and she spun, flaming at the figures.

Hubric cried out to my right and I saw him in a deadly lock with the leader, both men wielding knives and tangled around each other like wrestlers.

"Where's the girl?" he demanded.

I dodged a second man at the last second, narrowly missing his grasping arms. I wasn't much of a fighter, but I stabbed out frantically with my knife and felt it hit something. It stuck for a moment and I wrenched it loose.

There was a cry as the man who attacked me fell into the shadows. Was that blind luck?

I didn't have time to register what just happened or how Hubric was doing when a second man lunged forward. A magenta burst of flame left his hand, flashing toward me. I dove to the ground. Wincing at the hard smack of my body against the rock. I'd landed on something metal.

My heart was pounding so hard it was difficult to hear. I felt like I should be looking at everything at once, but my eyes were too slow and my hands too shaky.

I heard a squeal of pain as Hubric repeated himself. "The girl! Tell me!"

"North, she went north!"

"Like Granton did?" There was a note of warning in Hubric's voice.

Another squeal of pain. "With friends. She went with friends."

Behind me, heat and light burst in steady flares. The dragons were fighting. No time to turn to look. Saboraak could look after herself.

I guess I'll have to if that's the best you can do.

I grabbed at the metal lamp pole I'd landed on, hurrying back to my feet just in time to see a second fireball streaking toward me. I never signed up for magical battles! This was madness!

I leapt to the side and then darted forward, striking the Magika with the heavy lamp pole and then spinning to find Hubric in the mess of the battle.

His attacker was on the floor whimpering, but a second man raised his lamp pole and green mist stretched out from the lamp like tentacles, clawing toward Hubric. Hubric's eyes narrowed and his hand darted out like a viper, the knife flying from it to lodge in the throat of the Magika. He fell to the ground, his lamp and the green mist falling with him.

"Run!" I yelled, taking my own advice and dashing toward our dragons. I grabbed Hubric's arm as I passed, spinning him around to run with me.

"They always forget that a simple thing can defeat all their flashy magic."

"They aren't the only ones who made a mistake here. Why didn't you realize right away they weren't your friends?" I asked, ducking under the swinging arm of a fresh attacker and letting his arm clang against the lamp pole. That was going to hurt him in the morning. I could still feel the vibrations of the hit twanging through my arms.

"I was curious."

Curious? He risked our lives because he was curious? Hubric threw a second knife barely missing my face. I gasped. What in the –? The sound of something heavy hitting the floor behind me cleared up my confusion. The crazy old man just saved my life. Again.

Hurry! There are too many to hold off forever. I've never seen magic come from objects before.

I was hardly an expert on magic. Although I already knew I didn't like it. I was an expert at not liking it, if that counted.

There was a path clear to Saboraak and I rushed across it, leaping up on her back as if I mounted dragons every day. She was so busy flaming shadow after shadow that I thought she hadn't noticed until she launched so suddenly into the air that I fell backward, barely catching myself on the saddlebags.

Next time worry about clipping in and not about what I'm doing. We can't be a team if you're second-guessing me.

Fair point.

The lights below faded as we climbed into the sky. Where were Hubric and Kyrowat?

Right behind us. They're fine.

So much for hot food and a warm bed.

Stop complaining. You aren't the one with a bleeding tail and lightning welts.

Was she okay?

Please address all comments to me directly.

It was just a thought!

Please address all thoughts to me directly.

I didn't know if I was clenching my jaw in frustration at her constant orders or at the frustration that I still hadn't received a proper meal even after selling my soul to the twin devils of Hubric and Saboraak but if I clenched it any harder it would probably crumble like rock in a landslide. Maybe I should have taken my chances with those madmen below. They probably had hot food and they weren't any crazier than my current companions.

A growl rippled through Saboraak, shaking me in my seat.

Skies and stars! These two were going to be the death of me!

Chapter Ten

WE FLEW FOR SO LONG in the dark that I had no idea where we were when we finally set down in a cluster of thick trees.

"Get some sleep. We'll talk in the morning," Hubric said, but it barely registered as I slid off the saddle and fell to the frozen earth.

Ugh. I should find somewhere warm, so I didn't freeze to death, but I was so tired ... so very, very tired.

Something leaned up against me and then warmth flooded me. Oh, soup and biscuits – yes! That was nice. Mmmm. I was mostly asleep before I realized that I was being warmed by a fire-breathing dragon. A cranky, demanding fire-breathing dragon.

Just give the attitude a rest for a few seconds and get some sleep.

I woke to the smell of a wood fire.

I rolled over, regretting it immediately as the cold hit me like a vengeful hammer. Ngh! I blinked life into my eyes, scrubbing the crusty sleep out of the corners and sitting up.

We were camped on a rocky hillside looking over the pine forest below. Hubric was busy with a tiny wood fire and a kettle. It looked promising. I gathered my cloak around me and stood. Both dragons lay with heads on their forepaws, eyes shut to the world.

"They flew hard yesterday and both need to heal," Hubric said, blowing gently on the tiny tongue of flame he'd created. "Caf?"

"Do you have any food?" I asked hopefully.

"Check your saddlebags. Remember when I filled them at the cabin?"

I walked stiffly to the Saboraak's side, trying not to disturb her as I rummaged in the bags. Skies and Stars! There was food in here!

He couldn't have said that before? There was also that cloth package Ephretti gave me. I grabbed it, too. This was the first chance I'd had to even look at it.

My stomach rumbled so loudly that I was afraid it would wake Saboraak as I returned to the fire, hard crackers and dried meat in hand. I was already stuffing them in my mouth as quickly as I could.

"Go easy on it," Hubric warned. "I had expected to resupply at the post last night."

I was holding more food than I'd seen in a week. There was no way I wasn't going to eat it. I'd worry about finding more after I was done eating what I had.

Hubric cleared his throat and I looked up guiltily, my mouth stuffed so full with food that I could barely chew. He was only offering me a steaming tin mug. I accepted it gratefully, ducking my head in thanks since my mouth was full.

"What did you learn from last night?" he asked when my mouth was empty enough to talk.

Last night? I'd been too busy surviving to learn much – except that I was really beginning to hate Magikas.

"Those Magika guys are trouble. But if you're fast you can get past their defenses."

"And?"

"They said that they didn't know who I was, but they seemed to have an interest in you." Although, if Ephretti was to be believed, they had an interest in me, too. I would just have to keep my eyes open to see for myself. No point mentioning that, though. It would only make me sound crazy.

Hubric sipped his caf. "No surprise there. I've been more in the eye of the public than I ever asked to be."

"I thought you were a spymaster."

He laughed. "That's still new. And I'm going to have to become more forgettable to make that work."

"They took that friend of yours, didn't they? Do you think they have her back at that house?"

"I don't think so," Hubric said thoughtfully. "That place was clearly a trap. They can't stay there for long. There are only supplies for a short stay and no way to get more when they are on the run."

"So where is your friend?"

"With other Magikas, somewhere in the north of here like they said. The man who admitted it was in too much pain to be lying." I shivered at his words, remembering those squeals of pain. Hubric didn't notice my reaction. "She's a smart girl. Her name is Zyla. About your age. I recruited her as soon as I could trust her. Her parents were traders. They traded oddities all through the northlands as well as the Dominion. But in the war, a loose Ifrit slaughtered them in front of her."

I shivered at my own memories of the dust demons. "Thank the skies and stars those things are gone now."

Hubric frowned. "For now. There are other enemies and other dangers. Don't get too comfortable or they'll sneak up on you."

"So, I should count on ulcers and digestive problems then, should I? A life of living on edge? No, thank you. I didn't sign up for a life of terror."

His smile was wry. "Zyla is the perfect recruit to spy on Ko'Torenth. I was planning to pair her up with you and send you both to Ko'Koren - one of their larger cities. She and I are already working on communication routes and protocols. But I expected to have time to help the two of you ... get to know each other."

"And now she's been kidnapped. Are you saying she can't be rescued?"

"I'm saying that I'm not the one who can rescue her. They know me."

They certainly did know him. They'd set that trap for him. The old codger must be more valuable than I ever thought.

"Worse," Hubric continued. "Did you see that rod they used?"

"The one that hurt Saboraak?" I asked, glancing over at my dragon. She looked better in the morning light, but I hadn't had a very good look at her wounds in the dark.

"Dragons heal remarkably quickly if they can get deep sleep," Hubric said, sipping his caf. "And yes, that's the one I mean. I've never seen an *object* that was magical. Magic is something that Magikas use to tap the life force of the earth and use it to alter the world."

"Mostly with colorful fireballs. Yes, I've noticed." My tone was dry.

"That is a weak use."

"You sound like an expert. And a fairly haughty expert at that." I tried the caf to hide my grin at calling him out. Skies and stars, it was bitter! Who *chose* to drink this stuff? I put it down and grabbed the cloth packet Ephretti gave me.

"I've seen things that would make your hair curlier than a sheep's, boy. Magic great enough to level armies and build statues as tall as a sky city."

"Keep talking old man," I said with a laugh. I could use some entertainment. I loosened the strings on the cloth packet and carefully unfolded it. The cloth was white and of a fine weave. I was going to keep it as a handkerchief. It had been a while since I had one of those.

"You saw what Ephretti did when she saved Vanika. She rose up out of fires that should have killed her and saved us."

Point for Hubric. I couldn't deny that what Ephretti did was somehow magical. I paused in unwrapping her gift.

"She fulfilled a prophecy."

Hubric nodded, his eyes serious. "I've seen bigger prophecies than that fulfilled."

Now I was feeling awkward. "I don't know about prophecies."

"Maybe you should learn." He reached into his pocket and pulled out a slender book, bound in red leather and shoved it into my hand. A book? Really? For all my spare time?

"What's this?"

"The Ibrenicus Prophecies. This copy belonged to Savette Leedris."

"Never heard of her."

Hubric rolled his eyes. "Just take it and try to learn something from it. At any rate, there are other magics, like I was saying. Truth magic – which is a powerful bending of what is to what should be. And deception magic, a mirror magic. There are others still that I've never seen. Tonight, I saw what I think might be artifact magic. The magic of ancient items. Someone needs to fly south and warn the Dominar that it is loose in her lands. Maybe that someone should be you."

Was he kidding? I was meant to have adventures, not get myself stuck helping fancy court ladies in and out of carriages. "I'm not going to talk to any Dominar!"

Hubric laughed. "Well, someone needs to do the harder task. Someone needs to fly north to the border of Ko'Torenth and the Dominion. There is a camp of Magikas there. Someone needs to sneak in and rescue Zyla."

"That's not a tall order or anything."

"Or they could attack the camp head on and hope she survives the carnage." The glint in his eye told me he was teasing. "But don't worry. I knew you weren't up for that."

"How many of them do you think there are?" I looked back at the package to avoid his gaze. Inside the cloth was a fine silver chain with an oblong stone the thickness of my thumb hanging from it. It rippled in the light from golden to dark brown like a boiled candy.

He shrugged. "More than there are here. Is that Tiger's Eye from Ephretti? It seems to suit you."

I slipped the chain over my neck and hid the stone in my shirt as I thought. No one had ever given me such a fine gift. It was a reminder that I was in this now. I'd made commitments I couldn't wriggle out of and people were counting on me. And if I was stuck helping people out, I should at least find a way to do it my way. Something inside me seemed to solidify.

"Stop and think, Hubric. Which of us is better at hiding? Which of us has a chameleon for a dragon? It's not you, old man. You go south and bow to Castelans and Dominars. I'm going north to rescue the girl."

"If that's how you feel about it." He was watching me sidelong as if he was waiting for something. If he thought I was going to chicken out or change my mind, he could think again!

"And how will I know this Zyla girl?"

"She has golden eyes like that stone you just put in your shirt. That's the only distinctive thing about her."

"You must just kill with the ladies using those complimentary descriptions."

"I don't compliment people."

"I've noticed."

He looked awkward for a moment as if he was thinking of something else but then he turned back to me.

"If you succeed in rescuing her, she'll know what to do next."

"And if I don't?"

"Saboraak will know what to do next."

I rolled my eyes.

"You know, Hubric, you could go ahead and tell me. I'm great at keeping secrets. I can even keep secrets from myself if you want."

"Best to focus on one thing at a time."

"And if I end up separated from both Saboraak and Zyla?"

Hubric's eyes narrowed. "Then you'd better be dead, or I'll make you wish you were. They are your responsibility now."

I sighed. "I don't like responsibility."

"I know."

"Then how do you know that I won't just get up and run." I tried to make my voice sound defiant, but I knew it was no use. I was tangled up in this now.

He smiled. "I have my reasons to believe in you, boy. Oh, and Tor?"

"Yes?"

"Not to put to much pressure on you, but the world might hang in the balance. What we do now, could push it one way or another."

Yeah. There was no pressure there. None at all.

Chapter Eleven

I SHOULD PROBABLY HAVE asked him why he wasn't the one taking care of me when it was literally only yesterday that he vowed to do that. But if I said that I'd have just sounded like a whiner. Besides, I'd asked for this mission and I could do it without anyone's help.

And you already whine enough. AND you're doing it with my help.

Saboraak and I had been headed north all morning. I rubbed at the sore spots on my inner thighs – still no leathers to protect them – and tried to concentrate on the horizon, but it was all a blur of trees and hills and sky and had been for hours. We'd stopped at a creek just before noon and even that had looked about the same as everything else.

City eyes.

Is that some kind of insult? Or are you just terrible at nicknames?

It's a statement of fact. You have city eyes. You don't know how to read the forest.

Has the forest written something worth reading?

We hadn't even seen Magikas on forest paths like we had yesterday.

Which is good. Hubric told me to keep you away from them. It will be harder to sneak in if they know we're coming.

Because disguising a dragon was so easy.

You did see me change colors and shapes, right?

She was still green except for the burn marks and jagged pink scars from last night's battle.

You were lucky to get out of that unhurt. Are you a good fighter?

I was just lucky. Did her wounds keep her from chameleon-ing, or whatever that shapeshifting thing was? I hadn't seen her change again since the first time.

I can change. I just don't want to right now. Hubric said to conserve my energy.

I looked back over my shoulder as if I could see Hubric back there. Unlikely, since he'd flown south at the same time we flew north.

Impossible.

Thanks for chiming in. I chewed my lip, hoping I'd see the camp before long.

I can already see the smoke from the cook fires. It's a large camp. They must be planning something big.

Other than kidnapping, rebellion, selling Dominion secrets, and trying to suck the last magic out of the world?

Yes, other than that.

Saboraak had no sense of humor. I was going to have to help her with that.

I was still straining to see the smoke. Nothing. Either she was imagining things, or her eyes were better than mine.

I have a sense of humor.

Oh yeah? Prove it.

She was silent for long minutes and my smile was beginning to get smug before I saw the smoke. There was a ridge of hills between us and the smoke, but the smoke was clear enough.

I'll land on this side of those hills and we can decide what to do then.

Hopefully, they weren't too far from the camp. I didn't want to hike.

Hold on. I'm going to change into something that blends into the sky better.

I held on, not knowing what to expect, but even though I was braced for it, my skin still felt like insects were creeping across it when she changed shape underneath me and her skin went from brilliant emerald to a bluish grey.

Perfect. Keep low over my neck. They'll never see me now, but you still stick out like a long nose.

Long nose? She was one to talk.

On me, it's called a snout.

Minutes stretched to hours before we reached the hillside. Saboraak landed close to the top, taking care to stay low, but even so, I had to creep up the last few paces on my own. My legs ached from sitting so much for the past two days. I concentrated on that ache and I swallowed hard to push away the fear creeping up my chest. All I had in my hand was my dagger. I should have asked Hubric for a better weapon than that.

What would you call me if not a weapon?

Too far away to do any good right now.

You insult me.

I held my breath as I reached the summit, kneeling and then folding down to press myself against the earth before I crept over the horizon and looked down.

Below me, a massive camp sprawled - striped silk tents, bonfires, covered wagons, strings of horses, and masses of people filled the bowl of a valley. From the camp, a tired road wound north, its poorly maintained surface rife with plants and moss. No one left the camp to travel the road. So – what were they doing gathering in this place?

There's water there. A spring, I think.

How did she know that?

I can sense the bones of the earth. Can't you?

No, I hadn't been gifted that particular skill set. What would you even do with that?

Mine ore. Find water. Locate important tunnels or warrens.

Maybe it wasn't as useless as it sounded.

I felt Saboraak's mental sigh. *It's going to take a lifetime for me to educate you, human.*

There was a stir in the camp below and a small figure was taken out of one of the tents and marched through the late afternoon sun, her head held high. If I'd been a betting man – oh wait, I was! – I would have said that they were under orders not to hurt her because while they pulled and prodded, the weapons stayed in their belts. Was that a glimpse of gold I saw in her eye? It could have just been a trick of the light.

Whoever she was, she was thrown into one of the central tents and left there. I licked my lips and thought about what would happen if I just rushed in.

You'd be quickly dispatched.

You think?

No need for sarcasm. Let's think this through.

I smelled something like sulfur and rotten fish. I was about to turn to look for it when I felt a heavy jowl rest on my shoulder.

Oh gross! Her breath was awful and if that wet sensation was saliva, she could just bury me now.

You're a skittish little thing. I'm only here to help.

Then let's get to the helping part, shall we?

Hubric suggested that you had ... skills.

Well, of course I did! Didn't I mention that you were lucky to have me?

She ignored my boasting.

And your scales are not unlike theirs.

Scales? Did she mean my cloak?

Yes. Similar color and shape.

But underneath I was dressed in commoner clothes and these Magikas had heavily embroidered robes.

The ones who attacked us last night didn't.

Only because it was a trap.

Then go down there and claim to be one of them. They can't have made it this far yet. Tell the guards that they captured Hubric and that you were sent ahead with the news.

I rubbed my chin feeling the light stubble growing there. I hadn't seen a razor in months. Fortunately, my beard didn't grow very quickly.

Do you need me to flame those scraggly scales clean?

No! Keep your flames to yourself!

It was only an offer.

She sounded hurt, but seriously, she'd burn my skin off and leave me to dance in my bones. What kind of partnership was that?

I didn't realize you were so fragile.

It was like she'd met her first human yesterday.

Actually, it was nine days ago.

I felt my jaw drop. I shut it with a click. Her suggestion for infiltrating the camp was a good one ... especially for someone who had just met humans.

I read a lot. She sounded proud.

Okay.

So, I needed to sneak down into camp, trick them into thinking I was one of their own, cause a distraction of some kind and then grab the girl from that central tent. No problem, right?

I shall wait on the hillside and camouflage myself. When you need me, call. I will come immediately.

That was as much plan as we could hope for. I was more of an improviser anyway.

I slid back down the hillside and hurried to rummage in Saboraak's bags for anything I thought I might need. There was a leather satchel with a waterskin and some food. I took out most of the food and put it back in the saddlebags to make room for a blanket in the satchel. I needed to look like someone who was traveling. I added a flint and knife and carefully strapped the dagger to my belt before smoothing my hair back and making sure it was all in place.

You look dapper.

I squinted at her. What was she saying? There was another dragon sigh.

I'm saying you look fine. Go get 'em!

I swallowed down my nerves. It was just another con. Just another gamble. And gambling was my life. I could do this.

I started my climb around the peak of the hill, careful to stay low enough not to make a silhouette against the sky.

You'll do just fine. Try to look more confident. Push those shoulders back.

She was worse than a mother. I skirted a thorn patch and slid step by step down the steep hill.

Whose mother?

Anyone's mother. She'd better come if I called her. That was all there was to it.

Chapter Twelve

BY THE TIME I REACHED the edge of the camp, it was deep into the heat of the afternoon and winter or not, I was sweating. I wasn't used to walking so far and particularly not through nature. Nature hated me. Every dip, furrow, and root there was had sprung to life and tried to kill me on the way down the hill.

Don't be so dramatic.

Worse, Saboraak's voice was still loud and clear. I'd been hoping for a bit of a break from that.

If I thought I could trust you on your own, I would, but so far, your thoughts have not been very reassuring.

There was a loose string of guards around the camp at various intervals, looking bored but alert enough to catch me should I try to sneak in rather than going through on the main road. I didn't even try. Instead, I ambled up to the cluster of five guards on the main road and knuckled my forehead like commoners did. I never did that. No one was above me, no matter how rich, no matter what title.

Is your arrogance a species thing or is it particular to you?

At the last second, I realized my error. These weren't full Magikas and if I wanted to pretend to be one I shouldn't be behaving like a commoner.

"Where are you coming from, Apprentice?" one of the guards asked. The others barely looked up from their card game.

Oh good. The slip had made me seem like an apprentice, which was probably a better idea for me anyway. And these guards seemed too lazy to care. They probably didn't see anyone but Magikas come through here, anyway.

"We had a trap laid at the house south of here-"

I was cut off by another guard – one of those sitting at the makeshift table. "Hold your tongue, boy! If your master was with you, he'd give you a thrashing for speaking about secret things where you shouldn't!"

He looked sharply behind me and I turned to see another traveler stopping behind me, waiting his turn with the guard.

"You'll give your report to Shabren the Violet or to no one at all, understood?" the guard said.

I nodded. A name like that didn't sound very intimidating. *The Violet?* Sounded a bit girlish, really.

"Here, stand aside and let this Magika pass and then we'll deal with you."

I stepped to the side, edging close to the barrel where the cards were laid, and the guards posted.

"Magika, welcome to Caravan City. If you could please provide your name for our book of records, by order of Shabren the Violet."

My hands sweated nervously but I kept an easy expression on my face. No need to let them see that the longer I waited with the guards the more worried I got about whether they would let me in. I leaned against the barrel and looked at the cards laid out.

"Triple pass?" I asked. I knew that game. Trump games were fun, but hard to win money on. Games of chance were better for that.

"You play," the guard asked. He was a wide fellow who looked like he was incapable of standing on his own without the barrel for assistance.

I doubt he'd be a guard if he couldn't move.

So now I couldn't even exaggerate in my own mind?

I prefer accuracy.

There was something strange about the Magika who had just arrived. He was fishing around for something in his cloak and for a second, I thought I saw a gleam of silver in his eye.

I squinted at him. He wasn't the same man as at the house or in Vanika. How many men could there be with swirls in their eyes? And why did they all seem to be near me? Could it be true that they were looking for me? I felt a little tingle of fear. I didn't like the idea of being hunted.

The first guard – a lanky fellow with yellow hair – had a book and quill out. "Name?"

"I have it here somewhere, here ... somewhere ..." The Magika reached in a final pocket and pulled out a bowl.

"We just need your name, honored one."

The guard frowned, and I felt myself frowning, too. Why wasn't he giving his name? And what would he need a bowl for?

The same thing they used a rod f-

I was leaping behind the barrel as soon as I registered her thought. Lightning burst from the bowl in every direction, striking the ground and the air with cracking sounds. Flames burst up into the sky where the random strikes hit tents or wood.

The yellow-haired guard stumbled backward and froze mid-stride. A wrist-thick bolt of lightning hit his chest with a crack so loud that I jumped. He fell to the ground faster than I could gasp and for a half-a-second everyone was silent.

Screams and shouts erupted from the camp and as if a spell had been broken, the other guards leapt to their feet, drawing their weapons.

Before they could do anything else, silver pooled in the Magika's eyes, flowed down his cheeks and to the dust around his feet. I knew I should duck and cover my head, but I couldn't help but watch as three little bursts of dust and dried grass rose up from the ground around him, swirling and growing until they were twice the height of a man and half as thin. Arms spread out from them and howling mouths appeared and then they leaned in around him and began to rip at the Magika. Shreds of cloth flew out in every direction, their actions a whirlwind of fear and destruction.

This time, I did duck – just in time to escape the worst of it when they moved from shredding cloth to shredding flesh. His howls filled me until I thought I must be howling, too.

Stop cowering and look! You need to get out of there!

I couldn't!

Be brave!

I ripped my hands from my face and ran, half-crouching, half running, haunted by the hollow screams. I didn't know where I was running, only that it was away from the magical fury behind me. I didn't stop until I collided with a tent. I threw myself into the dark entrance, not caring who or what was within.

First Vanika, now here! I'd thought I was seeing things back there!

It's real.

And it was coming for me. But what was it?

Evil.

Chapter Thirteen

THE TENT I'D STUMBLED into was clearly for storage. Crates and barrels were stacked haphazardly, some open and others nailed shut. Out of curiosity, I looked into the first open barrel. Grey dirt. Weird. I took a pinch between my fingers, rubbing it between them. It was more like sand, though I'd never seen such uniform sand particles before.

I left it to look at the next crate. Something was packed in dry lamb's wool. I pulled out the wool to find a simple metal rod. Better put the wool back. I didn't trust these artifacts. As far as I was concerned, anything old might spit lightning bolts at a moment's notice.

The rest of the barrels and crates were the same. Useless junk. No food. No water. No clothing. No weapons. Just old things packed in wool, weird grey sand, and colorful glass bottles also packed in wool. The wool might work as Firestarter. It was bone dry and plentiful, but otherwise, this was just heavy junk.

It might be safe to go back outside.

I snuck to the edge of the tent and looked out. People swarmed across the camp, toward the road I'd arrived on. There, where the lone Magika had lost his mind, there was nothing but a smoking heap of ashes, a bowl still rolling across the road, and three dead guards slumped in uncomfortable positions. The man who had looked like he wouldn't move had moved just fine. He alone of the guards was still on his feet – at a tent as far from the barrel as the one I occupied. I swallowed. I could have been one of those poor fools.

You still could be. I can see you all the way from here. Either get back in the tent or step all the way out. You look suspicious half-way in the door.

Well, that was embarrassing – being called out by a dragon.

I coughed awkwardly and left the tent with a purposeful stride heading into the camp. People rarely questioned anyone who looked like they knew what they were doing. I kept my gaze forward – a man on a mission – but watched everything from the corners of my eyes.

It's going to be hard to help you become the best version of yourself. I swear you're prone to self-sabotage.

Who said I wanted to be my best self?

Doesn't everyone? If you don't want to be the best version of yourself, what do you want to be?

I want to be the real version of myself. This one. The one who has a bit of fun and doesn't worry about 'best.'

The real version of myself was starting to draw attention and I still had to get to the center of the encampment. Despite the milling movement toward the road, eyes occasionally followed me, squinting in thought. Did I stand out too much?

Maybe it's because they are all going one way and you are going the other.

That seemed reasonable. I smiled at the squinters. It wasn't the first time that I'd drawn attention in a crowd, but there was something strange about this crowd. What was it?

For starters, there were no children. No one at all younger than me – and I was about twenty.

A dragonlet. We'd barely trust you to control your own flame at that age. And I'm pretty sure you're lying about being twenty. Hubric said you were seventeen.

There were also no elderly people.

I heard a rumor that Magikas don't get old.

That would be handy. Or maybe they died young, which wouldn't be handy at all.

And there were very few women. I knew for a fact that there were female Magikas, but there were more males in this camp. They were dressed in a fashion that to me meant, 'try to pick this pocket.' It was all I could do to keep my itching hands to myself.

You saw what that bowl did. Pick the wrong pocket around here and you might end up with your own mobile storm.

The entire place smelled strange. Spices I'd never smelled before filled the air and made me twitch my nose irritably.

At one campfire, rather than food cooking, there were a variety of glass vials set up on a twisting metal arch over the fire. They bubbled with liquids of various colors and consistencies under the keen watch of a female Magika.

Someone enterprising was selling herbs and cloth from the back of his wagon. The Magikas buying from him pretended that they weren't buying at all, "just looking" and then would slip him a coin and walk away.

I let my eyes wander over the oddities. Maybe there would be a clue about how to rescue Hubric's friend. I was starting to think that was a fool's mission. Maybe I should fly away and rethink this.

I'm not a horse. You can't fly me where I don't want to go, and I have committed to help Hubric. I met your Dominar when she visited our Queen. I was impressed. I agreed to help her efforts.

We could do that from Dominion City or anywhere else in the Dominion. We didn't have to die saving a girl we'd never met.

I was asked to help this way. I am committed to this.

Just my luck. The fire-breathing dragon had more moral fiber than I did.

Perfect.

I turned a corner around a yellow and black striped tent and saw the central red and white tent stirring in the breeze. Almost there!

Just find the girl. First things first. Then look for an ally. I can't arrive on the scene until the last minute and you could use someone to help you.

And how did she expect me to do that?

Use your brain. Look around. There are always people with goals that don't line up with their communities. Use that.

It sounded so easy when she said it, but it wasn't like people just raised their hands over their heads and volunteered to help you betray their group.

I'm sure that if you keep your eyes open a likely option will present itself.

Well, it would have to reach out and grab me, because I wasn't seeing anything. Everyone on the road between the tents and around those cook fires looked content and purposeful.

Just have a little faith.

A hand reached out of the yellow and black striped tent and yanked me in.

Chapter Fourteen

I STUMBLED FORWARD as the pull on my cloak suddenly released, tripping and falling to the floor. Rugs of various sizes, shapes, and colors overlapped across the tent floor. Closed chests and folding chairs served as the only furnishings other than the braziers of coals scattered throughout the tent. They gave off just enough light and heat to see in the dim interior.

A man stood at the center of the tent with arms crossed over his chest. He wasn't much older than I was, though he had an air of a foreigner about him and around his head, four leather bands were tied, almost completely covering his forehead. His hair was cropped short and his clothing was not Magika clothing. He had the rakish look of a noble out for some fun in the gaming houses.

"You are no apprentice," he said, his smile growing, like he was enjoying catching me out.

"You're no Magika," I countered.

He wore a long vest with tasseled ends and a heavy belt over it. His loose trousers tucked into high leather boots and a light scarf was wrapped around his neck and shoulders. I wouldn't mind clothing like that. They looked easy to move in.

"If you were an apprentice, you would know who I am." He was testing me, of course.

"I just arrived," I said. "My master said that I was to pass a message to Shabren the Violet."

"You arrived with the man who died in the commotion?" He tilted his head to one side, testing me.

"Is this your tent?" I asked. It didn't' seem to suit him. It felt ... feminine somehow. Maybe it was the embroidered pillows on the folding chairs or the way someone had placed a jar of dead flowers on one of the chests.

His eyes narrowed. "You're here for something. The man at the gate was a distraction to get you in. I've been watching you walk through the camp. You don't belong here. You're just trying to fool your way in to see Shabren."

I hoped he couldn't hear my heart thudding in my chest. Already called out! Already discovered! I wasn't much of a spy, was I?

He's the perfect one to make an ally.

Was she kidding? He was a threat. I should con him and get out of here.

"That's nonsense," I said. "And I don't have to stay here and listen to it. You're the imposter here. This is not your tent and you're trying to trick me into telling you secrets about our Order that you don't have any right to. I won't be fooled so easily!"

I put on an indignant air, held my nose in the air and whirled to the tent door. A rock-solid grip on my upper arm spun me back around and I clenched my jaw as I faced him again. I didn't want to fight – but I would if I had to.

Don't fight! It will only draw attention!

"Order?" the man asked.

A lie, if it is to be believed, must be spectacular.

"If you don't know about the secret Order of the Nine Bowls, then I won't break trust by telling you." I made my tone as haughty as Saboraak's. "And now, I need to go about my business."

I turned again, shaking off his grip and stepping toward the entrance of the tent, when something whizzed by my head, leaving a stinging burn across my ear. I slapped my hand to my ear at the same moment that I saw the flying knife strike the side of the tent and slide to the floor.

"It's funny," the young man said. "It would lodge right in your back if I wanted it to, but the tent has so much give that it just slows the blade. It's hardly even hurt by it."

I felt blood rush to my face and I spun. He'd outmaneuvered me!

The man held two more throwing knives. One in each hand.

"Who are you?" I asked grimly.

"A guide. These men want me to lead them through the desert north of here."

"What do you want?" Was he a prisoner then? But he had the freedom to roam the camp.

But would they let him live if he tried to escape? I told you there would be someone unhappy here! He's the perfect choice.

"I'm stuck here." He said. "Stuck in this camp. When you go, I want you to take me with you."

"If you don't like it here, just leave," I spat. Saboraak might like him, but he posed a risk. He didn't know me, and he was telling me all of this. Who else would he talk to if I told him anything about myself?

"It's not so simple. I want your word."

I frowned.

"Or," he added, "I'll tell everyone that you don't belong here. It's obvious to me, but I'll admit that Magikas can be in their heads a bit. They don't notice what is right in front of them ... unless someone points it out."

"What's your name?" It was a good threat. But I needed to know who I was dealing with beyond just 'a guide.'

His smile returned. He was almost as charming as I was and with his added good looks, he probably did well with noble ladies to boot. I had a better face for the street, though. It was unmemorable. The kind of face you forgot. Good looks were a liability if you needed people to forget you were ever there.

"I'm Bataar Bayanen and I could be your friend – if you don't put a knife in my back."

Say yes! You need an ally and he's perfect.

He was going to be trouble.

Just listen to me for once! If you don't make a deal with him, I won't fly in there and rescue you when you call.

I sighed and Bataar raised a single eyebrow. I felt like he was trapping me somehow. He'd better not be, or Saboraak would pay for forcing me into this.

"I'm not the one throwing knives around like seeds, friend. You want out of this place? Fine. Then you're going to help me get what I came here for." I crossed my arms over my chest.

His eyes glittered with anticipation. "And what are you here for?"

I laughed. "Like I'd tell you that! No, your part will be to provide the distraction."

He frowned. "I'm almost certain that will take me away from where you are. How will you help me escape if we are separated?"

"Trust me. I can find you." Saboraak certainly could.

Yes. I feel every beating heart in that camp.

Because that wasn't creepy or anything.

He swallowed. "I'm going to need some way to trust you. Tell me your name, at least."

I hesitated. But then again, who here would know me by my name? And this really was a two-person job. And Saboraak was going to be obstinate if I didn't work with him.

"I'm Tor Winespring," I said. "And if you fail me in this, you will wish you'd never heard my name."

Good work. The two of you are off to a great start already.

Was that sarcasm? Had she finally found that missing sense of humor?

Chapter Fifteen

WE WAITED UNTIL DARK – though not in the tent. I was right that it wasn't Bataar's. It belonged to a female Magika.

"She'll be back soon," Bataar had said after I laid out what I needed from him. "She's studying these new trends from the Kav'ai people."

"Trends?" There were a lot of books in the tent. Some had illustrations, but they looked more like grisly monster books than like geography texts. Not that I knew what those would look like. I could read, sure, but I didn't do much reading beyond signs hanging from inns and taverns.

We will need to see to your education as soon as we can. Reading is essential to the forming of a refined philosophy.

Another thing I had no need of – philosophy.

"The Kav'ai traditions are all the rage these days," Bataar said. "You should see what the nobles of Ko'Torenth are like around them! Wander into any Ko'Torenth city dressed as a Kav'ai on a flying Oosquer and you'll be mobbed by excited fans. They dress like Kav'ai, do the Kav'ai morning rituals, drink tea in the Kav'ai way and now everyone wants to know about the Kav'ai magic – Smoke Magic."

"Don't worry about her studies, just grab one of her cloaks to disguise yourself and let's go."

If my plan worked. Bataar would provide the distraction and in the chaos, I would dive into the central tent, rescue Zyla, and call Saboraak to come and get us all.

Three people is a lot for me to carry. Try not to pick up any more strays, okay?

I couldn't help which way the adventure took me. After all, I didn't even want to be here. Rescuing girls wasn't really my thing. Weren't they supposed to rescue themselves? I thought someone told me that once.

If I believed the things you think about yourself, I'd think you were a terrible person.

We needed the cover of darkness to make the plan work. Along with the cloak, we stole a pair of lanterns, hiding them behind the tent. As long as no one saw them there and replaced them before dark, we should be fine.

After that, there was nothing to do but wait.

Waiting together would have been asking for trouble, but I wasn't longing for Bataar's company anyway.

I sat near a cookfire until someone offered me a bowl of stew and tried not to look like a half-starved wolf when I gobbled it up. After that, I spent the rest of the afternoon pretending I already knew about all the things I was carefully observing. If I had known Magikas were so interesting, maybe I would have chosen to join them instead of the Dragon Riders.

A lost cause. Their power dwindles, and they revolt against that. Fighting the inevitable is a losing battle. It's better to adapt.

That was harder for people who couldn't just change who they were on a whim like Saboraak did.

I was most interested in the smoke magic Bataar had mentioned, but I didn't see a trace of it. What I saw instead was Magikas practicing light tricks and fireballs. Magikas brewing potions and testing droplets of them for effectiveness. Magikas deep in discussion about things surrounding magic.

"... lucky we found this well of power," one told another. "Imagine the chances of setting up a camp here!"

"There was no chance in it," his friend replied. "It was all careful planning. We always knew there was a risk to joining the Dusk Covenant in their efforts."

"Risk, yes, but no one could have predicted what happened. Truth magic? I'd never seen it before."

"And hopefully you will never see it again. It can't be controlled. And you saw what it did to the Ifrits! Until that point, I thought they were the most powerful magic to ever exist. But this attack today ..."

"You don't think they know about us, do you?" the man sounded jumpy.

They noticed me watching and I moved on, keeping my gaze to the ground to avoid suspicion.

"...at the gate," a woman was saying at the next campfire. "Do you really think there might be more artifacts like that? I didn't know such magic existed."

"I've heard rumors," a man replied, "but all of them lead to Ko'Torenth and you know how those people are – cold and hard as their mountains."

I heard the same conversations again and again – resentment over their loss at Dominion City, hope in Ko'Torenth, and all of it laced with rumors of strange magics and fear about what had happened at the road.

Eventually, dusk fell. I almost breathed a sigh of relief at the single rising star.

It was time to begin.

I moved nonchalantly through the camp, smiling when anyone looked at me. I'd grabbed a basket from beside the entrance to a tent, playing the role of apprentice as well as I could. I'd been watching other apprentices all day and they'd been busy delivering things from tent to tent for their masters. There was nothing strange about one more apprentice on an errand.

"Are you headed to the center of the camp?" a breathless voice asked.

I managed to keep myself from jumping and instead adopted an easy smile, shoulders relaxed. Nothing to see here.

When I turned to look, the voice belonged to an apprentice. He was about my age with dark, brooding brows and a thick thatch of hair.

"Sure," I agreed. "I have a basket to deliver for my master."

"I've been given too many tasks and all need to be done before dark!" He had a leather satchel stuffed with cloth over one shoulder, a second one with loaves of bread peeking through the top of it over the other shoulder, and a wide basket in his arms. Whatever was in the basket must have been heavy. He was sweating and shifting from foot to foot.

"It's dark already."

"Exactly! Can you help me?"

I didn't have time for this. I frowned.

"Please? If I fail at this ... I've failed the last three tests. This is my last chance!"

"Fine," I growled, reaching for the basket, but he set it on the ground and handed me the leather satchels instead.

"They both go to Shabren the Violet's tent. You know the one? Red and white?"

"It would be hard to miss." I couldn't keep the wry sound from my tone and he looked at me sharply. I sighed. "Don't worry. I'll get it done."

"Right away?"

"Before I deliver my basket," I agreed. I needed to get moving again. I was running out of time. Bataar was going to start that distraction any time now. And I was heading to Shabren's tent – though not to deliver satchels.

"Thank you!" The apprentice grabbed his heavy basket and hurried off.

I looked both ways before stashing the basket I had under the corner of a tent. These satchels were a better cover anyway. And they needed to go to the very place I was headed. Lucky, that.

Perhaps you are touched by a great story. Sometimes, what looks like luck is just a great story catching you up and propelling you along. Like how we came to be bonded together, or how you escaped our first battle unscathed, or how you ran into Bataar when we needed an ally ...

I hoped not. People in stories had the worst time of things. They never had enough to eat or a comfortable bed or a bit of fun. It was just work and sacrifice all the time.

You mean like now? Don't forget, Tor. The world hangs in the balance. Hubric said so.

I tried not to curse.

I hurried through the camp, the very picture of an apprentice on a mission. With the rise of the dark, the Magika camp seemed busier than ever and their bright fire-displays in red, magenta, and emerald were pretty enough that I would have stopped to watch them practice if I wasn't in such a hurry.

I felt sweat cooling on my brow. Great. Now I was nervous, and I never let myself get nervous about anything. Things either were, or they weren't. No point fretting about it all.

You'd be a fool not to be nervous. Now that I see those Magika light displays, I'm worried that your distraction won't draw the attention you were hoping for.

She was worried?

I was worried!

She was the one safe on the hillside while I was the one risking my neck!

I rushed through the traffic of people moving between the tents and breathed a sigh of relief when I was finally just outside the red and white tent. This was madness. I should be far away from this camp by now, heading back to Vanika.

Where men with swirls in their eyes stalk you?

She knew about that?

You think about it a lot.

A pair of guards stood watch at the entrance, but that wasn't how I was planning to go in anyway. People always forgot that tents were just made of cloth. A cloth wall was nothing to a man with a sharp knife.

I quickly scurried around the back of the tent. It backed against two other tents and the second that I thought no one was looking, I snuck between them, hiding from view in the small space between the tent backs.

I could hear the murmur of voices from the white and red tent as I slipped the satchels off my shoulders. If I got a chance, I'd take the one with the bread with us. We could use the extra food.

Okay, now's the time, Bataar! Bataar? If only he could hear me like Saboraak could.

Give him time.

Or, maybe he was betraying me. Maybe even now he was telling the Magikas that I was here and that I was trying to take something from them. Maybe I should go without his distraction.

Wait.

You couldn't trust people who just turned up out of nowhere. That just didn't make sense. It was too convenient, too easy. I'd been a fool to trust him.

One more second ...

A fool! I should be found out and tortured by magic. It was what I deserved for being such an idiot!

BOOM!

The sound was so loud that I fell to the ground, landing hard on my rear and for a moment, everything was silent.

Chapter Sixteen

UP! UP! HURRY!

What happened?

Bataar lit the storage tent on fire just like you asked him to.

A simple tent fire was a good distraction, but I didn't expect ...

Stop thinking and act! Bataar is in trouble and I might need to fly in sooner than we expected.

Don't hurry just for him. He'll be fine.

Don't be heartless! I certainly will not wait if he needs me! We promised him a rescue, too. Now, get moving. I can only give you a few minutes.

I leapt to my feet, slashed the back of the red and white tent with my knife and rushed in through the slash. The old expression 'A fool rushes where a blind man is too wise to tread' came to mind.

As soon as my head was through, I froze.

The tent was full of people, most of them clustered at the entrance, looking out at the distraction. There was a pair of burly guards close to the entrance and a few Magikas of various sizes, shapes, and colors. But what caught my attention was a man with a heavy, curving blade in one hand who stood at the center of the tent looking out. He wore bright purple Magika robes lined with strange symbols and scrollwork.

Maybe that's why they call him Shabren the Violet.

He was a bit ostentatious. Could anyone be taken seriously in clothing like that?

They can when they carry big swords and perform magic. And the girl? Where is she?

I heard a small sound and looked right below me.

Skies and Stars! I could have cut her with the blade!

Gold colored eyes glittered in the light, just as Hubric said, and I started to smile. My smile melted when a second set of gold eyes turned to me. There were two girls – both with hands tied and both with imploring golden eyes. I looked from one to the other. They were mirror images of each other, each with dark skin, freckles, golden eyes, and short, curling hair. They looked about my age, maybe a year or two older, but delicate and slight. They were mirror images of one another and I found my eyes quickly looking back and forth from one to the other as if to compare each set of features to the other. Hubric never said anything about *two* girls!

I blinked, but there was no time to second guess. Hubric could figure it all out later.

Carefully, I eased my way through the gash in the tent and slipped in behind them, slicing the ropes that held them tight. All attention was still on the tent entrance but at any moment it could turn back to us.

Skies and stars! Rescue missions were not my thing.

"Stop!" the word thundered from the center of the room and I looked up, knife in hand. I pulled my dagger awkwardly from its sheath, licking my lips.

"Run," I whispered, hoping the girls would listen. They scrambled behind me without a word.

Shabren the Violet raised his curved blade, but humor painted his face.

"And what are you, little mouse? More boy than man, no proper weapon, and I can sense ... no magic. What do you think you'll do here? Gnaw at my heels?"

Saboraak had better hurry!

I told you not to pick up more stragglers. What am I supposed to do with four people?

It was her idea to include Bataar, so she could figure it out. Besides, there was no way to tell which girl we were here for.

I could feel my legs trembling. I willed them to stop. You were only as big as the image you projected. I straightened my shoulders and lifted my chin. Focus on looking big and bold!

Behind the Magika the others fanned out like an audience trying to get a good spot to watch from. No one bothered with weapons, though there was a grin or two from the audience. I shifted my grip on the dagger and glanced quickly over my shoulder.

"Oh, they ran out the back like you wanted, boy. Two more mice running out of the trap – but a mouse won't get far in a camp of traps. Someone will scoop them up for me. You, on the other hand, you interest us." Shabren smiled. He was even bigger than I realized and his smile was a little too easy, a little too charming, a little too handsome, like the smile of a man who always got what he wanted.

"Us?" I hated that my voice wavered. I wasn't afraid. Of course not! I'd seen worse. I clamped down on my own mind as it tried to feed me images of a burning city and people screaming as they were engulfed by flames. I wouldn't think about that. Couldn't.

"Davorek here had been asking me to demonstrate a new trick I learned," Shabren the Violet said. Maybe they called him that for the purple shade across his cheeks where blood vessels had burst and left their spider lines across his skin. They didn't quite mar his otherwise good looks. I'd known my share of men with faces like that. They liked to drink.

A man with dark hair set off by wings of white over the temples smiled slightly. Davorek. He carefully circled, blocking the rip in the tent where I'd entered. I'd remember him. He looked like he'd eat horses if he got the chance. Horrible man.

Don't knock it until you've tried it.

Was that her first joke? Now is not the time for jokes!

I lifted my dagger a little higher.

"I won't be using the blade," Shabren said. "Except to direct the flows of magic. Did you know you don't need to actually hurt a man's body to make his mind think he's hurting?"

That didn't sound good. No, no it didn't. What was I doing here? Facing evil people face to face was not my deal!

Wait.

What *was* I doing here?

I leapt at the same time that violet bands of energy – horizontal lightning – reached for me. That's how he got his name! The lightning flashed over my head as I hit the loose rugs on the floor with a thud, but I wasn't done. I scrambled forward, one thought in mind.

I crawled to the corner of the tent, ignoring the cursing behind me. There! In the corner of the tent. I sawed at the rope holding the edge of the tent out. If I could get out under that corner I could cut the ropes and collapse the tent. That was more my style.

My knife dropped from limp fingers. Wha-

And then pain hit like I'd never felt before. Horrible, wracking pain. I fell backward, writhing and tossing on the floor like a strong wind was whipping my rag-doll body across a field of rocks. I couldn't make out the words or sounds above me, couldn't even see the world except for in glimpses.

Panic washed over me like waves. Horrible, squeezing waves, snatching my breath, filling my lungs with water, battering me back under just when I thought I might escape.

Darkness filled my vision and then a quick glimpse of the interior of the tent, the hole I'd cut in the side flapping in the wind. I wished – pain took the wish right from my mind like plucking a leaf from the grasp of a toddler.

Saboraak! Help! Help me!

Darkness again and then a glimpse of Shabren, Davorek and the others standing over me, looking down. I needed – thought left again.

Saboraak!

Darkness and then faces, but over their heads the cloth of the red and white tent tore apart, flames licking the edges. Burning ash rained down over us.

The faces vanished and through my shaking and twitching, I thought I heard screams and the scent of burning flesh. There was the sound of something heavy hitting the ground and then a wet white muzzle drew close to me. One burning eye was inches from mine.

Still alive?

If she drooled on me, I would make her haul a cart for the rest of her life.

Our relationship doesn't work that way. Besides, you called me. I came. End of story.

Someone was calling my name. I was too disoriented to know who – and then rough hands were lifting me, and I was thrown over someone's shoulder. Oof! The breath knocked out of me as his pointy shoulder dug into my diaphragm. Would a little care be too much to ask?

I was thrown roughly over the saddle. There was a sense of being crowded, like people's legs and rears were closer to my limp body than I might like. All I could see was the pattern of the rug on the ground below us. There were holes in the pattern where the burning ash had seared it.

Screams and smoke surrounded us.

"Hurry!" A female voice shrieked over me. It pierced my skull, reverberating through my brain. I tried to slap at the sound, but my hand barely moved.

We lifted into the air suddenly, but with more wobble than I was used to with Saboraak.

Four is a lot!

I remembered Kyrowat carrying six people.

Males are stronger.

The carpet was suddenly far away and instead I was watching a burning encampment, fire everywhere. Balls of fire in green and magenta streaked toward us from the ant-like people on the ground, but bright orange flames consumed the tents below. One here, one there, and where the supply tent used to be was nothing but a black crater.

"You almost killed me with that brilliant 'distraction,'" Bataar said as we rose higher in the air, so high that even the fireballs couldn't reach us. He sounded annoyed.

"Mnph," I replied. Yeah! Take that comeback!

"If it wasn't for this dragon, you'd be useless."

Ha! Joke was on him, because I was alive and while there was life, there was ... something. Not hope, obviously. Utility? Use? Life?

Get some rest. I'll find a relatively safe place to take us and then we'll worry about your ability to mangle old wives' sayings.

I couldn't afford to sleep. I needed to keep everyone safe. Not that I would, of course. That wasn't my deal. I wasn't the hero type.

Just go to sleep. Hero.

I wasn't going to sleep, and she couldn't make me. And I wasn't a hero.

And yet, you act like one constantly.

Exhaustion hit me like a sledgehammer and everything went black.

Dragon Chameleon: Paths of Deception

Chapter One

"THEY'RE FOLLOWING US. A fire is a bad idea," a girl's voice was saying.

Why did she have to be so loud? I just needed one more minute of sleep. Just one more minute to clear my head a bit.

Wake up, trout, or you won't get any say in what happens next.

Memory crashed in like an uninvited guest. Oh yes, my bossy dragon friend, Saboraak. It sounded like her threat skills were as bad as her joke skills.

I felt the equivalent to a mental sigh.

I'm looking out for you. Do you want others to decide your fate for you, or do you want to be master of your own fate? We are ruled by our choices, but also by the choices of those around us. As much as possible, we should influence those choices for good. We must refuse to only look out for ourselves.

It would be nice to be master of *something*. Other memories were flooding my head now. Had my heroic moment really been when I ran away from a guy named Shabren the Violet?

Precisely.

Ugh. It would be hard to hold my head up high with that on my mind. But I'd never pretended to be a hero.

I think you will find that character isn't always what's impressive about a person from the outside. It's an inner mettle they possess that shows itself in the middle of great difficulty. Together, we will hammer some character into you.

The only thing inside of me was a trace of beef jerky. My stomach rumbled to emphasize the point and my eyes shot open.

I was lying against something hard and hot – Saboraak, no doubt. She was faithful, it would seem. I had no idea before meeting her that dragons were so affectionate to humans.

Don't mistake my nurturing spirit for affection, trout. It's not about who you are. It's about who I am.

I also had no idea that they were so bad with nicknames. Trout? Really? Just because my eyes went big *one* time?

Flames licked sluggishly along wet wood in a circle of rocks just in front of me. Bataar – my new ally – leaned over the flames, blowing into the embers a little too aggressively. We had a dragon here. Why didn't he ask her for a fire?

He is too independent to ask for help. A trait you both share.

Beside of Bataar, a pair of girls watched nervously. They were mirror images of each other from their tousled curly hair – barely brushing their chins in length – to their wide golden eyes. I'd never seen girls like them before. And they were a puzzle. They were holding hands as if they were afraid of letting go.

Well, first things first. Always lead with a grin.

I sat up, offering my very best grin. "I expected to rescue just one girl. Zyla."

The girls exchanged a glance, but they both looked away from me, as if they weren't going to say another word. So much for gratitude.

You need to get over yourself, Tor. This isn't all about you. Compassion is the door to wisdom. Open it, and you'll find that you see the world more clearly.

I didn't sign up for a second conscience. Saboraak could keep her moralizing to herself.

I'm not sure you have a first conscience! Stop whining about what you signed up for and step up! Start with compassion.

I drew in a deep breath. Skies and Stars! I thought nagging authorities on the outside were a problem but now I was going to have one inside my head for the rest of the foreseeable future.

The rest of your life.

Don't remind me!

I must have been silent for too long because Bataar stopped blowing on the fire and spoke.

"The other girl is Zin. They're sisters."

"I can see that."

They were staring at me with twin glares, like cats who had just been doused with water.

"And are we being followed?" I asked Bataar.

"It seems like it." He looked over his shoulder nervously and I stared past him, assuming he was looking in the direction of the camp. How far had we flown? It was too dark to see anything, so it must still be night.

Not far. I was worried about you. We fled less than an hour ago.

"So why the fire?" I asked, standing up. "Won't that show them where we are?"

There was a gasp when I stood, and I turned to see the girls with mirror looks of surprise on their faces. Seriously? Did they do everything in tandem? Were they just one person in two bodies?

"Where did you get that?" the one on the right said, her deep voice musical. I could get used to that voice. Maybe she could sing ...

She was staring at me. Those golden eyes were like glittering gems. They were fixed on my chest, probably looking at the tiger's eye pendant that slipped out of my shirt, but I was very conscious that I was under her gaze.

"Well?" she asked.

Oh. Yes. Speaking. I should do that.

I *never signed up to deal with your hormones.*

"Ephretti Oakboon gave it to me. She's the Castelan of my city – Vanika."

Bataar shifted his weight and cursed quietly at the fire he was trying to build but the girl's eyes widened even further.

"Vanika?" she asked.

"Yeah." I scratched the back of my neck. Why did it itch like that when I was uncomfortable? It wasn't the new cloak. Even if it was, I wasn't giving up this cloak for anything.

"Hubric took me from there. He said I was supposed to find Zyla and that she would know where to go next. He didn't say anything about a sister."

"I think it should be obvious where we go next," Bataar said. In the moonlight, his chiseled features stood out starkly. I didn't like that he seemed so in control of the situation. Confidence was my thing. "We go further than this. Even taking the hills into account, those Magikas will be here before morning. Anywhere is better than sitting here."

"*If* they're following us," I said. Best to remind him who was boss here. "We don't know that they are."

You're boss now?

"They *are* following us," the musical voice of one of the sisters said again. There was a deep burr to her voice like she was always slightly growling. I could really get to like that...

Mind on the task!

"How do you know?" I asked.

"They ... want ... things from Zin and me." She looked down, her lower lip quivering.

Compassion. Remember?

"Look, ummm ... are you two okay?" That was my very best compassion. Saboraak should be proud.

That is your best? Skies and stars, Tor! We have soooo far to go with you. Courage in physical danger is a great asset – and one you possess – but courage in emotional danger is another essential for a life of bravery.

The girls both looked away. I ran a hand through my hair awkwardly. How did you even talk about this stuff?

By talking about it!

"Ummm ..." I looked to Bataar for support, but he was suddenly very interested in the leather satchels at his feet. The girls must have grabbed those two satchels I'd been delivering to Sabren the Violet as part of my cover. "Are you physically hurt? Do you need bandages or hot water or something?"

I drew in a deep breath. Eggs and bacon, how did you ask a girl if she had been tortured?

"No," Zyla said quickly. "The things they wanted weren't physical."

I shuddered. Why did her voice make it sound like that was somehow worse?

"So, umm, Hubric didn't say anything about your sister," I said, crouching down in front of the girls. Maybe if I was closer, I could do a better job at connecting. I felt so clumsy, like I was too tall – though I was only average height, too bulky – though I was slight in build, too full of thumbs – though I had the normal number of thumbs. Girls. They made you feel weird.

"He didn't know she was there. Neither did I. I thought Zin was dead," Zyla said. "I thought she died with my parents. I didn't know that she was captured by Magikas."

Zin's eyes were far away, not even acknowledging that we were talking about her.

I nodded, trying to look like someone you could talk to. Serious. Reliable.

You look like you have stomach problems.

What did Saboraak know? She'd only known humans for nine days.

Eleven days, now.

"And does she talk for herself?" I asked looking at Zin who wouldn't look at me.

Zyla made an exasperated sound in her throat. "Just leave her alone, okay? Talk to me."

"Okay, well, Hubric and I went to the House looking for you but there were a bunch of Magikas there with weird magical rods and stuff."

"Items with magic in them?" Bataar interrupted, suddenly interested in us again.

Zyla frowned, looking between us like we were discussing something we shouldn't. When her eyes caught mine, they looked intent, like she was trying to say something with them.

"Anyways, he sent me to find you. He had an important message for the Dominar so he had to go south."

"To Dominion City?" she asked. Those eyes looked so intelligent, like she was thinking a thousand things at once. I nodded, distracted by the way her lips made a perfect archer's bow at the top. "Then he won't be back here for two weeks at the very least. Maybe more. That means we need to make our own decision about what to do."

"And it needs to be fast," Bataar said, offering us torn pieces of bread from the loaf he was holding. I snatched the one he offered me quickly, gulping it down as he raised an eyebrow.

"What?" I challenged. Couldn't a guy eat without being judged?

He shook his head. From the corner of my eye, I saw Zyla gently offering a piece of bread to her sister. Zin took it with a faraway look in her eye.

"We have a little while to decide," I objected.

Bataar shook his head. "Look south."

I stood and followed his pointing finger. I had no idea which way south was without his help.

In the distance, an eerie green light bobbed along the ground – like a lantern being carried by men hurrying.

"I think they want these girls back. Unless these bags have something more valuable in them than Kav'ai clothing and bread."

"They'll do anything to get us back," Zyla agreed.

I watched the bobbing green lights for a moment more. There were more popping into existence by the minute. Far too many to fight. I swallowed and looked at Zyla.

"Why do they want you so badly?"

Chapter Two

"IT'S NOT ME," SHE SAID, rising to her feet to join us. Bataar's smoldering fire popped suddenly and we all jumped. "It's Zin. We can't let them get her. Please!"

I scrubbed my hand through my hair again, thinking. We were north of the camp, which meant we were already in Ko'Torenth, a foreign country. There were four of us, poorly supplied for winter. Saboraak couldn't fly four people very far.

It's possible that I can take you in short flights, hopping along the ground little at a time like a chicken flying, but proper, eagle-like all-day-soaring is out of the question. I may even manage a few hours in the air – if I truly must – but I can't fly all day.

"Where would we go if you were just following Hubric's plans and not trying to outrun and outwit Magikas?" I asked Zyla.

"Ko'Loska. A smaller mountain city north of here. It's a single day's journey by dragon. From there we were to make our way to the capital."

In continuous flight it would be a day's journey, but not the way we are doing it.

"Okay. Then let's go to Ko'Loska. We can hide in the city."

Bataar barked a laugh. "Four foreigners on a dragon? Hiding? I think not. We'll stick out like sore thumbs."

He was going to challenge me? As if he had a better idea? I didn't like that scornful look he was giving me or the way he was looking at Zyla as if he could bring her in on the 'mocking Tor' festival.

I frowned.

"Didn't you say you had Kav'ai clothing in that satchel? Is there enough for four?"

Now it was his turn to frown thoughtfully. "Maybe."

"And do dragons sometimes visit Ko'Loska?"

"Often," Zyla said. "It's a hub for trade to the south. There will be people of the Dominion there with dragon riders. Not many, but some. Or, we could try to disguise this dragon as an oosquer. One of the flying creatures of the Kav'ai. They're smaller. Grey. A bit ... ratty looking."

No, thank you! I am not ratty looking!

"That's a possibility," I said.

No. It is not.

If I needed to learn compassion, Saboraak was going to have to learn a little humility.

"Then we will travel to Ko'Loska. Where is it, exactly?" I kept my voice firm and even. No need to show them how uncertain I felt about all of this. If I was being honest with myself, I still thought turning back to Vanika would be best.

Not an option.

But I preferred lying to myself, anyway. It was usually easier than being honest with myself.

I could pretend to be a hero – at least for as long as it took to bring Zyla and Zin somewhere safe. Bataar could take care of himself, but I didn't like the way Zin's eyes seemed too large for her face. She didn't blink enough. It was like she'd seen something that she couldn't stop seeing even though it wasn't there anymore.

Zyla didn't quite roll her eyes but she looked like she was barely holding it back.

"Ko'Loska is northwest of here – in The Devil's Ribcage – a mountain range that rivals anything you've ever seen. The high deserts of Ko'Torenth start just north of that range."

I nodded as if I had any idea what 'high deserts' or mountain ranges looked like up close.

"Are you two about done?" Bataar asked. I didn't like the gleam in his eyes.

It might just be the firelight.

"We're just making plans."

Bataar stood up and started to kick out the fire. "If you're just about done making plans, then we need to hurry."

"Don't kick out the fire!" Zyla protested.

"The Magikas are a lot cleverer than you two," Bataar said. "I don't think those green lanterns are at the front of the group pursuing us. I think they're at the back."

A snap of a stick in the trees propelled me into action. I grabbed the items strewn over the ground - saddlebags, flint and striker, blankets – ignoring my pounding head, and began to stuff them into Saboraak's saddlebags. Why *was* my head pounding so much?

Do you remember being knocked unconscious by the pain when they tortured you?

I was trying very hard to forget.

Head injuries don't just go away.

"Come on," I said, turning to find Zyla right behind me. My turn brought us nose to nose. If I moved an inch forward, I could kiss her.

"Don't even think about it," she hissed, shoving her sister into my surprised arms. "Help Zin up. She rides in the front."

"That's my seat!" I protested as I helped Zin climb up the stirrups onto the front of Saboraak's saddle.

"Where are the reins?" Zyla demanded.

"Nowhere you can find them," I said. She grabbed my shoulder and began to scramble up into the saddle, her whole weight on my shoulder as if I was nothing more than a rock to climb all over. "Oof!"

That's exactly *how I feel! Four is too many.*

And Saboraak called *me* a whiner.

"Hurry!" Bataar demanded, following Zyla up into the saddle. He sat pressed tightly against her so that his legs wrapped right around Zyla's hips and still there wasn't room for me on the saddle.

With a sigh, I scrambled up awkwardly onto the saddlebags and sat between them. It was lumpy here and difficult to find anywhere that didn't hurt my tailbone.

"Everyone try to strap in," I said irritably. "They make these saddles with so many extra straps that there should be enough for three people to secure themselves."

"What about you?" Zyla asked in a sudden burst of consideration.

"There are baggage straps for him," Bataar said.

Oh yeah. Thanks, guy. I'll just strap in like a spare blanket, shall I?

I saw a glimmer of movement in the trees and then everything went green. My eyes widened at the fireball sailing right for my head. Even though I ducked, I knew it was too late.

So long, fair life. It was nice to live you.

Chapter Three

DON'T BE SO DRAMATIC!

Saboraak dodged the fireball and then scrambled over the rock. Her tail swung back and forth, and it felt as if we were almost out of control as we slid on her belly down the hillside, swiping trees as we went. Each jostle to her backside sent us all reeling back and forth like we were being shaken by a big dog.

You're too heavy!

I looked back to where the Magikas stood in the moonlight, my view careening wildly with our flight. I only saw snatches - one of them was standing on the log Zyla and Zin had been sitting on. He raised a hand and it bloomed with light. Others were racing in from the trees, shouting and gesturing.

We needed to get into the air and fast!

My heart was racing as I reached forward to brace myself.

"Keep your hands to yourself!" Bataar sure was jumpy!

Saboraak's powerful wings gave a flap and we jumped into the air a few feet before falling again. My teeth smashed together as the landing jarred me, triggering that awful headache. Pain and light ricocheted through my skull. Ugh! How could a man stay upright with so much pain in his head? I gripped the saddlebags with all my might, hoping Saboraak could launch in the next flap.

There was a yell from the Magikas. "On my count! Three ..."

Saboraak tried to lift again, her wings beating at the muddy ground as she fought for lift. We slid further down the hill, but her belly never left the earth. She was panting so loudly that I could hear it and now I was starting to worry ...

"Two ... "

Come on Saboraak, you can do this! Come on, you old girl!

"One!"

Five fireballs launched toward us at once. Magenta, green, and fuchsia, searing through the night sky like a celebration of Spring.

Saboraak twisted jarringly and just when I thought my spine might have snapped from the sudden movement, we were tumbling forward again. Has she lost her grip on the hill?

A fireball splashed on the ground behind us – a little faster than the others. One of the larger sparks hit Saboraak's tail and she hissed so loudly, it sounded like opening up a furnace.

Her mighty wings flapped and her tail seemed to push off on the rocks and then we were bobbing into the air, the fireballs splashing uselessly in the ground where we had been.

Got it! There's a trick to taking off with four people!

Our flight was erratic, up and down, left then right, as if Saboraak was struggling to gain enough height to get over the trees. And then we were up! Her feet scraped the top of a spindly pine, but a moment later we were bobbing above the forest.

I breathed a sigh of relief.

I'm not old, by the way. I'm not your 'old girl.'

Of course not. She was anything she wanted to be – especially if that thing could fly just a little faster.

I do appreciate your confidence in my ability to do the impossible.

Just keep doing the impossible, Saboraak. That's all I ask.

Trying. You guys really are heavy. Are you sure you need all that bread?

I rolled my eyes, but I felt warmth rising up in my chest. Saboraak had just risked her life to save us – and I kind of felt that she probably would have done that for just me.

You're my human as much as I'm your dragon.

Well, stick with me and we'll keep pulling ourselves out of impossible situations.

Is that a promise?

Sure. I was getting good at surviving deadly situations. Maybe that could rub off on her. I felt heady and confident up here in the air with the wind in my hair.

That's called an updraft.

And Magika fireballs falling uselessly beneath us made me feel even better. For people with magical fire ability, they sure were useless in a fight.

You only say that because we escaped. If they'd hit you with one and burned you alive with that sticky fire, you wouldn't be so confident. The others are scared out of their wits. I can hear their hearts pounding and their breathing coming way too quick.

I wasn't scared.

You should be. This is scary stuff. Look! They lit the forest on fire. They're like hatchlings who haven't been fire-trained!

She was right. Below us, orange flames licked up along the edges of the pine forest where we had been a moment before. It was only a few trees, but a fire like that could spread fast.

The wind is not in our favor. It blows west and we are headed northwest. It speeds our journey, but the fire could easily spread northwest and follow us.

Let's hope it doesn't come to that.

"Tor?" Zyla asked from the front of the dragon.

"Yeah?"

"Do you think they can follow us?"

"They don't have dragons," Bataar said arrogantly. "Not like us. We are in a superior position."

I wasn't so sure. They didn't have dragons, but Saboraak couldn't keep this up for long, and now there was a forest fire to worry about. I didn't like fires. They still filled my nightmares almost every night.

I know.

How did she know?

I heard them the last time you slept.

She could hear my nightmares? Ugh.

Don't be so bashful. We have a special kind of relationship. With it comes a predictable intimacy.

Intimacy? She was making my skin crawl. Why couldn't I have had a boy dragon like everyone else? I bet he wouldn't use a word like 'intimacy.'

Most certainly not. But he also wouldn't have my kind of patience for your shenanigans.

Zyla spoke again, her voice raised to be heard over the wind. "I'm just wondering, how far can the dragon take us?"

"Her name is Saboraak," I responded. They should call her by name. She deserved that.

Thank you.

"How far can Saboraak take us before she needs to rest?"

I didn't even want to think about that. Not yet.

At most, I can fly like this for a few hours. I see the foothills of the Devil's ribcage up ahead. I might be able to make it that far.

I couldn't see anything in this dark except the people I was traveling with.

Trust me.

"A few hours, maybe," I said.

"And when we land, can we sleep? I'm not asking for myself," she said hurriedly. "But it's been a while since Zin had a rest and she needs it."

I looked anxiously at the fire behind us. I could see the glow of that still. It wasn't that big. Maybe it would just burn out.

"Of course," I said absently. After all, who cared what I said? I wasn't in charge of their lives.

But I watched the glow behind us anxiously as we flew. It wasn't getting bigger ... was it?

Chapter Four

SABORAAK FLEW FOR AS long as she could – about three hours by my guess. I watched that forest fire swell through the entire night. With every passing moment, I felt my own anxiety rising, bubbling up like boiling tar and occasionally bursting in a quick-breathing fear before I brought it under control. I kept seeing visions of Saboraak tiring and of setting down only to be unable to rise again and then of the flames coming and swallowing us up.

I do *have to set down. I am too tired to go on. But those flames are far away and panicking about them won't make things any easier for you.*

I scowled. I wasn't panicking.

What would you call those little breathing attacks?

Realism.

Get a grip. Zin is asleep. Zyla is holding her in the saddle. They need rest and so do I.

I really wasn't panicking.

The moment Saboraak's feet hit the ground, I loosened my straps and leapt off her back. The ground was rocky and uneven, and I nearly twisted an ankle.

Remember when I told you to look before you leap?

I rolled my eyes.

But it's good that you have lots of energy. You have an important job.

I sure did. I needed something to eat and then a nice long sleep.

No. I need to sleep so I can fly us again in a few hours. I'm going into a deep recovery sleep. It will heal my wounds and rest me enough to be able to carry four people again. That means it's up to you to keep watch for enemies and to wake me if there's trouble.

What would she do if there was trouble?

Bataar slowly dismounted as we were communicating, dragging the saddlebags down after him.

Flame it, obviously.

You didn't flame the Magikas back there!

I didn't want to start a forest fire.

Well, nice work. There's one anyway.

I was busy trying to fly with four people on my back!

You could have bought us some time!

"I'm not building a fire this time. I'm just going to curl up in a blanket and go to sleep," Bataar said sleepily. "Don't wake me unless we're under attack."

"Can I get a hand here?" Zyla asked and I rushed to help her. She could twist an ankle if she got down too quickly. She needed to be careful. "Zin fell asleep. Here. Help me lift her down."

"There are only two blankets here," Bataar said from where he was squatting over the saddlebags.

"Well, excuse me for not anticipating the need to provide for you," I said irritably.

"Zin and I will share one," Zyla said as I helped her carry her sister to a flat area near where Bataar had arranged the saddlebags.

We laid her down and Zyla took the offered blanket, covering her sister and then snuggling in under the blanket with her. The ground was damp. No one was going to be very comfortable. I noticed Saboraak move a little closer to the girls, bringing the heat she gave off a little closer.

"I get the other blanket," Bataar said.

My eyes narrowed. Maybe he should keep the blanket. We didn't need to fly with four people. We could fly with three and go a lot farther. He could use the blanket to keep warm while he hiked through the mountains.

Tor?

I was surprised by how vulnerable my big dragon sounded. I spun to look at her. Was she okay?

I have something to admit.

Was that all? Girls! They were so dramatic.

I don't like killing people. That's why I didn't flame the Magikas back there. I ... I don't like it.

I frowned, but inside I felt a burst of affection for her. She was really too soft-hearted to be a dragon. Go to sleep, Saboraak.

Goodnight.

There were already snores from where Bataar was huddled under his blanket. Of course. He stole my blanket and now he was sleeping like a baby. The other blanket was still and motionless, too. I saw the tip of Zyla's nose peeping out of the blanket. I sighed. and the nose twitched. I'd better stop sighing. I didn't want to keep her awake.

But now that everyone was quiet and motionless, exhaustion began to creep over me. I yawned, letting my eyes drift over the hillside we were camped on. The rocks were so large where they peeked out of the hillside – as large as dragons – that it would be nearly impossible to see if anyone was coming. I'd have to keep a close watch.

I fished some bread out of the saddlebags and began to eat. Only to keep myself awake, of course. My stomach rumbled the moment I smelled the bread and it took everything I had just to eat slowly and prolong the moments. Minutes dragged like hours. The cold damp had crept into my bones, making them feel brittle and sore.

I alternated between sitting and standing, stomping my feet to get them warm and looking often at the pendant Ephretti gave me. It seemed to catch the moonlight in a strange way, reflecting back on me. I even pulled out the small book Hubric had given me and flipped through it. I couldn't make out the words by the light of the moon, but there seemed to be drawings, too. Sketches and maps. I would have to look at them better later. I tucked the book in an inner pocket of my trousers. I didn't want to lose it any more than the pendant. I didn't own much, so what I owned was precious.

The cold bit at me, leaving my breath in wispy clouds and clinging to any exposed skin so that I huddled deeper and deeper into the cloak.

It wasn't like I hadn't slept in the cold before, though now I couldn't sleep at all. That figured. Tor has to come up with the plans and do all the work, but then he doesn't get to sleep. Oh no, Tor gets to stand out in the flaming cold and freeze.

I circled the camp, letting those thoughts stew as I looked at the scraggly bushes surrounding us. The trees had petered out leaving hard, leafless bushes and scattered tufts of grass. This place was mostly made of loose stone and dirt. What a miserable land. No wonder it wasn't part of the Dominion. We had proper dirt for growing things back home, and proper trees that could make a fire. I couldn't even see enough trees to find firewood here.

I kept watching for the forest fire, but it was still only a far-away glow on the horizon. It had better stay like that.

My circles grew larger and larger. Moving helped. It kept me warm and awake, though my mind wandered a bit from tiredness.

It didn't really matter, did it? As long as I kept the others in sight – or at least sort of in sight. They disappeared when I went around the larger rocks and then reappeared again when I made my way around the obstacles. That was what you did as a guard, right? You guarded things. And with these larger and larger circles, no one could sneak in and surprise us.

My circling was closer to the camp when I was above it on the hillside. The slope was too steep there to climb far without resorting to hands and knees – which I was not going to do – but when my circle reached the point below the camp, I found it widening and widening.

The rock formations and bushes were interesting, and I might even find a creek if I looked hard enough. It beat sitting around the camp listening to everyone else snoring or mumbling in their sleep – Zin did that, though her words were too muddled to be understood.

It was on a particularly wide arc below the camp, that I stumbled across a narrow opening between two dragon-large rocks. The roots and deadfall above them were so tangled that I hadn't been able to look down behind the rocks from above, but this crevice between the two rocks was almost like a door.

I shouldn't go in the crevice. Even with my brain this tired, I knew that. I shouldn't even be this far away from camp. I was supposed to be guarding the others, and I was getting too far away from them.

And yet ... there was something about that little hole in the rocks that longed to be investigated. Maybe, if I just lit a torch and held it in the crevice, it would be enough to satisfy my curiosity.

I grabbed a likely looking bush, cursing when ripping it out of the ground tore my skin. Who would have known that the trunk of it was lined with talon-like thorns?

It was dry as the inside of my mouth and twice as dusty. Maybe there would be a well or a spring in those rocks. I'd heard of water coming out of rocks in dry places.

It was long minutes before I managed to really light the shrub. I had two others ready in my free hand. When this one burned down, I could light the next and then the next. I didn't admit that I was planning to enter the rock crevice until I was jamming my body through and wishing I'd eaten less bread.

Chapter Five

I DIDN'T NEED TO LIGHT those torches.

That was the first thing I thought when I squeezed my way through the crevice and into the space beyond. But anyone could have been forgiven for not expecting this.

Someone, a long time ago, had been very clever.

They had laid out a dais and then put a door? Arch? A something like a door at the top of it. And then, cleverly, they had laid mirrors out around the dais and they reflected the moonlight back and forth, amplifying it so that this little, hidden space was almost as bright as day.

How did they get all this past that narrow crevice in the rock? And what kind of thing is so important that you would go to all this trouble to hide it after you built it?

I yelped. Pain shot up my hand and I dropped the branch. I'd forgotten about the licking flames in my wonder at the cavern.

How had this place come to be covered by deadfall? I squinted up at the roof. Was that a wide mesh net that covered the ceiling? It was hard to make out with all the light below, but I thought that perhaps whoever had put this dais here had covered it with that net.

Those super clever people had a secret. And I just found it.

Excitement filled me. After all, people only hid valuable things, right? They didn't hide things they thought were worthless. This was going to turn out to be amazing! I just needed to follow their lead and find whatever treasure they had here.

I took a step forward, cursing when I kicked a rock.

"Skies and Stars!"

It was a rock, alright, but more of a marker stone than a random rock. Something was written on it, but the writing was filled with moss and worn by time. Either that, or it never meant anything at all, and I was just imagining it as writing. No one hid treasure in rocks anyway.

I shrugged and hurried to the stairs leading up the dais.

No one had been here in a long time - or at least, that was the impression I was getting from the dust and woody debris that lined the stairs to the dais. Had people forgotten about this place? Maybe its creators had hidden it too well.

Whoever had built it must love stairs. I was twenty stairs up and my legs were starting to ache before I reached the top of the dais. The crumbling rock of the floor was arranged in a mosaic pattern so that the floor looked like a rising sun. In the center of the sun, the strange empty doorway stood. It was large enough for a dragon to walk through – if a dragon ever wanted to walk through a door to nowhere.

It was difficult to make out fine detail, despite the light from the mirrors, so I stepped in close, looking at the frame. It was shaped like an arch and the stones that formed the doorway fit together so tightly and were cut so precisely that it was hard to make out where one stone ended, and another began. On each stone, symbols were carved. I squinted, trying to make them out. One looked like a stylized sword, another like a tongue of fire, a third like a blowing wind.

I circled the doorway, looking at it from all angles. It seemed normal enough. I could see through it to the other side, no matter what side I stood on. Why build a doorway to nowhere?

I tilted my head to one side. I liked puzzles and I was bored. Maybe there was a way to make this door into more than just a door. Maybe it had to do with the symbols in the frame. I reached toward the nearest one, but a strange chill washed over me and I froze.

What was that feeling? It felt as if every hair on my arms were standing up straight. I swallowed. Maybe I should take my time and choose my symbol more carefully.

There were many to choose from - at least twenty. It made it hard to pick one, but as my eyes ran over them again and again, I kept being drawn back to one that looked like swirling smoke rising upward.

Well, I could stand here all day, or I could do something. I reached for the smoke symbol, letting my hand trace over the carved surface of it. I felt icy chills run up my fingers and into the bones of my arm - but that was it.

I'd been wrong about the symbols, I guessed. Oh, look! There was another smoke symbol. With my other hand, I reached out and touched it, too. I could reach them both at once but touching them both didn't do anything. Too bad. I'd hoped it would open a secret compartment or something. A freezing burn suddenly shot up both my arms. It swirled around them, filling them with icy pain.

I pulled my fingers back and the pain subsided.

Skies and stars! Was this some kind of torture device? If it was, then no thank you! No wonder they hid it down here! Someone should smash those mirrors so that no one ever found it.

I should be getting back, anyway. I should be guarding the camp.

I stepped forward, planning to walk through the gate and down the stairs, but as I stepped, my foot disappeared, and a wave of heat washed over me. It was as if the doorway had eaten it up. I pulled my foot back before I'd even completed the step, my heart racing and almost melted with relief when it came back whole and fine.

I should try an arm. I plunged my arm through and watched it disappear with the same wave of heat, counted down from five and then drew it back. I had felt nothing strange except for that wave of heat. Strange. Was my arm okay?

I rolled up my sleeve and gasped. A swirling symbol identical to the smoke symbol on the doorframe marked my arm in a silver pattern. I scrubbed at the skin, trying to smear or remove it. Was that from dipping my arm through the door? Nothing. It was as if the design was part of my skin now.

Anxiously, I rolled up my other sleeve. My jaw dropped. My eyes widened so far that tears formed. The same silver design wrapped itself around that arm, too.

I was marked.

Not by going through the arch, but by touching the door. What would happen if I touched any other symbols? No, no, slow down, Tor! No more touching things that left permanent marks.

I took a deep breath. Well, while I was here, I should do one more thing. I should stick my head through that door. Then I could see what was on the other side. But I had to be sure I could come back. What if I stepped all the way through and the door - or whatever it was - closed behind me?

My mind filled with worse scenarios. What if I couldn't breathe on that side? What if nothing on that side existed and if I plunged my head through, I wouldn't have a brain to tell my body to pull back?

I'd just have to risk it. If I didn't, then I'd spend the next days and months - maybe even years! - wondering what could have been behind this door. I swallowed and leaned forward, closing my eyes and my head slowly pushed through a fiery burst of heat. It was still burning around my neck when I opened my eyes. I gasped and nearly fell backward before I remembered that my feet were on solid ground, but my belly reeled, queasiness filling me.

The other side of the arch opened on the side of a mountain and under the edge of the doorway was nothing but a sudden drop down the side of a snow-coated mountain into nothing at all.

Chapter Six

ONLY AN IDIOT WOULD jump off a cliff.

I stumbled backward, falling to my backside and scrambling backward across the dusty dais until I could get my breathing under control. A few minutes later, I pulled myself to my feet.

This had been a mistake.

I would just go back to camp and finish guarding everyone and pretend this never happened. I could be dreaming, anyway. After all, I was very tired, and I hadn't slept.

I scrambled up, dusting myself off, and carefully maneuvered around the door. The key thing was to stay as far away from that flaming door as possible. If I just watched my step and stayed far away, then ... that's right. Just like that!

Only heroes messed with magical doorways, and I was no hero.

I eased my way around the dais, almost sneaking as I carefully took each stair to the ground. I didn't breathe again until I had squeezed through the crack in the rock and back to the night beyond.

I leaned against the rock, closing my eyes for a moment. No real harm done. My sleeves covered those silver markings, and who knew, maybe they would wash off later. Or maybe they were just my imagination or a trick of the eyes.

I started to climb back up the hill toward camp when a cracking sound arrested me.

I froze.

What was that?

After a moment, when nothing else happened, I started to climb again.

The moon hadn't moved, and the air was still cold. I couldn't have been gone from camp for long. I was just jumpy and nervous after my close brush with disaster.

But now worry gnawed at me. I was supposed to be standing guard over my friends and I'd wandered off.

But guard against what? There hadn't been anything there to worry about. The Magikas were far away and the fires - even if they had grown - would still be hours away.

There was nothing to worry about.

A scream pierced the night.

Was that Zyla? I increased my pace, tripping over a log and catching myself at the last second. My dagger was in my belt – I was smarter this time about remembering to carry it. But what good did that do in the dark and so far from whatever was happening?

A second scream made me leap forward, running up the hill now, ignoring the scratching and clawing of the rough bushes and shrubs. What was happening?

Where are you?

Saboraak! Uh oh. She was supposed to be sleeping.

You were supposed to be standing watch!

Well, I had been standing watch until I got too bored. What was happening up there?

I rounded a rock and gasped.

Small fires ringed my friends, as if someone had lit the nearby bushes into fiery torches. Saboraak squatted low on the ground, neck extended and at that moment, I noticed the dark shadows in the bushes. She flamed wildly, her head swaying back and forth as her fire surged toward the shadows. Beside her, Bataar crouched as if he was waiting to fight, too. Where were the girls?

Who are these people?

How should I know who they are?

I woke up to the attack. They were already here!

There was a shuffle in the bushes beside me and then a blast of green light lanced toward my friends. The light of the burst lit the face of a man who fired it. He was standing only one rock over from where I crouched. He held out a metal device about the size of my palm, shaped like a metal spider, its legs reaching outward. His hand fit into the spider, like it was made to be held that way.

He was focused on my friends. He didn't know I was here ...

We're surrounded and they're closing in.

They were completely distracted by Saboraak ...

Hurry!

I was sick of them turning these weird devices on us. I was sick of not knowing what they were or how they did what they did. I slid slowly towards him, clinging to the shadows as orange and green flames danced in front of us. No one knew I was here ...

There's no more time!

The figures in the shadows were closing in on Saboraak. I watched as a bolt of lightning burst from the perimeter and struck Bataar's leg. He slumped to the side, but Zyla reached down from Saboraak's saddle, grabbing his hand and yanking him back upright. She was trying to pull him up the side of the dragon.

No sudden moves, Tor. Ease your way along. I was so close ...

A twig snapped, and my quarry spun, raising the spider-device, his eyes widening in the flickering orange and green light.

I leapt forward with all the speed of my youth and fearlessness, grabbing the spider with both hands and twisting as I rolled to the side. I heard a cracking sound and a yelp, but in the dark it was hard to see clearly.

We were both on the ground, rolling over dirt and rock. I pulled my arms down. Raised a foot. Found his wrist. Shoved it as hard as I could with my foot while I pulled with my hands. For a moment we were motionless as muscle fought muscle and then his grip broke and I tumbled away, spider in hand.

Success!

If you make me wait five more seconds, I am leaving without you! One.

I scrambled to my feet, running almost before I was upright.

Two.

I saw a burst of lighting arching toward me and leapt over it, feet barely gaining enough height to dodge the bolt.

Shouts filled the air and with them came the snapping, sizzling feeling of lightning all around me.

Three.

I leapt over a slumped body on the ground. How did that get there?

Four.

Dodged a green fireball. I'm telling you, those things are useless!

Five.

I'm here!

My hand smacked her side playfully as I threw a foot into the stirrup. Bataar was slumped between Zin and Zyla, his head lolling to one side, but they were all strapped in.

We were in the air before I was the rest of the way on Saboraak's back, gaining height as I hung from one stirrup.

Serves you right for wasting time and getting Bataar hurt.

She was getting better at these four-person launches.

I told you there was a trick to them.

Uh oh.

What?

Was there another dragon out there?

Chapter Seven

I DON'T SENSE ANYONE...

Well, something was moving in the sky and it wasn't the fireball that Saboraak just dodged.

I didn't dodge it well. It hit my foot.

It's surprising they hit anything at all. Those things are terribly inaccurate.

It hurt! You can be flippant about it when it's your foot!

Look! There it was again, something rising in the sky.

"Do you see that?" Zyla called down to me.

"It's not a dragon," I called back. "I don't know what it is."

Now that we were gaining height, I could see that the flames had spread. The forest fire was working its way toward us, leaping from one clump of bushes to the next. It would be here by morning.

Magikas combed the foothill we had camped on waiting to launch inaccurate bursts of magic on anything that moved.

I think they were camped on the other side of the hill. They were there all along. I'm surprised you didn't notice them sooner. You were keeping watch, right?

Was my face flushing? It felt hot suddenly.

"That's a rug!" Zyla called down. "Are those Magikas sitting on it?"

Impossible! Rugs didn't fly!

It is a rug. And there are two more. I don't know how fast those things are, but I'm slow with you four on my back.

"They're blocking our route northwest!" Zyla called. "Can your dragon outmaneuver them?"

The nearest carpet crackled with light and then the Magika at the front of it – was that the front? – lifted his hands and lightning shot toward us. Saboraak shuddered.

That hurt!

Quick! Fly down the hill from our camp until you see a cluster of rock with a bunch of deadfall at the center.

What? That's heading towards danger! I won't do it. I've never been hurt so many times as since I met you. I need to stay with the Whites for a month!

Listen to me! I have a plan!

Your plans always involve ridiculous risks!

My arm was getting sore holding the strap and dangling from the stirrup and her last dodge had left me flapping in the wind in a way I didn't even like to think of. Worse, that Magika was lifting his lightning-hands again. How could I get Saborak to trust me?

Ask!

Trust me!

I felt her mental sigh.

Where are these rocks?

A second flash of lightning crackled toward us and Saboraak swung wildly. I couldn't prevent a very unmanly screech as the stirrup swung outward and my grip slid a hand's width down the strap I was clutching.

Skies and stars! I can do the flying, but I can't hold on for you, too. Take some responsibility – for your own life, if nothing else!

Demanding, arrogant, self-righteous dragon!

Silly boy!

There it was! I could see the heaps of deadwood below me. I wouldn't be able to get a dragon into the crack in the rock, but if she burned through that wood ...

She was flaming before I explained my idea, her steady stream of yellow-hot flame ripping through fallen logs, rotting branches, and dead leaves. After a moment, the netting below gave way and the deadfall dropped in a free-fall of burning wood, popping sparks, and wet debris.

Follow it down!

Saboraak dove and I gritted my teeth as the stirrup followed her movements. It felt like I was falling, too.

You sent me down a dead end!

Go through the door!

"What is this place?" Zyla asked from up in the saddle. She had her hands full keeping Bataar and Zin safely in place. As usual, Zin didn't seem to even know where she was. And Zyla had to push and pull her and the unconscious Bataar back into place every time Saboraak moved.

We needed to find a place to get these two some help before they dragged us down so far we never recovered.

Lightning hit the rock wall beside us as Saboraak made a wobbling landing on the edge of the dais. I glanced upward and fought the instinct to duck as I saw three rectangles blocking the bright moonlight above. How many of those carpets did they have?

"We're getting out!" I called to Zyla. "Hold on tight!"

Trapped!

Just go through the flaming arch!

It's not flaming. It's made of stone.

Flaming is a curse word you dense, flaming dragon!

I think your language gets worse under stress. And for the record, I object to your choice of curse. I 'flame' things and you benefit from that.

Just go through the door!

The rectangles were getting bigger as they descended, lighting crackling down from them and striking the dais around us. If she didn't hurry, we were going to get hit any time now...

It's going to be tight! Hang on!

Saboraak crept forward and I tried not to gasp as her head and shoulders disappeared. Zyla made a strangled sound in her throat but her expression was determined. She forced Zin and Bataar's heads down, so they wouldn't hit the top of the door.

I finally did gasp as they went through into oblivion and then I moaned as the doorframe scraped across my back. Agh! I was going to come loose! I redoubled my grip, pressing my face into Saboraak's side and hoping we could squeeze through. The breath was knocked out of me and I felt as though I was being wrung of every drop of blood and then burning pain washed over me followed by an icy burst of wind.

We were through!

Almost.

Pain struck my heel and I reeled from it, my body temporarily frozen and my grip on the leather strap loosening for just a second. A second was too much.

I fell away from Saboraak's side.

Chapter Eight

I WAS YANKED BACK – suddenly – by my cloak around my throat. I fought for a strangled breath as my hand fumbled for the strap again. There! I grabbed it with both hands and the pressure on my throat eased.

"Almost lost you there," Zyla said from above me. Her face was pale. She must have amazing reflexes to have caught me so quickly.

Saboraak spun and dove suddenly, her neck arching around and her jaws snapping at something below us.

Do you still want this spidery thing?

Yes! Wait – why didn't you grab me when I was falling?

Zyla is a very capable woman. She didn't need my help.

My heel was throbbing painfully. I had a bad feeling that the burn was severe.

Don't be a baby. You didn't let me whine about my burnt foot.

Skies and stars, it flaming hurt!

Language!

I looked down, trying to distract myself, and then immediately regretted it.

Oh.

Oh.

Oh.

We were very high up.

Maybe my shortness of breath wasn't just from being strangled by my own cloak. Icy air bit into every inch of my skin from hair to that flaming heel.

I give up. Just remember. Words shape us. The ones we use shape the way we see the world and what we value and those things shape our very souls.

It was just a word. A useful word for channeling anger and frustration.

And your soul is just your soul. But it's the only one you get. Guard it well.

Beneath us – far beneath us – white plains lapped at the edge of the mountains and a hazy blue and white horizon drifted off to the wide expanse beyond. But up here we flew between the peaks of a delicate crown of mountains. There must be a hundred peaks – their tops craggy and white with snow. The nearest three seemed to be smoking. I squinted at them through light-blinded eyes. The rising sun glittered diamond-bright off the white-crusted shards of mountaintop.

"Legendary Ko'Koren," Zyla breathed from above me.

"I thought we were going to Ko'Loska," I said. But none of us had bargained for that arch, had we?

"We were," Zyla agreed. "But this is even better. I know someone here who will hide us and send word to Hubric on our behalf. The further we penetrate into the depths of Ko'Torenth, the better, and it will be easier to hide a dragon here. Ko'Koren is the heart of Ko'Torenth culture, a city known for arts and trade. There will be visiting Dominion dragons here, sentries from Baojang, oosquer of the Kav'ai and adelini of the Westlands. Saboraak can hide among them."

I swallowed.

A city.

A huge city to be learned and conquered. I would plunder her secrets. I couldn't keep the excitement out of my mind any more than I could keep my lungs from burning in the cold. I leaned in close to Saboraak, trying to absorb her heat.

There was a cry from behind us and I looked back. On the mountainside behind us, I could still make out the small doorway on the edge of the cliff, at the very peak of the mountain. A carpet loaded with Magikas was crossing through – but whatever they used to fly it failed as it rolled through the doorway. It crumpled, a normal carpet once again, leaving its cargo to fall to earth. The Magikas fell, looking like tiny specks as they disappeared into the blue haze below.

I swallowed down bile and looked up at Zyla. Her face was green.

"Which of those mountains is the city?" I asked faintly. All three peaks were smoking – from fires, I guessed now. And all three had structures clinging to them, like barnacles on a rock. I'd seen a sea-rock with barnacles being sold as an oddity in Vanika once.

"All three," Zyla said, her voice shaking. We didn't turn around when the second set of screams began. We didn't want to see that. After all, we couldn't stop it and we couldn't catch them even if we wanted to.

I can barely carry four. Don't ask me to do more.

I wasn't asking. Boy, she was touchy.

It's my conscience. I don't do well with needless death. There should *be something I can do.*

Why? It wasn't her responsibility. We could only be responsible for ourselves. And even then, well, accidents happened.

Compassion means taking responsibility for all other people.

Ugh. That sounded awful.

It will make you a fuller person.

Or a deader person. No one could live like that.

I disagree.

I sighed. "Which peak should we aim for, Zyla?"

"The closest one." Her voice was very certain. "That's Eski. The other two are Ziu and Balde. The three peaks of Ko'Koren."

"Is that where your contact is?"

"No. It's the closest place to not freezing to death, which I think should be our main priority right now."

Agreed.

"Is your dragon slowing down?" she asked.

Yes. The cold makes it hard to fly.

Skies and flaming stars! Out of one mess and into another!

I warned you about your language!

Chapter Nine

"WE SHOULD STOP OFF somewhere quickly along the way and pull on that Kav'ai clothing," Zyla said after long minutes.

"Why?" I asked. "If there are people of the Dominion here, and Saboraak can't change anything but her color, then why change what we are wearing?"

"If she stays a pale grey and we cover the front of her head, and if we sneak through a back way into the city so that no one gets a good look, she can pass as an oosquer."

"I still don't know what those are."

"They're hard to explain. Ask the dragon if she would please set down on a mountainside - if she can."

There's nowhere to set down and I need to take the shortest route to the city. I'm worried I can't fly even that far. Can you put on your disguises while we fly?

"She says we'll have to get dressed on here," I said.

Zyla sighed. "Then you're going to have to climb up behind me. I can't reach into those saddlebags and hold these two in place at the same time. Bataar's not doing well. He's going to need a sickbed when we arrive."

Scrambling up onto the back of a dragon from the stirrup while she's flapping like an eagle with a tick burrowing in his neck was no easy matter. To my embarrassment, I needed help from Zyla.

"Grab me around the waist, it's the only way you'll be able to get your leg up."

I tried to reach for a far strap. I really shouldn't be grabbing her waist or any other part of her. Especially not when that waist looked like the absolute perfect size for my hands. I swallowed.

"Stop being so thick-headed and just do it," Zyla insisted.

I lifted my leg up behind her, wiggling to try to reach it further, but I really did need to hold on to something if I was going to swing up on to the saddlebags behind her. She sighed, shifting Bataar to one arm and then grabbing my wrist with her other hand. She planted it on her far hip.

"Grip here and use it for leverage!"

I felt my cheeks growing hot – far too hot in this frigid, icy air.

Even I can feel the blood rushing to your head. Cool down, Tor. You're climbing a flying dragon, not asking a girl to dance.

I didn't know of any dances that would end with me tucked in so close and with my hand on her hip.

Don't humans have any fun?

Surprise distracted me for just long enough that my muscles worked on their own. I slid into place and then pulled my hand back like it had been bitten. It still felt warm from her touch. Maybe one day ...

Just find what we're looking for in those saddle bags! We'll worry about your mating dance later.

No one said anything about a mating dance! Now my cheeks were throbbing from blushing so hard.

What kind of dance were you thinking about, then?

A social dance! People danced in the city square on Sata Day and High Spring.

Dragons only have one kind of dance.

Earth swallow me! I wasn't safe from women anywhere!

I fumbled in the saddlebag and pulled out the over-stuffed satchel.

"I'm surprised you all remembered to gather this in the excitement," I said, reaching into it to pull out a loose hooded tunic, heavily embroidered and woven of a coarse fabric.

"We didn't leave anything behind," Zyla said, turning to look at the tunic. When she looked down her dark eyelashes looked longer than usual and when she looked back up, they shaded her cat-like eyes in a way that made me swallow all over again.

"Is this for you or me?" I asked.

"It would be best on Zin. If I dress her as a Zyvaar, no one will ask any questions if she doesn't speak. Here. Pass it to me."

"What's a Zyvaar?"

"One of the silent practitioners of the Kav'ai ceremonies," Zyla answered. "Here, Zin, wear this."

Her sister obeyed silently, looking off into the distance as if she hadn't heard at all, even though she was complying.

"What's wrong with her?" I asked. I needed to know and there was no delicate way to ask. If we were going to sneak into this city, then we had to plan around ... whatever.

"Nothing," Zyla snapped.

"Can 'nothing' be healed?" I pressed.

"No."

"Can it be reasoned with?"

She made an exasperated sound in her throat. "Listen, boy. I don't have answers to all your questions. I was in that house where Hubric left me when I was surprised by those ruffians who call themselves Magikas. They hauled me off to the camp you found me in. I was there for one day before you showed up and your dragon saved us."

Someone knows who to credit.

"That's where I found Zin. I thought she was dead with my parents. So, I don't have answers to all your questions – or any of them, really. Zin will talk when she's ready."

"She's not even talking to you?"

"She'll talk when she's ready!" Zyla's voice had a snap to it that made me think of a whip cracking. "Now, reach into that satchel and see what else there is."

I reached in.

"A leather harness."

"With a wide piece of leather at the center?"

"Yes."

"We'll use that to disguise Saboraak. What else?"

"An embroidered scarf. It's kind of filmy." I said. I felt weird doing this with her. "How do we sneak into the city?"

"The scarf is for me." She took it and wound it around her head and face, so I could see nothing but those mesmerizing eyes. "And it should be easy to sneak in. The Festival of Lights started yesterday, and it will go all week. Everyone will be distracted by the feasting and parades. We won't interest anyone. We'll fly in from the craggier side of Eski and try one of the smaller entrances."

"We're flying a dragon. We don't need to go in through a gate," I objected, pulling from the satchel a wide embroidered belt with a sparkling silver buckle and a long leather strap with feathers sewn along it.

"We do if we don't want the city guard searching for us. All visitors pass through a city gate or don't pass at all. We'll find an inn there and lie low until I can meet my contact. And that belt is for you. The leather band is looped around your forehead four times and then tied."

"Like Bataar's?"

"He's dressed like Kav'ai, isn't he?" She sounded impatient.

"How should I know?"

She turned to gape at me. "You didn't know?"

"Of course not!"

"Then why did you agree to help him? How did you know he would be on our side?"

"It seemed like a good idea at the time. Why would a Kav'ai be on our side."

The look of fury on her face was only overshadowed by shock. "You mush-headed, sewer-dwelling, think-with-the-hair-on-your-chest ..."

Had she run out of insults?

"What?" I asked, letting my eyes go wide so I would look innocent. She was alive and out of the hands of Magikas and so was her sister. What more did she want?

She took a long breath. "You need to learn to think before you act."

"If I did that, we'd still be fleeing from a forest fire and a bunch of guys on flying rugs. Instead, we're on our way to a Festival." I gave a bright – albeit false – smile. Maybe she could be distracted.

Zyla rolled her eyes. "The Kav'ai hate Magikas. They found Bataar trying to sneak into the Dominion and snatched him up. They were hoping to get information about the rumors of Kav'ai magic. Everyone is saying they have an alternate source of power – one the Magikas are desperate for. I thought you knew that."

The city was growing closer and I focused on it instead of on her accusing eyes. Anyone could have made the same decision I did. After all, I needed an ally at the time, and Saboraak had insisted on Bataar.

Don't drag me into this.

"So," I said eventually, "what you're saying is that Bataar doesn't need any more disguise than what he has."

Zyla sighed so loudly that I was sure it was meant for me to hear. "Just listen to me from now on, okay?"

Like I was going to promise that! I did what I thought was best, not what other people told me was best. Let their decisions kill or beggar them. That was their business. I looked out for me and I made decisions that kept me alive, and that was that.

I huddled against the cold, doing my best not to touch Zyla despite the tight squeeze on Saborrak's back. My heel throbbed uncomfortably. She was busy trying to get the headpiece to fit my dragon while Saboraak flew, and both of them were too occupied with that – a nearly impossible task – to berate me. For now.

I crossed my arms. I never signed up to work with a bunch of girls who always thought I was the one to blame for everything. Shouldn't they be glad to have me around? I'd saved both of their bacon more than once now. That doorway trick was ingenious.

Ahead of me, the city grew closer and closer. It didn't sprawl so much as climb. Who thought it was a good idea to build a city on an almost vertical mountainside?

The buildings clung to the sides of the rock like nesting cliff swallows. Spiraling stairs and steep ladders led from building to building and formed soaring bridges from cleft to cleft.

The buildings almost looked like tiny sculptures of the mountains. Their roofs were peaked and so steep that they were far higher than they were wide with round windows and many struts keeping the buildings in place along the steep mountainsides.

Scores of people filled the ladder-and-stairs streets and narrow boardwalks between buildings, many of them carrying something that smoked in their hands. My feet were already itching to explore a new city. Would it be like Vanika with hidden spots only a few knew about? Could there be secret trade, and back alleys, and underground business in a place like this?

I couldn't wait to find out.

"Here's the gate," Zyla said briskly. "Remember, let me do the talking."

Chapter Ten

THE 'GATE' - IF THAT was what it was - was three times as tall as it was wide, but four different boardwalks passed through it – two on one level and two beneath them, not quite parallel, but squeezing through the structure. Two guards were posted at each boardwalk, looking outward and stopping each person to note their names in a logbook.

Stairs climbing from below or descending from above or winding up in spirals led to the boardwalks and where they surged through the gates they were straight and flat. Everywhere else they were more vertical than horizontal.

My eyes stung from opening so wide. I wanted to see everything at once. I'd lived in Vanika while it was still a skycity. I shouldn't be impressed by this – but I was. I was imagining what it would be like to pick pockets and try a round of 'find the weevil' in this city.

Wait. Observe and think. You'll only get us in trouble if you rush in without watching first. When you live to deceive, you'll often find you are as much the victim as the perpetrator.

Dragons sure were a stuffy breed.

Saboraak descended to the lower level of boardwalk and tucked in next to the rock wall. I could see why. Here, in the shadows, she was less conspicuous. The guards would notice her, but I doubted anyone else would pay her much mind.

Animals, carts – how did they move carts up the stairs? – and people filled the boardwalks despite the early hour. Their backs and beds were heavy with packs and loads. And the animals were not horses, as I would have expected but a creature that looked like a large mountain goat.

Those carts move on rails. Do you see that? The animals and people pull them along those metal rails. I see them going up the slopes, too.

How would that help anything?

Maybe they have a system that keeps the loads from slipping backward once they reach a certain level.

If Saboraak could think like that, then maybe she should have been planning better dragon cities instead of careening through the countryside with me. Did dragons have cities?

Our cities would make your eyes pop right out of your head.

Yuck.

Your brain would get so hot from overuse that it would melt out your ears.

That was so gross.

I am not prone to exaggeration. I merely state the truth.

Then keep me far away from dragon cities!

"What's that creature pulling the cart?" I whispered to Zyla.

"A yudazgoat. They are native to these mountains."

We fell in line behind a cart and my eyes squinted as I looked for the rail Saboraak had seen. There it was. It made the load less maneuverable, but the path was also more predictable. I could see how that would help but there had to be more going on to make this possible. What if two carts wanted to go different directions on the same rail?

Did you notice that everyone on this boardwalk is walking in the same direction? The other boardwalk on this level is walking the other direction.

Weird. How did they get people to agree to that? If you told someone from Vanika that he could only walk in one direction on a road, he'd laugh in your face.

This is not Vanika.

Clearly not. Vanika made a lot more sense.

From what you've told me, Vanika is a ruin on the edge of starvation.

It still made more sense than this place.

The guards pulled the cloth covering off the top of the cart, searching through the bags of cloth inside before letting it pass. The guard was still writing in the book he carried when his partner motioned us forward.

Zyla sat up very straight in the saddle, a bright smile on her face.

"Purpose of entry?" the guard asked.

"We are here to do business with your potters' guild," Zyla said with a smile.

"You look like you're dressed for the festival," the guard said smugly.

"Do we? What a strange coincidence," Zyla said with an equally smug smile.

I felt my face contorting in confusion. Why did it sound like the guard knew she was lying and liked it? Why did it sound like she was teasing him with it?

"And this creature?" he asked, poking Saboraak. I saw her head dip like it did before she flamed and I hoped she could hold in her temper.

"My oosquer," Zyla said.

The guard made a note in his book, but his eyebrow quirked like he knew she was lying. "Then you're from Kav'ai?"

"From the northern reaches of Kav'ai where the cormorant nests," Zyla said.

He looked up sharply when she said cormorant and nodded before returning to his writing. "And the man? He is ill?"

"Only injured. We seek the fine healers of Eski for help with him."

The guard snorted before running his eyes over Zin. "Honor to the Practitioners. Thank you for entering our city."

When she didn't speak, that seemed to please him and he turned to me. "And you, boy?"

I waited for Zyla to make an excuse for me, but the guards eyes tracked up to me and met mine. He made a motion like he wanted me to get on with it.

"Yes, Kav'ai," I said quickly.

The guard rolled his eyes. "And you are from ...?"

I was supposed to say which region? I didn't know what regions there were in Kav'ai!

"Ummm the ... region ... of ..."

Zyla's left hand, hidden from the guard, pointed urgently at my boot where the lightning had struck the heel. Was that a clue? Was there a boot region of Kav'ai? That didn't make any sense.

"Lightning," I said in a rush.

The guard looked up sharply and I felt Zyla tense in front of me.

"You're from the Lightning Region? You're sure?" His eyes narrowed.

Well, the best thing to do when you're caught lying is to double down.

"Are you calling me a liar?" I asked.

I didn't expect the gasp. Zyla's gasp was to be expected. But both guards and every person in earshot gasped in unison before the guard flushed, his eyes flashing with anger.

"Report to the central guardhouse in the pottery district of Eski by noon tomorrow to confirm your identities. Next!"

Well, that didn't seem so bad. I half expected him to challenge me to some kind of duel with that reaction.

"You fool," Zyla whispered the moment we were past the guards. "You're going to get us all killed."

Chapter Eleven

SABORAAK WAS RIGHT about the rails. The carts on the rails had little hooks that were loose and mobile in one direction, but which caught on a ladder if they tried to roll backward. It was an ingenious way to deal with the steady verticals in this strange mountain city.

Along the road, there were hawkers, like in every city, except these hawked wares through windows instead of from carts on the streets. Prospective customers would line up along the rungs of ladders for their turn to buy from the steaming warm windows and merchants with sleeves rolled up despite the cold were quick to take orders at one window and deliver the wares through the next one further up the ladder.

Zyla avoided the roads with the rails and merchant windows, quietly directing Saboraak to a series of back ladders and staircases that seemed to lead deeper and deeper into the hidden parts of the city. I thought we should avoid ladders altogether. Saboraak's approach to them was to simply hop to the next level and avoid them altogether. I wasn't fool enough to speak that thought out loud.

We found a back alley buried inside a stone crevice, and by the look of the debris on the staircases, it was meant for waste and hidden dealings.

"There's an inn somewhere along here," Zyla muttered a few minutes after we found the back way.

I didn't want to say anything out loud, but I had no coin for an inn, and I doubted she did, either.

"I can't believe the guards thought we were from Kav'ai," I said, hoping to soothe whatever was irritating her.

"They didn't. They thought we were Ko'Torenth nobility dressing up as Kav'ai for the festival."

"Then what was all that about cormorants?"

She sighed. "It's the traditional Noble Code of Ko'Torenth. We are expected to lie and to do it well and they are expected to pretend our lies are true but listen for the hidden code behind our words."

"That's ridiculous!"

"That's culture."

Ha! The joke's on you, Tor. It's hard to ply your trade as a liar when you're in a whole city of people who lie better than you do.

I felt as though someone had thrown a bucket of lukewarm water over me. Great. Just great. I was like a declawed cat in a city of tigers.

Apt.

She could laugh all she wanted. She'd have to lie low in this city of few dragons, and from what I could tell, that meant spending her time in these back alleys that smelled like vomit and last night's dinner.

They also smell like blood. Violence has touched this place.

"So what did the cormorant comment mean?"

"He was asking me what level of noble I am. I chose a low house symbol – cormorant."

"And what did it mean when I said 'lightning'?"

"That you think you're royalty. You're lucky he didn't kill you for the audacity of such a lie. Here we are," Zyla said. "The Leaping Lizard Inn."

Would Saboraak consider herself a leaping lizard?

I most certainly would not.

"Okay," Zyla said, as she leaned Bataar over the saddle and dismounted. "You bring Zin and Bataar inside and find a place for Saboraak. I need to go find a healer for Bataar."

"Whoa," I said, leaping off of Saboraak's back. "You're the one who knows the people here, and I don't think it's safe out there. I have a bad feeling about this place."

"Then what do you suggest?"

I rubbed the back of my neck. "I'm worried about leaving Saboraak here in the middle of a strange city. She sticks out like ... like a massive dragon. Anything could happen."

Noble. But I assure you, I will be fine. I can flame this whole city if I need to.

"But," I continued. "I'm also worried about you. How do we know who we can trust? What if someone tries to grab you out there? They did once before."

"Stop fussing. Your dragon will be fine." As she spoke, she tapped twice on a door that looked like every other back door along the alley. "But we need a healer here immediately and we need to negotiate with the innkeeper and manage the injured. If you're too worried to let me go find a healer then you will have to do, mud boots."

"Mud boots?"

"It's a word we use for yokels."

"I'm from the city!"

Zyla ignored me, helping Zin down as she waited for the door to be answered. "You need to follow this alley until it comes out to a main square. Go up a few levels until you see a tall building with green doors and shutters with oak leaves carved into them. That's a house of healing. They're scattered throughout the city on the upper levels. Bring a healer here however you can. Can you do that?"

I felt myself pull back. She didn't think I could handle a simple chore?

"Obviously," I said, offering her an elaborate bow. "Whatever the lady wants, she shall have."

And this way she and the others would be in one safe place and not wandering around the city like vulnerable chicks away from the hen.

I am no chick.

"I *want* six trained warriors, a bag of gold, and a man who speaks every language of Everturn, but I suppose I will have to make do with you," Zyla said. I didn't like the way she raised her eyebrows when she spoke like that. It was like she was judging me.

"What's Everturn?" I asked.

"The name of the world we live in," Zyla said, rolling her eyes and then, as we heard the door opening, she waved a hand in a hurrying motion. "Now be off with you!"

And don't forget this spider.

I had completely forgotten about the spider! I hurried to Saboraak's muzzle, taking the proffered spider from her snout.

It was sticky.

I've been carrying it for hours. What did you expect?

Ugh.

Behind me, I heard Zyla speaking urgently to a man with a long apron and a close-fitting cap. I ducked out of sight and scurried up the alleyway – everything was 'up' in this city – shaking the spider to get the spit off of it.

At least I was going to get a good look at the city! I couldn't help the itch in my feet at the thought of that. It even blotted out the pain in my heel and the cold in the air.

Just try to be careful. I'm beginning to get attached to you.

I could even win dragon hearts in a city like this!

Keep telling yourself that.

Chapter Twelve

I EMERGED FROM THE alley just like Zyla said I would, and I barely managed to hold back a gasp as I stepped into the square. It was formed in a crevice in the mountain. Tall, sharply vertical buildings surrounded three sides of the small square, climbing up into the sky as if five or six of them were racing to grow above the others. I saw windows six or seven high and people in every window.

I studied the square while I turned the metal spider around and around in my hands. It was a strange little thing. It hadn't spat out sparks or felt warm to the touch, but its metal surface sometimes felt ... spongy ... under my fingers. Like it had a bit of give in it. I wondered what it would take to trigger those lightnings. What one man could do, another man could do. I'd just need to pull it out in a sticky situation and see if it would do for me what it had done for the Magika back on the hillside.

In the alleys, lines of clothes drying intersected with one another, but here in the square it was lines of small bells and every wind that whistled through the craggy open area jingled tunes unique to itself.

The building nearest me was a bakery and the smells coming from it made my mouth water. I could spend a day in the square and be happy to have spent it here.

People filled every inch of available space, even rubbing up against the raised statue at the center – a rising creature portrayed as rocketing skyward on a carved trail of wind and ... ash? It was hard to tell.

I couldn't stay here all day. I couldn't learn the ebb and flow of the city like I might want to. I needed to get up two levels and find this house of healing.

I scanned the square looking for the closest ramp, or stair, or ladder. A likely looking spiral staircase - packed with people going up while a parallel one was equally tight with people going down – was only accessible by crossing the square.

Taking a deep breath, I jammed the spider inside my shirt, wrapped my cloak around me, and plunged into the mass of bodies. The spider's stiff metal legs dug into my chest every time someone bumped into me, but I didn't dare lose it. I'd seen what it did in battle and I was too curious to lose it before I tried it myself.

I tried to find a shoal of people moving in the direction I was going, but everyone was intent on their own business and none of them moved with the purpose I needed.

In the end, I shoved forward, maneuvering step by step across the square, dodging one person only to have to plant myself in the path of another. There! An opening was forming in front of me. I leapt into it, surprised when no one else filled the gap. I teetered for a moment on one foot before catching myself and looking around.

The crowd had parted around the central statue, leaving a space almost three people wide around it. As I stood motionless in the gap, I watched the crowd draw back further.

How were they even finding room to pull back – and why now? Was this statue a fountain about to rain down water?

I glanced around, trying to make sense of it until I realized that as many people as were staring at the central statue were also staring at me, eyes wide as saucers. I scrambled backward, trying to join the crowd. How did people go from loose individuals to an impenetrable wall?

There was a gasp from the wall. I spun around to look up to the statue, desperate to know what was coming next.

A man stood at the base of the statue, his eyes turned upward as if looking at the sky. Well, there was nothing strange there. It must feel claustrophobic to him in the middle of these tall buildings and people.

He moved so suddenly that I jumped. He spun in place, his head snapping down to look at the crowd below – no, not the crowd – at me.

Our eyes met across the gap and my breath caught in my throat.

In the depths of his eyes, light swirled like a silver tide rising. It blotted out his irises and pupils until his eyes were nothing but silver – liquid, shining, but possessed of an otherworldly quality that made me shiver.

I wanted to run, but my feet wouldn't move. I reached into my shirt and drew out the spider. Would it even work for me? It looked like nothing but a wrought metal spider in the light of day. My hands shook as I held it up in front of me. Okay, spider, work your magic!

Nothing happened.

The man raised a hand, his index finger pointing right at me.

Gasps filled the air as every eye swiveled to where I stood.

My mouth was suddenly dry.

"You!" he breathed. "You have it!"

Maybe I shouldn't have taken that spider after all. Not only was it useless, but now it was drawing attention.

The man's index finger began to tremble and then the silver in his eyes burst, splattering across his face and hair and dripping like hot wax in long trails to his feet. It pooled there, as if each drop was seeking out the others, not random, but alive.

I was tumbling backward before I realized it. But everyone else was pushing backward, too. Somewhere behind me, the screams started.

And then figures erupted around the man as I knew they would. They formed out of the heavy snowflakes in the air, swirling messily around him. Like small, personal demons formed of snow and silver, they whirled and grew.

I knew I should shut my eyes.

I'd seen this twice before and that was twice too many times. But my eyes would not shut even though they burned, tears streaming down my face from the wind and the cold. Not tears from stress or fear. Just from the wind and the cold. That's probably why I was frozen in place. I was just too cold.

What's happening? What's wrong?

Trouble, Saboraak. Stay with the others! No one else needed to get hurt. Not when I was pretty sure it was me that they wanted.

The snowy creatures pounced on their creator. A ripping, wet sound end in a high-pitched squeal that went on and on. Then, like a snowball breaking against an old wall, the creatures burst into a puff of snow and steam.

When the cloud of their remains settled, there was nothing left of the man with the silver eyes.

I didn't wait for someone else to break the silence. I didn't dare wait. I ducked under the arm of a man right behind me, quickly bent double and began pushing my way through the crowd, head down and refusing to be stopped. The insistent drum of my heart filled my ears and guided my feet. Forward. Forward. Forward.

Yells and curses followed me. I didn't dare turn to see who was following them. Whoever they were, they weren't going to be friendly. I pressed on through the crowd, weaving and dodging.

Were those faces I was passing? All I saw were expressions: confusion, surprise, hate. Did they see what happened? Would they turn on me?

I didn't dare stay long enough to find out. Just another corner and I'd be only another member of the crowd. I pushed harder. I wished that I could run forever until there wasn't a single man left with silver in his eyes. What could I possibly have that they wanted? I was poor as mud without even a decent set of clothes to my name! Unless it was the spider. I could see wanting that – though it hadn't produced any lightnings to defend *me*.

I shoved it back in my shirt as I finally reached the spiral staircase leading upward. I pulled the hood of my cloak up over my head, joining the slowly ascending line of people. Was that man pointing to me as he spoke to a man dressed in dark emerald? How about the woman with the wide apron frowning in my direction? Everyone I passed was a potential threat.

I didn't breathe a sigh of relief until I reached the second level and left the slow train of people to push onto a narrow boardwalk above. I needed to get a hold of myself. I needed to find that house of healing. That was all. Whatever happened in the square had nothing to do with me. No one could blame me for it.

Now, where was this green-doored building?

I saw it as soon as I scanned the boardwalk – a tall white building with green doors and long green banners hanging from the upper windows. Perfect. I'd do my job and get out of here like nothing ever happened.

Was that a man pointing to me? Nonsense. He must mean someone else. For a moment, I almost thought it was the same man in the green coat I'd seen a level below. But no, it must be a uniform.

That had better not be the city guard of Eski! I did *not* want to get on their bad side the second I set foot in their city.

I sidled nonchalantly to the first green door and then, as soon as the crowd surged and took me out of the gaze of the man in the emerald coat, I slid to the door.

I took one last look back before I shut it behind me. A flash of purple caught my eye. It couldn't be ...

The crowd shifted again, and I caught a clear look at the face of a man in a purple Magika robe. Across the sea of people, our eyes met. I gasped, ducking in the door, my heart pounding. That was impossible! He couldn't possibly be here!

But I'd never forget the face of the man who tortured me.

Shabren the Violet.

Chapter Thirteen

"WELCOME TO THE HALLS of the Oak," a voice said, and I whirled to see a man smiling gently at me. He was dressed in white furs and wore a wreath of oak leaves around his neck. "Can I take you to see one of our healers?"

I glanced back at the door behind me. I needed to get further into the building. Shabren and the guards would not be far behind.

"Yes, please," I said.

The room we were in was some sort of anteroom. There were chairs and a fire and a wide stone basin full of glowing embers. All of it clean, fresh and tidy. Dax the White – one of the Dragon Riders I'd known in Vanika – would have loved this place. As a healer, he was always very specific about keeping things clean and well recorded.

The man smiled gently. "If you'd follow me, then."

He moved gracefully, but slowly, down a smooth-walled hall and I nearly stepped on the backs of his heels in my hurry to go faster.

"I need to see a healer right away," I prompted.

"Yes," he said with a smile.

"I'm in a hurry!"

He frowned, still gentle like a beloved uncle. "Hurry helps no one. What causes this haste?"

I opened my mouth, but I felt suddenly tongue-tied. I was used to spinning out a lie at a moment like this, but these people were used to liars. Maybe the best thing to do where they were concerned was to surprise them with the truth. I looked over my shoulder, worried that Shabren might be right behind me.

"I have a hurt friend," I blurted out. "He needs help right away."

"Is that why you came here wearing a black cloak?"

"What?" I was so confused. What could he possibly mean?

Tor?

Saboraak! She needed to know that I'd seen Shabren in the crowd.

Tor, there's trouble here!

My eyes lost focus for a moment as I tried to turn inward to sense what emotion that was filling her words.

I sensed a movement out of the corner of my eye and came back to focus just in time to see the man with the oak leaf wreath heft an axe from off a bracket on the wall.

"I'm taking you to the authorities, boy. Don't try to run. I'll make as much coin from bringing you dead as I would alive."

I spun, looking for an escape route and he rushed toward me, brandishing his axe.

I stumbled to the side, barely dodging his wild blow as his axe crashed into the stone, sparks flying where its edge hit the wall.

What in the-

Bataar is a wanted man! Somehow word is out that we have him and that we will be looking for a healer. Don't go to the house of healing.

Too late. And I looked a lot like Bataar with this band wrapped around my head! I ripped it off and threw it to the ground.

The wild healer was charging for a second attack and I scrambled down the hallway, pulling a vase down from an alcove and throwing it behind me. Anything to gain a few strides on him and that axe!

There was a cry from behind us at the entrance and a deep shout. That wasn't Shabren, was it?

I launched forward at twice the speed. I needed Saboraak! I couldn't manage this part on my own. I rushed to a circular metal stairway, pounding up the steps, my legs on fire with the effort. They were going to be strong after a week in this vertical city.

You're going to have to manage on your own. I'm busy here.

Well, that was convenient. She was busy, was she? Maybe I'd be busy the next time her life was threatened. Maybe I should have been less worried about her safety in Eski and more worried about my own.

Don't be childish. You'll be fine. Just don't die.

Yeah, that was the plan.

I could hear footsteps right behind me and my breath came faster and faster, searing my lungs with fiery pain. But that was nothing compared to the pain that would greet me if that axe hit me. There was a door at the top of the stairs and I rushed through it and then threw myself against the wall right beside the doorframe.

This was another hall. I didn't know where it led or how to get out of this place or who else might be looking for me with axes in their hands.

Below me, I heard footsteps pounding up the stairs and shouts. Shouts meant more people. People with axes. My chest was heaving, and I tried to calm my breathing down. What was the best way to deal with a problem?

One step at a time.

Good advice. Step one: deal with the axe. My pursuer had an axe. I did not. This needed to change.

I took a deep breath as the footsteps grew closer. The second the door beside me was flung open, I launched myself forward, head curled down so I could hit him in the face with my skull. I felt the crack on the top of my head, but I gritted my teeth, refusing to recoil from the impact. My attacker stumbled to the side, colliding with the half-open door and falling to one knee. His axe fell from his hand, skittering across the stone floor and into the hall.

I scooped up the axe and plummeted down the hall.

Step one, complete.

Now the man chasing me was down one axe and I was up one axe – not that I planned to use it. I shuddered at the thought of cleaving a person like one might cleave wood.

No time for that!

There was a window at the end of the hall. I could try one of the heavy doors along the way, but I had no idea what could be in them and I could end up trapped in a room with no exit.

There was a shout behind me and I risked a glance over my shoulder. Men with oak-leaf wreaths around their necks were rushing through the door and down the corridor. No time to make plans. I was a betting man. It was my fault and also my strength.

Time to bet that I could jump out a two-story window and live.

Don't do it! Human's are fragile! You will break yourself!

Not if I did it right.

I sped up, excitement coursing through my veins. I never felt so alive as when I was being chased. I jammed the axe handle into my belt. It had better hold! That thing was heavy.

You're crazy.

The window loomed ahead, big and bright – easy to vault through. I measured my steps by eye, counting, ready ...

"Stop!" That was Shabren's voice. No time to turn and confirm.

I reached the ledge at the exact right moment, letting my momentum help as I lifted both legs while my hand found its place on the ledge.

I leapt, flying through the window, spinning to turn toward the wall.

Was I right?

I'd better be right.

Yes!

A green banner hung from just below the window, exactly as I'd been betting on. I grabbed it frantically, sliding down it as my grip slowed me. There!

I slowed to a stop, dangling free over the side of a building set in the side of a cliff. I could see the little boardwalk below and below that vertical city falling down, down, down beneath me – and below that clouds, and below that ... who knew? Death, perhaps.

One step at a time!

Oh yes. This was the step where I got to the ground faster than they did.

I let the fabric slide through my hands, dropping me down until I was almost at ground level. I'd have to drop free the last few feet. I let go, falling into a crouch on the boardwalk.

Around me, people gaped, stopping to stare at my sudden acrobatics.

No time to stare back.

I sprinted down the boardwalk. I needed an alley. Preferably one with laundry hanging to dry. There! I paused in the entrance, glancing backward and nearly froze like the crowd.

Something was coming out of the same window I'd leapt from – not a man, or at least, not only a man. It was a flying rug with three men sitting on it, and one of them was Shabren the Violet.

Chapter Fourteen

I DUCKED INTO THE ALLEY, running as fast as I could. I'd done this before. I needed to remember that.

I'd run from the city guard, from merchants, from angry citizens, from fire, and from dust demons. I could do this.

Step three, change how I look.

There! A washing line hung along the alley, some of the clothing hanging low enough for me to grab them. I snatched anything I could reach and kept running. The alley was dark and grimy, but there were fissures in the stone wall it butted up against. I was looking for one the exact right size – big enough to hold a man.

The first one was occupied. Someone about my size was curled up in the shadow there, sleeping. Good to know that people like me lived here, too – people surviving on luck and brashness.

There was another crevice up ahead. Unoccupied. Good. My luck hadn't run out yet.

I ducked inside and examined what I had. A light red cloak, threadbare and not nearly as warm as the dark one Hubric had given me. Reluctantly, I exchanged them, hiding the axe and the fancy belt beneath the cloak.

The other garment was black and loose like a long scarf. I tangled it around my head like I'd seen some of the visitors at the gate do. It covered my face except for my eyes. Perfect. No one could tell who I was beneath this.

Now, the cloak. If I left it here it would be a dead giveaway ...

With a flash of inspiration, I backtracked, dropping the cloak over the sleeper in the other crevice. He could use it. Sleeping outside in this cold couldn't be easy. And if someone was looking for that cloak, he'd make a good distraction.

I hurried further down the alley. That flying rug would be here any minute and before it arrived, I needed to get further away. No ... wait. They would just expand the search farther. What I needed was a place to hide. Then I could hunker down until dark and give them the slip under the cover of night.

But this was a foreign city and I didn't know the back ways yet. Going down would be easier than going up. I should drop down a level.

Don't drop down.

Why not?

We are dealing with our own situation here and I can't allow you to bring trouble back with you.

She had to be kidding me! Was I not in trouble, too?

You're on your own, kid. Hold them off. Don't die. I'll let you know when you can come back.

Rejection and betrayal filled me as I hurried up the alley, looking both ways in the street beyond.

Don't take it personally. I have a lot of responsibilities to juggle here.

The problem with compassionate people was that sometimes they were so busy being compassionate to strangers that they made bad friends.

Ouch.

I almost didn't see the green embroidered sleeves of the guard at the end of the alley. I drew in a deep breath when it finally registered. His back was to me, standing guard over the alley. There was no way to slip around him.

I stumbled backward, wincing as I hit my heel on a stone. I didn't dare make a sound. I wasn't going to have anyone to save me if I messed this up. Those traitors!

Get over yourself. Zyla and I were betrayed. Since then, we've changed locations, changed disguises, and found a friend. We've been a bit busy. But we're still being hunted, and we need to find a safe place before we're discovered. Do you know how hard it is to hide when you're a dragon?

Didn't Zyla say there would be dragons here? Why didn't she go hide in a dragon cote? She could pretend to be a purple. They were notoriously reclusive. Zyla could be her rider and they could tuck Zin and Bataar into the saddlebags until things settled down.

That's actually a very good idea.

I was known to have those. I eased myself along the wall of the building behind me. It smelled like rat. Why was my stomach rumbling? I had better not have developed a taste for rat. That would be awful.

Why didn't you suggest this plan before?

I'm running for my life, remember?

I leaned back and took a second step backward, back brushing the wall. My footing felt spongy – and then suddenly I was falling. I gritted my teeth to keep from screaming as the ground gave out beneath me. I must have stepped on rotten wood. Skies and stars!

Terror shot through me as visions of falling forever filled my mind, but I landed before I could flesh them out.

Ngh!

I clenched my whole body against the impact. My hip throbbed like I'd bruised it, but I pulled myself to my feet.

I was in a cellar, or maybe a storeroom. Crates and barrels were scattered around the room with old sacking and straw strewn untidily about. Someone wasn't keen on housework. Not that I minded too much. I hadn't slept in almost two days and even then, I'd been unconscious. Maybe this was a good place to lay low. No one was going to find me here.

I gathered the loose sacking and straw, found a dark corner and wrapped the old red cloak around me. I already missed the black one. I had a bad feeling I wasn't going to be able to replace it any time soon.

The axe dug into my side as I settled in, but I didn't adjust it. I liked the reminder that I had a weapon now – even if I had no idea how to use it.

Sleep came quickly.

Chapter Fifteen

WAKE UP! WAKE UP!

Skies and stars, she could keep the flaming yelling to herself!

Your enemies are upon you!

I scrambled up from the cellar floor, my heart leaping into my throat at the scurrying sounds around me until my brain supplied me with a reminder – rats.

I stood still and silent, listening. It was strangely quiet for a city, no sound of bustle or business outside.

You slept the day away. Darkness falls.

The barest glimmer of light worked its way down from the rotten wood I'd fallen through. Could I climb back up through it? Yes, if I used the barrel. I heard a scrape from further into the room. Maybe Saboraak was right. There might be someone coming down here.

Of course, I'm right.

I grabbed one of the barrels, rolling it toward the hole. The movement sounded loud in the silence. Are you nearby, Saboraak? Can you hear that? There was a knot forming in my belly.

Hardly. We followed your plan. We're in the dragon cotes three levels below you. Zyla is trying to sort out Zin and Bataar without a healer. We really could have used one.

You wouldn't have wanted me to send the one I met ...

I climbed up on the barrel, steadying myself and ready to climb through the hole. Why was it so silent out there? Sweat formed along my brow. The scarf wrapped around my face wasn't helping with that.

The Cantata is about to begin.

Cantata?

Cantata of Lights. It's part of the Festival.

And that made the whole city silent? If I climbed through here, it was going to be noisy enough in all that silence that I would certainly draw attention.

It won't be silent for long. Move.

Light flared into the room as a door opened. I hadn't even realized there was a door there. A guard held a bright lantern up.

"There he is!"

Not for long! I leapt up from the barrel, grabbed the lip of the hole where I fell through only hours ago and dragged myself up over the jagged wood. The edges of it bit into my belly as I wriggled across and I knew they would leave marks. But those guards with the axes would leave far worse marks.

What was with everyone and their axes around here? I hadn't seen a decent tree in days.

The axes appear to be of ceremonial importance. Perhaps they think they can divide the lies they tell with such tools.

I was sprinting down the alley, not bothering to look behind me. I already knew what I would see. So much for sneaking out after they'd given up looking for me.

I'd need a different plan this time.

I adjusted the scarf around my head, making sure it covered my face. Okay. If there was still a guard at the end of the alley, I'd have to take action. Violence wasn't really my thing, but neither was dying.

Yep, there he was, still standing at the mouth of the alley. I yanked the axe free from my belt. I didn't want to do this.

Axes have two sides.

Why hadn't I thought of that?

I turned the axe around, trying to be careful not to hit too hard as I struck the back of his head. The guard fell, and I bit my lip, trying not to look at him as I stuffed the axe back into my belt. I didn't want to know if I'd accidentally killed him.

There was a shout behind me and I dashed out into the boardwalk only to draw up short. Wha - ?

The Cantata of Lights. I told you it was starting.

People lined the boardwalk, motionless, looking out into the sky beyond. From where I stood, I could see that every boardwalk, every staircase, every open window was filled with silent, statue-like people. Cold ice whirled around them in the black of the night and then, as if by magic, lights sprang up on the lower level, spreading one after another to light the entire city.

I almost jumped as a crackling sound started over my head. A spark sped up a line above me, lighting each candle in blue lanterns above me as it ascended.

From below, a ghostly sound began. No time to listen. I edged my way up the line of people, sneaking behind them, hoping they were too absorbed in their silent celebration to notice. The sound was growing louder. Voices, I thought.

I dashed to a staircase, climbing behind the backs of the silent crowds.

Was that singing? Wordless – or with words I didn't understand – the song grew. Layer upon layer of harmonies rose level upon level through the city.

Below me, the guards dashed out of the alley. I caught a glimpse of purple in the blue lights. Shabren.

He opened his mouth, but at that moment the people nearest me began to sing, their powerful voices drowning out whatever he had meant to shout.

I continued my climb, speeding up until the muscles in my legs burned from the effort and my lungs grew ragged from sucking in the icy air.

I didn't have a plan. I was only running, running, running. I needed some burst of genius to help me, but nothing was coming to me as I rushed up the stairs.

What was this festival for? Between the eerie blue lights and the focused singers, the whole mountain seemed to be caught up in the drama of the moment. Across from our mountain peak, the other two cities lit up in a wave of blue just as ours had and my imagination made me think that I could hear their singers, too – though in reality, all I could hear was my own heart beating so hard it was going to rip my chest in half.

Zyla left me with the others. She is looking for a healer. You are still on your own.

Great. Just great.

The city grew more decadent the higher I climbed. Carved arches were spaced out across the boardwalks, both suspending them and adding beauty to the structures. The buildings on either side were carved out from the rock – likely there were few alleys here – and the skill involved in carving the intertwined knotwork that decorated them was something I'd never seen before. At this rate, I'd never seen it again.

Shabren was gaining on me. Every time I glanced behind me, he was closer, forcing his way through the well-dressed people on this level, their long vests and wide belts trimmed with ermine and fox. The women's hair was elaborately dressed and some of the men wore scarves around their faces and heads just as I did. Good. That should make me blend in more – except for the threadbare cloak. When the time was right, I would need to slip that off.

Why hadn't he brought his flying carpet?

Too conspicuous in the middle of the celebration. He would be seen, and such an offense would alienate any allies he has here. This day is sacred to Ko'Torenth.

I was looking desperately for an opportunity, now. I glanced down every walkway, into every window, dodging people like a fish dodged seaweed, but looking, looking, looking until my eyes streamed with tears from looking too hard. If he caught me, there would be no escape. Saboraak was stuck helping the others. Zyla didn't even have the connections to help her sister. Bataar was a wanted man and Hubric didn't know where we were. I was on my own and I didn't know the city. This one, wild chase was my only remaining hope.

I was running out of time and running out of city. The crowds thinned as I gained another level, getting closer and closer to the apex of the city. Despite fewer people, the sound of their song filled every available space. It reverberated through me like I was a part of it, it was rushing into me – a waterfall into a basin.

At the very peak of the city, a strange structure loomed. It was like a great three-pronged arm that extended out over the mountain city. It rose in the center of the curve of the mountain so that anyone standing on the platform at the end of it would be standing over a drop that went all the way to the foothills below the mountain. How would you build a thing like that? What was it for?

You will have to ask Zyla. I do not know of this thing.

All three arms led to that circular platform. A pair of intersecting arches towered over the platform, serrated along their edges. Arches were interspersed all along the arms, a long beam running along the peaks of them as if it was part of the structural integrity of the network.

In my experience, strange things like that led to nothing good.

Except for the time you thought we should fly through one that was like a door.

I saved our lives, didn't I?

Technically, that was me.

Fine. Then if you're the savior around here, then get out of that dragon cote and come lend me a hand. I hadn't wanted her in danger before, but now things were getting ... dire.

I turned a corner only to find my way blocked by guards. I pivoted at the last moment, rushing up a spiral staircase instead. Great. The guards had joined the chase again. I was like a prize fox in a hunt. Everyone wanted a piece of my hide.

Chapter Sixteen

I HAD A TERRIBLE FEELING that they were herding me upward. That, or they figured I would collapse if I kept climbing.

I was close to collapse already, my lungs heaving and the taste of blood in my mouth. I was no quitter. If they wanted me, they'd have to come and get me.

On my way.

Really? I breathed a sigh of relief as I turned the last spiral in the staircase and then gasped. If the level below had been rich, this level was palatial. The boardwalk wasn't boards but woven metal strands in vine-like patterns. The rail along the edge was equally decadent and by the knot-and-scrollwork around every door and window and the carved friezes on the walls, I had a terrible feeling that this might be the kind of place where a king would live.

There were only about a hundred people standing around the railings on this level. Their song seemed to be almost a trance. But their guards were alert. They were charging towards me.

Nice work, fellas. Who said that guards were unobservant?

I turned. Better to take my chances below. Movement made me stop just in time. The pair of guards from below were rounding the last turn on the spiral staircase.

Skies and flaming stars! I was in trouble now!

Language!

She could say whatever she wanted, but she wasn't here.

I told you I was coming, I just need to work on a great disguise, so no one recognizes me ...

Yeah, you work on disguises, I'll work on not dying.

I was going so quickly now that my feet were slipping and skidding on the icy woven walkway. I nearly skidded into a girl with flowing golden hair and huge eyes. Her mouth formed a perfect 'O' but there was no time to admire pretty faces. I was surrounded.

The purple of Shabren's robes rose over the lip of the staircase.

There was only one path left to me – the nearest arm leading to that center platform. I was already squirming inside as my feet hit the edge of it.

If you are going to die, do it spectacularly. Like everything in life, you have a better chance of pulling it off if you add the right level of drama.

What do you mean 'pull it off'? We all die.

I mean that if I can, I'll find a way to cheat death.

If that was possible, no one in Ko'Torenth would ever die. I feel like I should walk through this city blindfolded and with wool in my ears. No one is who they pretend to be!

I sped up, my lungs screaming in protest as I raced down the arm. Something was digging into my chest uncomfortably. What was that?

The spider! I'd forgotten about it in my hurry. I reached into my shirt, fumbling for it as I ran. There!

I pulled it out of my shirt. It was hot to the touch and glowing.

Uh oh. I never wanted to be in a place that made magic things start working again. That was for heroes and I was definitely not hero material.

I should throw it off the side of the arch. And yet, somehow, I couldn't bring myself to do that. I knew this thing could shoot lightning. I'd seen it before, hadn't I? Maybe it could shoot a little lightning for me.

Be careful! Things that are done remain done. You can't un-kill someone.

Oh, trust me. I won't want to.

Have you ever killed?

I'd gotten pretty close.

You won't like it. When you kill someone, it feels a bit like cheating.

I liked cheating. I did it at every conceivable opportunity.

And yet, here you are being faithful and loyal when you could just turn the rest of us in for the reward.

Shabren stepped onto the arm. I could finally hear him.

"I knew you'd be trouble," he said. "The second I saw you, I knew you were a street curr."

His flattery would get him nowhere. I backed up as I fumbled with the spider.

"You're dipping your toes in pools that you have no business even knowing about. Hand me that artifact."

Yeah, and I'd go ahead and give him the axe, too. Did he always deal with idiots or did he really think he could charm me out of my only weapons?

The tiger's eye pendant on my chest vibrated.

"Do you know what it means to step on this walkway, boy? Do you know what will happen when your feet hit the Ko'tor'kaen?"

I didn't even know what that word meant. Now, how did this thing work? You pointed it at your enemy ... I lifted the spider up, aiming the legs at Shabren.

"This is the seat of judgment, boy. This place was made to judge truth. And you are no son of truth."

So, what? If I had to guess, I'd say that the only truthful person in this city was Saboraak and she was no one's son.

Your acknowledgment means a lot to me.

Uh huh. Enough to fly up here and get me out of this mess?

I'm stuck here. I can't leave until Zyla returns.

Just get me out of here before Shabren remembers he can do those lightning tricks.

"The Ko'tor'kaen judges the destiny of a soul. And on this day – the Festival of Lights – the day that Ko'Torenth celebrates how each person holds within him a spark of Truth – on this day, walking onto that platform has a special significance."

"Did you know that you look smaller without your pet rug?" I asked. It wasn't my best insult, but I was feeling a little out of my depths.

I took another step backward and stumbled slightly. It was a step down. I pulled my other foot down to quickly stabilize. Whew. It didn't feel like I'd hurt my ankles. That was a close one!

When I looked back up, Shabren's eyes were wide with shock.

Chapter Seventeen

I FELT A TINGLING IN the air. Without realizing it, I had stepped onto the platform. I could see the other two arms branching off next to the one I'd followed. Guards stood at the edges of the arms as if they were afraid to step on the platform, their eyes wide and their faces tight with fear.

Above me, the tingling air leapt and jumped along the intersecting arches, sizzling with leaping blue light.

"Where is it?" Shabren asked quietly, as if he was afraid his voice would shatter our special moment.

"In my hands, genius."

Beneath me, the song in a thousand throats caught for a moment before morphing into something brighter, something almost triumphant. I didn't understand it. But one thing I did know – I was glad my face was covered. I had a terrible feeling that every set of eyes in the city could see me right now.

"Not the spider, the book. Hubric didn't have it when we caught up to him. There's only one person he could have given it to."

Caught up to them? Did they have Hubric? Was he okay? And what book was he talking about? Did he mean that weird prophecy book Hubric gave me before he left?

The spider pulled upward, as if being sucked up to where the arches intersected, but I held on tight even when it yanked my arms above my head and my sleeves fell down around my elbows. I wasn't letting go of this thing. It was the most valuable thing I owned – or at least, I thought so. I was going to have to look at that book again.

There was a gasp – a gasp like the rush of the tide, a gasp torn from several thousand throats. Shabren's eyes were locked on my arms above my head. I looked up. The silver tattoos glowed in the blue light of the arches.

At the arms of the other two arches, the guards dropped to their knees.

"The Ko," Shabren breathed.

Run. I sense … terrible evil.

Run where?

The spider ripped from my hands, rocketing up to the apex of the arches and sticking there as if by magic. I'd lost my only hope of fighting back – not that it had been working for me anyway.

Run anywhere!

"You'll never escape now, boy."

I let my eyes narrow and clenched my jaw. I'd never been a hero. I kept telling people that.

Then be a gambler. It's what you keep on saying you are! Take a gamble. Do something no one would predict.

Okay, Saboraak. It's now or never. You want to be my dragon? You get one chance at this.

I smiled at Shabren. "Watch me."

I turned my back on him and ran, jumping through the arch and leaping out into the empty air beyond. If you're going to die, do it dramatically.

My legs and arms wind-milled as I dropped, a meteor falling from the sky. My heart was in my throat, tears streaking down my face. What had I done? This gamble was too much!

It might be my last big bet.

The wind whistled around me as I dashed past thousands of horrified faces, past level after level of mountain city. My heart was pounding too hard. It was going to burst before my dice pips could be counted and the bet decided …

I crashed into something hard.

It dipped under me, leveling off as I was still grasping for a hold of the saddle. A massive red head and neck spun around to give me a baleful look.

You can always bet on me, kid. Although, for future reference, I'd prefer that the risks you take be a little less suicidal in nature. I was thinking that you'd dart over the heads of the guards or try a spinning kick, or something …

I had bet my life on my dragon.

And when I was done having a heart attack, I was going to feel all warm inside that my bet had paid off.

I'll show you warm! I'll toast your heels if you ever pull a stunt like that again!

It was actually kind of fun now that it was over ...

I'll roast you like a pig on a spit!

And it was the first time I'd ever completely trusted someone else with my life.

Saboraak's rage stuttered and was gone.

I'm starting to love you, too.

No one said anything about love.

I just did.

Dragon Chameleon: City of Ice

Chapter One

NOW WE'RE IN TROUBLE. Every single person on Eski has seen us and they will be looking for us.

My dragon was right, of course. She was more than just a thick scaly face.

I don't need compliments. I need a plan.

Well, lucky for us, Saboraak could change shape and color. We could hide, and she could just pop out again as another dragon.

And you don't think they'd be looking for that? They're looking for a dragon with a boy riding her. It doesn't matter what color I am, they'll be looking for me.

You really haven't been around humans long, have you? We don't know that female dragons can change colors. If you show up as a different color, they will think you are a different dragon. And I had a scarf over my face. They don't know what I look like under the scarf.

They saw those arms, though.

Don't remind me.

The city was shrinking as we flew outward.

Hurry! Dive.

Why?

We needed a place to hide while we changed appearance. Maybe there would be a crag in the mountain below the city where we could hide out and then we could change our appearance and re-enter the city.

She was diving before I finished my thought. I wrapped my whole body around her like a squirrel hugging a tree. She could have at least worn a saddle!

I was in a bit of a hurry, as you might recall. You leapt from a platform at the apex of the city.

It was hard to fly like this! My palms were slick with the sweat of anxiety and her dive was making them worse. What if I lost my grip and fell from her back to the rocks beneath.

That will not happen.

I wanted to wipe the sweat from my brow, wanted to squint my eyes shut, but neither was an option in the middle of the skin-crawling anxiety of the moment.

You were the one who told me to dive.

I was. What a terrible idea. Why did she listen to me?

You're hard to ignore.

Maybe you should practice!

I'll take that under advisement.

We leveled off so quickly that my muscles were still wobbling like jelly when we were finally slowing toward the underside of the city. The dwellings here were more scattered and in poorer repair. There was a ramp system from the ground below and a steady flow of traffic following it, but the people here didn't look at us. They were working hard to pretend we didn't exist.

I wonder if you would judge me if I read their minds.

Why would I judge? I'd read everyone's minds if I could. I hated secrets - unless they were mine. It only made sense to learn as much as you could about everything – including other people's thoughts.

It's considered ... unethical ... to read human minds indiscriminately.

What about dragon minds?

We all read each other's minds all the time.

I straightened. I mean, obviously, they must, right? She was reading mine all the time. She never asked if she could. Kyrowat hadn't asked either. They just did it. But Ephretti's dragon didn't do that.

All dragons can read each others' minds. Only some dragons can speak to human minds. But all dragons can speak to dragon minds.

Weird.

It's called communication. It's the foundation of a functional society.

And we'd done enough of it for now. We needed a place to hide out and change. I felt a pull to the left. Could that be a good hiding place there? It was hard to tell. As we descended, the fog grew thicker. Was that a crevice underneath a wide overhang? There was no ramp under it, though a wide rope cable hung from a trapdoor. It looked like the bottom of a building built into the rock. It was very tall – three levels at least – and the doors and windows were on the upper levels. My unconscious mind must have noticed the perfect spot and drawn me to it.

Or you just like to tell yourself that.

Either way. This was a place to hide and we needed to take it. Then Saboraak could change colors and shapes and I could ditch this red cloak and face scarf.

What about the axe?

It was my only weapon other than a belt knife.

Do you know how to use it without chopping your own leg off?

Insulting!

No, I mean it. Can you be trusted with that thing?

I was keeping it. If nothing else, it might be valuable enough to sell and we needed money.

If you sell it, it will draw attention to us.

We eased into the fog, finding the overhang. Despite the trapdoor on the underside of the overhang and the thick cable hanging out of it, no one from up there would be able to see us unless they stuck their heads out and deliberately looked.

So, why did I feel so drawn to that building? I wanted – badly – to climb the cable and see what was inside.

Your sense of adventure will be the death of you. You're like a cat. You investigate everything and fear nothing. How many lives do you think you have?

Just the one ... obviously.

You don't act like it. You act like you have ten more lives in your saddlebags.

There was a ledge under the overhang and Saboraak maneuvered us to it, sticking out her feet and clinging to the wall like a bat.

I resent that comparison.

Stop being so oversensitive and help me think of a disguise!

In the morning. First, we sleep.

Sleeping on the back of a dragon as she huddles on a tiny ledge is no easy thing. First, Saboraak had to find a position where I could lie across her neck without falling off. Then, I had to convince myself to stop having panic attacks from the precarious position for long enough that I could sleep. Sleep came slowly and was intermittent. Not only was it a terrifying height, but the cold of the night bit into my exposed skin. I had to keep rotating myself to heat my body against Saboraak's hot hide.

It was almost morning when I heard a clunk in the building overhead. Something was coming down the cable!

My eyes snapped open and Saboraak jolted awake. I scrambled to hold on tighter to her.

At the sound of squeaking hinges, we froze.

Chapter Two

TWO VOICES GREW SLOWLY clearer as Saboraak and I leaned into the rock, trying our best to seem small.

"There are more coming today," the first voice said. A woman. She sounded irritated. "And we don't have room for the last ones. Someone needs to tell Shabren that even magic workers can't add more rooms to a house and we can't house them here. This is a shop and our enemies can easily send spies here."

Shabren? What did this place have to do with him? He seemed to have feelers out everywhere. How could he have established himself so strongly in a matter of days?

"I don't think he'll listen," the other voice said dryly – a man this time. "He says we need to move as many into the city as we can. You heard what happened to Aricas and Hriden. If we don't figure out what is causing the leakage, then we'll end up the same way."

"Stuffing the safehouse to the gills won't help with that, Cormaz."

"Bringing in more Magikas might."

The woman sighed. "Fine. I'll keep this room shut off for the rest of the day, but if our friends don't arrive by nightfall, then I need to open it up. We need the supply baskets that go through the floor here and without those supplies, we will all starve."

"You can buy food in the markets today."

Their voices were fading again.

"At those prices?"

A door shut behind them and we both let out a sigh of relief. I should look inside that trapdoor. Whatever was in that room was important. Perhaps it was a doorway like the one we used to arrive in Ko'Koren.

Or perhaps the woman simply meant that people would be coming up whatever baskets are cranked up the mountainside on that cable. We need to hurry, or we will be found.

Then we needed disguises.

Before I finished the thought, Saboraak was already morphing, her neck and tail extending and a wide frill sprouting out around her head. A pair of tentacle-like antennae grew out of her head and her skin grew a little less thick and burnished to a bright gold.

Perfect. Now it's your turn.

I tried to ignore the call of the room as I pulled the cloak off and fashioned it into a skirt around my waist. The scarf morphed easily into a veil. Like magic, I was a girl.

Saboraak turned to give me a very dry look with one of her huge eyes.

You aren't fooling me.

Yes, but she could read my mind. The key was to fool other people.

She kept staring at me.

Or ... I could go up that trapdoor and see what was up there myself. It was probably something amazing ... and maybe there would be clothing I could borrow.

No. Let's go.

But people would still be on the lookout for a single dragon and rider. Perhaps if I took a passenger? Two people would surprise anyone watching.

I don't have a saddle.

Then let's find someone who won't care. We flew slowly up out of the fog. Early daylight painted the cool tones of the city and snow had piled on the steeply sloped roofs and on the railings lining the narrow boardwalks.

We leveled off beside the ramps going up and down along the edge of the mountain. I scanned the up-ramp. The people with yudazgoats and carts wouldn't need us. And no one who was already in a group would want to leave their friends. I needed someone who wouldn't talk ... hmmm.

It helps to be a petty criminal when you are looking for a petty criminal. I noticed the signs immediately. One man walked on his own, his eyes on everyone but himself. He was likely a pickpocket or some other kind of thief. That was a man who would take a ride from a strange dragon.

Saboraak flew up to him and I gestured to him to join me on the dragon as Saboraak moved up to a bend in the ramp and settled down on it. The man looked around him, swallowing, watching to see who might notice, but after a heartbeat he joined us, a smile on his face.

"Are you offering me a ride?" I could see his eyes twinkling as he mentally added up what a dragon would be worth if he could steal it from an unsuspecting woman.

I was doing my own mental math. Older than me by at least ten years. No weapon, unless there was a knife hidden somewhere. He was heavier than I was, but I was faster.

How do you know?

I am always faster.

I beckoned with a hand and hoped my actions looked feminine enough.

You look ridiculous.

But not too ridiculous. The man shrugged and mounted.

"May I say what a lovely sight you are, my lady!" he said and when I didn't respond he tried again. "Are you by any chance, a Zyvaar? Do your oaths bind your tongue? Will you take me two levels up? The climb is difficult in the cold."

I nodded, hoping it would be enough as Saboraak launched into the air. The man behind me made a sickly sound in his throat as we slipped into the air. I turned back to see him green and sweating, but his eyes were still focused as he calculated his next move. Greed was a great lever. If someone wanted something – money, popularity, the good opinions of others, power – it was easy to use that as a lever to move them where you wanted them to go. He wanted something from me so I could convince him to mount a strange dragon. What lever would he try to use on me?

We were both silent as Saboraak climbed toward the dragon cotes.

"I don't know why you wished to offer me a ride up through the city, lady, but it is appreciated," the man tried to say. "Have you heard the latest news?"

I kept the alluring silence.

Good. Your voice would be the opposite of alluring right now.

Long minutes stretched as the man tried to make small talk.

"A person appeared in the city last night and displayed the Ko in the sacred place. You know what that means! He has declared his mastery of one of the sacred doorways. The Exalted are worried – and they should be. No one has challenged them in a hundred years!"

I could see a large structure ahead, shaped a lot like a honeycomb.

The dragon cotes. We will join our friends there.

"I am Apeq A'kona," the man said as the silence on my end remained. "I sell marvels out of my shop in the seventh level. Perhaps you would like to come and see them, lady."

If by 'marvels,' he meant items that had been pawned, I had no doubt he was telling the truth.

You might have need of someone like this, Tor.

Now that was surprising! Saboraak was the most straight-laced straight-lacer I'd ever met. Was she really suggesting that I maintain a friendship with a criminal?

I think he is more than he seems. And you only assumed he was a criminal by his behavior. You have no evidence. I'm starting to think you are tremendously lucky, Tor. First, you survive what should have been your death. Now, you run into someone who we might need.

Need?

Ask him about the cormorants.

I didn't dare ask him anything! He'd know in a second that I was not a girl!

I think he already does. I'm afraid your figure is not shaped like a human female's. Is that insulting?

No!

I think that Zyla's password with her contact is cormorant. She keeps using it when she meets new people as if she is trying to connect with them.

And what made Saboraak think this man was Zyla's contact? The man in question was rattling on about the various jade carvings he had bought over the decades.

You were right to think that he was watching people. But I do not think it's because he is a criminal. You were also right to think you saw a glitter in his eyes at our appearance. And yet. I think it was for a different reason.

Just spit it out! Saboraak could learn a few things about being direct.

I think he was out here looking for Zyla. I think he is wondering if you are her in disguise.

No ...

Whatever you do, do it quickly. We are almost at the cotes. If he is only a criminal, we must set him loose before we enter. If he is Zyla's contact, he should go straight to her. Either way, he has been a good cover. The guards hardly notice us.

It was true. The guards around the cotes did nothing more than glance in our direction. The place was guarded and tended by men and women in livery.

They are paid a fee for the care and protection of the 'animals' here. Tell me that isn't insulting!

I swallowed and then turned back to Apeq.

"Do you have any cormorants in your jade collection?" I asked in my sweetest feminine voice.

His mouth twisted slightly. I felt my face flushing. My voice work needed some improvement.

"As a matter of fact," he said with a smirk, "I do. And it's my understanding that I owe you some fine pieces."

Now what?

How should I know?

Can't you read his mind? Agh! Saboraak was frustrating. Why was she so tied up with ethics all the time?

It doesn't work like that. It's not that I won't get you your answer. It's that I can't.

If only he'd say something more. I licked my lips from behind the veil, nerves making them dry. Maybe if I held his gaze, he would say something more. People always wanted to fill in the gaps in conversation.

"After all, they were paid in advance on your behalf when our mutual friend was here," Apeq said with a smile.

I tilted my head to the side, urging him to continue. I was *not* going to risk speaking again. I sounded like a strangled cat.

Eventually, his face paling, he added, "Hubric."

My eyes shut for a moment in pure relief. We would have orders. We would finally know what we were supposed to be doing!

Chapter Three

I found our contact! I could hardly believe it!

Maybe because it isn't true, trout. I found our contact when you thought he was a petty criminal.

We flew into the dragon cotes, Saboraak's annoyance making her flying more choppy. I'd never seen a dragon cote before, though I tried to look nonchalant as the huge honey-comb structure filled my vision. Dragons filled most of the rock structures. Their scales were bright in the dawn. Who would have thought there were so many people from the Dominion in the city?

It's a huge city. You could live here for months and never meet any of them.

They dragons in the cotes seemed excited about something. Gusts of flames puffed from the openings and more than one snapped his jaws.

A sudden headache hit me and I put a hand to my forehead, but surprisingly, as it faded, so did the excitement in the cotes.

"If you aren't Zyla-" Apeq began.

I waved a hand irritably, cutting him off and spoke in my normal voice. "Hold onto your dragon, Apeq. Give us a minute and we'll get you to your girl."

His silence worried me, but our cote was close. I could see Zyla hurrying to the front of it, a lantern held high in her hand as Saboraak slowed, gliding on raised wings. Saboraak's huge foreclaws reached out and she grabbed the lip of the cote, pulling us into the open-sided room with the ease of practice.

Zyla bounced from one leg to the next, her face flickering through emotions as we dismounted. She must realize this was Saboraak to be so calm about our landing. When had she realized that Saboraak could change colors?.

"Rumors are tearing through the dragon cotes!" She said as soon as our feet hit the ground. "They say that the signs of destiny were revealed tonight – the Ko! I've been listening to stories about them all my life. Do you know what this means?"

"The time of Legends is upon us," Apeq said gravely.

Zyla met his gaze and they were both nodding – true believers in some faith I didn't share.

"Legends will walk among us, touching our fates and drawing us along in their current," Zyla agreed. Her eyes were bright, and her mouth trembled slightly. Somehow, the intense emotion made her look even prettier – and also crazier. Don't get involved with crazy, Tor. Crazy kills.

"The time when magic will change forever and a new generation will rise up to take the place of the old," Apeq continued.

"The signs will show us the way."

"You are Zyla Cloudbender," Apeq said excitedly. "I've been waiting for you."

"You are my contact from Hubric?" Zyla asked, her head tilted to the side.

"One and the same. The boy exchanged the password with me. I am Apeq A'kona of the Jadefire House of Marvels." Apeq's smile widened and I found myself looking him over, judging what I saw. He was about thirty, which was a lot older than Zyla or I. I figured she was about seventeen and I was only a hair older than that.

He shouldn't be smiling at her so confidently. That was my job, not the job of an old man who sold jade carvings.

Jealous much?

Of that old guy? Of course not.

But the way Zyla smiled at him stung. It made no sense. I'd only known her a few days. What did it matter to me if she wanted to smile at an old man? I bet he didn't jump off a platform last night and stun a whole city with the sheer guts of a move like that.

You should play that back for yourself in your mind. If that doesn't sound jealous to you then you need to adjust your mindset.

Dragons! And girls! Frustrating – all of them.

I stormed to the back of the cotes, wrenching the veil and skirt off. There was a half-wall set up. Maybe the saddlebags were back there. Last I checked, there was bread in one of them and I was still starving. Zyla could go ahead and get googly-eyed over Apeq – what kind of a name was Apeq? – I didn't care. I was going to find something to eat.

There was a pair of cots behind the half-wall along with a set of hooks for gear and a small cook area. Dragon Riders must camp out in these places when they didn't have coin for inns or anything else.

This place took coin. Surprisingly, Zyla had some hidden in her boot sole. Enough to pay for a week here. I think that was all she had.

Saboraak's tack was hanging on the hooks. I opened the saddlebags carefully, searching for bread. There was only a tiny piece left. Thanks, guys. It crumbled in my fingers, but I ate it sourly. Crumbled or whole, I needed the strength food could provide. I was dog tired, bone cold, and hungry.

There was a wide metal dish full of red embers between the two cots. A brazier. I guess they heated these places that way. What I wouldn't give to throw myself into one of those cots, but right now they were occupied by a snoring Zin and a sick looking Bataar. He mumbled in his sleep, tossing back and forth.

I wandered over to him curiously, still licking the crumbs off my fingers. Why was he so sick? Saboraak had been hit by magical lightning.

I'm a dragon. I am built differently than humans are. I'm stronger.

Way to rub it in. But that point wasn't valid. I had also been hit by the lightning in the heel.

I sat on a small crate at the end of the cramped space and pulled my boot off, looking at my heel. It still stung, and the skin on my heel was glassy and smooth, painful to the touch. It formed a circle about the size of my thumb. The boot leather was burnt in the same place, leaving a hole about the same size as the wound on my foot. It was healing like a burn would heal - hurting, but not insufferable. I needed new boots when I could get them. Hmmm...

The lightning that hit us was not natural lightning. It was magic lightning. Dragons can be hurt and die from that, but it takes a lot to kill us. A human? I am surprised that Bataar is still alive.

And me?

Perhaps it is your luck at play ...

If it was, then I was very lucky.

If it's not luck, then there is some other factor. Have you considered those marks on your arms – the ones that have the city in uproar – might have something to do with it?

I shrugged awkwardly and put my boot back on. I hoped that the marks had nothing to do with anything. I hoped no one ever brought them up again. I would have to be careful from now on. I would have to keep them hidden.

But if they provide you some shielding from magical attacks, that can only be to your advantage.

We had no proof of that.

You and Bataar were each hit by a magical lightning bolt at the same time. You have a minor burn. He's struggling for breath in a cot. Proof? If that's not proof, then I don't know what is.

She made a compelling point.

Chapter Four

I WOKE TO THE SOUND of someone quietly moving around the enclosure. I rubbed my eyes and Zin darted past me like a flash.

I froze. If I didn't move, then maybe she would feel safe.

She froze, too, chewing her bottom lip and watching me.

"Don't worry," I said. "I just ummm ..." I looked around. I had fallen asleep on the crate propped against a wall. "I just fell asleep."

She didn't move, just stood there, watching me from the doorway of the enclosure. I tilted my head to the side. I couldn't really move without seeming threatening and I didn't want to threaten her. Skies and stars, the girl had been through enough. I shifted my weight and she flinched. Great. She hadn't been this scared of me before.

She was always with Zyla.

A paper slid from my lap and I reached for it. The writing was flowing and elegant like how I expected a magic book would be written.

Tor, it began.

Apeq and I have gone to his Jadefire House of Marvels to prepare a place for Bataar and Zin. Do not leave them alone. Do you hear me? I don't like having to trust you with them, but I don't have any other options.

Zyla.

Really? She didn't trust me? After everything I'd done? Girls were the worst.

I had a flashing mental image of her huge golden eyes framed by too-long eyelashes. Well, maybe they weren't the worst, but they sure did make things hard for a guy. I folded up the letter while I leaned over to look at Bataar. He was sweating and pale, his breathing shallow. I ran a hand over my forehead.

He needed ... I didn't even know what. He needed something. And he needed it soon or he was going to die.

Something magical.

I still wasn't convinced of that.

I shoved the folded letter into my pocket and my fingers hit the book in there. Maybe I should read this thing that people wanted so badly. It wasn't like I could do anything else. I couldn't leave these two here on their own and there was no food around.

Irritably, I took out the book, glancing up to where Zin was standing on tiptoe, trying to get a better look at what I was doing.

At least she still had an interest in life. That was a good sign.

The book was handwritten in a flowing script and extra notes and maps had been shoved into the pages. One of the maps was of the plains around two sky cities. The only cities that close together were Dominion City and Sky City. I peered at the tiny notations all around the map. Was this a layout of the campaign in the war? It looked an awful lot like troop allocations and logistics scribbled in the margins. I tucked it carefully back into the end of the book.

The front of the book had a title written in it: Ibrenicus Prophecies.

These are the prophecies collected by Ibrenicus of Haz, son of dragons.

For the time comes soon in which these prophecies will be needed so that the world is not broken by a war between the earth and the sky. For long years we have fought, but peace is brokered, and we lay down arms. We shall grow sleepy in comfort and one day our children will have forgotten the grim battles fought for the peace they think they hold in their palms.

Boring, boring, boring. We get it. People are stupid, and they destroy themselves with their stupidity.

Without the Ibrenicus Prophecies, we would have lost the war against the Ifrit Scourge.

Had she been there?

No.

Was that chagrin I was feeling from my know-it-all dragon?

I wish I had been there.

Well, I didn't. I was no hero and I knew how wars played out. The innocent died with the guilty and everything of value was spilled out across the ground including human love and life. No, thank you! All I wanted was my next meal and a warm place to sleep. I was no hero.

Your display last night was a great start to your life of anonymity.

Sarcasm, Saboraak? From you?

I flipped further into the book. There were scribbled notations in the margins beside some of the dusty old prophecies.

Here was one prophecy:

Surrounded on every side, not overcome,

Light battles the depths, commands armies come,

Her battle not with mortal man, but earth and fire

And beside it, the owner had written:

Ifrits are made of earth and fire. Knowing that, where does their weakness lie. Is it in opposites or in a stronger version of their own strength? If light battles the depths, from where does our help come? Could it be the skies?

Wow, the owner of this book really took it seriously. I flipped a little further to where the flowing script of the Ibrenicus prophecies seemed to end with the words:

These are all the prophecies of Ibrenicus son of Haz, son of skies, concerning the Chosen One and the coming age.

But why did the book keep going? In a tight hand, similar to the flowing hand of the prophecies above, but more ... hurried? stressed? cramped? ... another series of prophecies were written. I began to read, barely noticing that Zin had crept across the small enclosure and was sitting on the edge of her cot beside my crate. Her head pressed in close to me, so she could read, too. I sat still, afraid that any movement would spook her.

I read:

These are the prophecies of Savette, daughter of the light, Chosen One about the day to come.

The day of walking legends comes. A Legend returned for the north to fill the breach, to stop the leak of souls and death of power. His sign the brand of smoke on skin.

Uh oh.

What? Saboraak asked.

I only knew one man who had smoke branded on his skin.

Me.

Chapter Five

"YOU," ZIN BREATHED so quietly that I wasn't sure she'd spoken at all.

I moved very, very slowly so I could look at her and she smiled slightly before motioning to me to give her the book. I shouldn't give it to her. Not only was it precious, but people were willing to kill for it. That made it dangerous.

"Please?" she motioned again for it, her big eyes and slight figure made her seem child-like in her request. How could she and her sister have identical features and still seem so different?

Reluctantly, I passed the book to her and her smile grew before she shyly looked away, hopping further into her cot and jamming her nose into the book. Well, someone was happy. And if I was being honest, it made me feel warm inside to make Zin happy. Her smile was like a tiny dawn.

I was just standing up and stretching aching muscles when Zyla burst through the door. She tossed a small burlap bag at me, keeping a larger one for herself, and began to speak as I opened mine.

"Word has reached Ko'Koren of the forest fires to the south. I don't know how they got word so quickly, but travel outside the city is being restricted and the city watches are being redoubled."

Great. As if things weren't bad enough already.

Inside the bag was a loaf of bread and three boiled eggs. I gently offered an egg to Zin who took it absentmindedly and began to peel the shell from it as she read. At Zyla's sudden silence I looked up.

"Is that all?" My own shell was coming loose, and my mouth was already watering.

Zyla startled and her mouth worked silently for a moment before her eyes narrowed and she began to speak again.

"The four Exalted families – the royalty here - are all searching for the man who showed the Ko last night. They have their house guards and spies in the streets everywhere. Apeq has given us clothing that marks us as from his house. It should provide us enough protection to get across the city to the Jadefire House of Marvels. He's already arranging for a healer for Bataar."

"What a hero that Apeq is turning out to be," I said sourly. Who did so much for strangers without payment? He must want something from us.

Or he is simply a compassionate person.

In my experience, those were rare. I popped the whole boiled egg in my mouth almost melting when I reached the creamy yolk. Oh, skies and stars, that was good!

"Isn't he? He's waiting outside with a cart and a yudazgoat for Bataar. Here, you should change outside." She reached into the large bag and shoved a ball of clothing at me.

I took the ball with a scowl. I had to change out in the freezing cold with no shelter just because I was male? Bataar might have the right idea. Dying slowly by magical wound didn't seem so bad after all.

So, you admit it's a magical wound?

I stormed angrily out of the enclosure and into Saboraak's cote. At least there were three walls here. I hid behind Saboraak, grateful that she shifted to shield me in a corner of her cote. Someone had spread out fresh straw on the floor and beyond the cold, it wasn't actually that bad in here. Would she be okay waiting here while we moved Bataar and Zin to a safer place?

For now, though I don't like the thought of staying here for long. I'm going to keep an eye on the comings and goings of the city from here. Maybe we can deduce something from the patterns in travel and flow of goods.

Smart thinking.

I shrugged into a pair of close-fitting breeches. They felt little too snug against my legs, but they were more than long enough. I tucked them roughly in my high boots, added a homespun shirt and a close-fitting grey jerkin with a green fire embroidered on the front, and then a thick charcoal cloak on top of that. So, this must be how Apeq's workers dressed. Fancy. Maybe he was more important than I first thought.

I gather his house is of the minor nobility and he mostly keeps them afloat with trade at this Jadefire House of Marvels. Do me a favor and keep in constant contact with me. I'm going to get bored looking out the window all day.

Like I had a choice. She would just read my mind anyway.

You owe me a favor. I caught you when you leapt from a ledge.

Fine, fine. I'd remember to keep in contact. I strapped on my belt and hid the axe around the side of it where the cloak would cover it.

It's too distinctive. People will notice.

It's an axe.

There are oak leaves on it.

Well, there was nothing I could do about that.

Hand it over.

Reluctantly, I moved to the front of her cote and laid the axe on the ground before her. Was she smiling? That grin looked wicked.

Stand back.

I stepped back as a small burst of flame seared across the axe and then her huge talon scored across it, flipping it over with a flick of her claw and scoring the other side.

You should wait for it to cool.

I gaped. The axe as unrecognizable. Not only were the etched oakleaves gone, but a black soot coated the axe and huge gouges marked the axe head. The handle was fine, but seriously, she completely maimed my weapon!

I marked it. Now it has your mark.

My mark? I'm not the one with talons!

We are one and the same. Your oath said as much.

Well, I couldn't say no to that. Not when I owed her. Not when I was starting to like her. I stamped out the smouldering straw around the axe and grabbed a rag from the hooks in the wall to scrub the soot off the axe. After a few minutes in the cold, it had cooled enough to be moved.

"Almost ready?" Zyla called to me.

"Coming."

I reached tentatively toward Saboraak and she met my hand with her snout.

"Call me if you need me and I'll be here in a flash." I felt guilty leaving her here, but I needed to help with Bataar and Zin. There was just no way that Zyla could move them herself.

I'm a dragon. You'll need me. I won't need you.

If that made her feel better, then she could believe it. I grabbed the axe, still warm to the touch, jammed it in my belt and hurried to help Zyla carry an unconscious Bataar out the door.

Zyla and Zin were dressed in matching grey cloaks, green scarves, and green dresses that had some sort of structure to them that pulled tight around the midsection. They looked very pretty, and the structured dress and green flames stitched into the dress drew the eye away from their faces – a good thing when we were being hunted.

"Help me with Bataar," Zyla said as she finished wrapping a blanket around him. I helped her lift him, noting that Zin still had her nose buried in the book of prophecies.

"Men are looking to steal that book, Zin," I said mildly. For a moment it seemed she hadn't heard, but then she tucked it in a pocket in her skirts and calmly opened the door for us. Maybe she'd recover after all. Despite her faraway look, she'd at least noticed the door.

My hopeful feeling faded when I saw Apeq standing outside the dragon cotes with an expensive-looking cart and a pair of those strange, shaggy yudazgoats.

His smile was smug and self-assured, and his black hair looked like it had been oiled. Worse, now that he wasn't trying to find us, he was dressed like the rich man I was beginning to suspect that he was, in a fine silk coat of broad yellow and white stripes and a black silk cape with a cord that tied across his chest. I doubted it helped much with the cold, but it made him look like a man who could buy and sell me.

I scowled at the way that Zyla greeted him. She didn't need to be so friendly. Scowled at the way he seemed so concerned when we laid Bataar in the cart. Scowled when he ordered a man dressed in his livery to get the yudazgoats going.

"You don't mind walking beside the cart to watch Bataar, do you boy?" he asked me. "As long as you are in my livery, it's important that everyone sees you serving me."

My scowl was so deep when I assented that I worried it might stay in place forever. My only comfort was the memory of his green face when he rode my dragon.

Jealousy will blind you. Ignore his wealth and power. Focus on his good points.

Like his ability to steal Zyla's attention?

He can't steal from you what wasn't yours to begin with.

Her reasonableness was getting irritating.

Chapter Six

THE TREK THROUGH THE city was worse than I had anticipated. By the time we were halfway to the Jadefire House of Marvels, I was already blushing red from chagrin. Without Apeq's help, we wouldn't have moved more than a single level out of the dragon cotes. At every stairway and rampway, there were guards or men from one of the Exalted families searching carts and bags and questioning passersby. They were looking for a lone man on a dragon and another man who was sick.

"The Exalted thank you for your help," they told each person. But the 'help' was not voluntary. The weapons of the guards were on full display. Their armor looked strange to me, as if someone had modeled them after the cliff birds of this region. Their helms had a metal feather sweeping up and back over the head and under it, a series of real feathers formed a swept-back crest. Large feather-like panels of metal comprised their feathers, layered downward in pairs over their chests and across their backs. Their faces were set in unreadable expressions.

Twice, I was certain they were going to hold us up because of Bataar, but each time Apeq flashed a charming grin, offered them a green-sealed letter and a bow, and each time they let us past. I watched Zin at every stop, worried that she would show the book and one of them would seize it.

Now that I knew those prophecies might be about me, I just had to read them. Losing them would be a terrible blow. Sweat formed across my back despite the cold air. I took care with every glance, every movement not to draw attention to myself. Skies and stars, but I hoped the others were careful, too!

We were only two levels down from the royal level and all the way across the Eski mountain peak when I saw a building in the distance that spanned two levels. The building was painted a dark charcoal with a roof so steeply pitched that it was almost a cliff-face and scrolling woodwork under the lip of the roof looked like golden lace. There was a wide door at the top level equally decorated in intricately woven golden carvings. On either side of it, green flames leapt a full pace in the air in golden braziers, and banners hung beneath each round window with the green fire picked out against charcoal. The windows were filled with wooden lattice and something obscured my vision when I tried to peer inside.

Paned glass. I have heard of this marvel.

No wonder Apeq looked wealthy! He was marvelously wealthy. Which begged the question: why was he working for Hubric? Because if he was Zyla's contact here, then he was a spy like us, a traitor to his country.

Don't jump to conclusions. Watch and wait.

I wanted to respond, by my breath was sucked away when a pair of men in livery stepped smartly in front of us, hands raised.

"Ex-"

"Soldier," Apeq interrupted with a smile. "How may I be of service?"

"Our apologies but the Exalted House of Tanagers seeks the Ko. We will search the arms of every man here, if it please you."

It was clear from their tones that they would do it even if it did not please him.

My mouth went dry, my heart pounding. I glanced quickly behind me at the pressing crowds waiting for their turn through the narrowing of the boardwalk. I would be hard-pressed to squeeze through those people if they wanted me to pass, never mind if I was trying to escape.

"Surely there is no need, Exalted," Apeq responded. "These men are in my employ."

"Our apologies to House Jadefire, but even you are not exempt. Please, Ex – "

Apeq interrupted him again. "We will roll up our sleeves." He laughed and seemed completely at ease as he rolled up his sleeves to show his forearms. "I've never been complimented on my fine forearms. Perhaps today will be the day."

Zyla joined his laughter and despite the tension creeping over me, I felt a stab of irritation at the laugh. The other man in Apeq's livery already had his sleeves rolled up and Zyla was hurrying to Bataar's place on the litter. Why wasn't she worried?

Why would she connect you to the man who dove from the arches last night? She has no idea that they are looking for you.

Wasn't it a little suspicious that Saboraak had to rush to my rescue?

She didn't know why. She thinks she has nothing to fear.

I swallowed, sweat forming at my brow.

She was wrong. We had everything to fear.

The Exalted's guard inspected Bataar's arms and then looked at me. I glanced around worriedly. What if I charged forward? But there was just as much of a crowd ahead of me. I couldn't move freely without being stymied by all the people. I could leap over the rail ...

No! I am not near enough to save you this time. Pull a hair-brained stunt like that again and I will roast you alive. Just show them your arms. Maybe something will come to you while they are in shock.

"Tor," Zyla was saying urgently. "Show them your arms."

They were right in front of me now, hands on the hilts of their swords. I cleared my throat. It felt like I'd swallowed a mug full of mud. I couldn't seem to breathe naturally.

"Tor!" Her urging this time was a sharp hiss.

Reluctantly, eyes still searching for an escape, I rolled up my left sleeve. I was waiting for the gasp or the shouted order.

"Both sleeves," the man demanded.

Stunned, I looked down. There was nothing on my arm but smooth brown skin. My heart was pounding so hard that I couldn't hear the man, but he seemed to be repeating his demand. Hurriedly, I rolled up the other one, too. Nothing.

The other guard inspected Bataar's bare arms and then they were waving us onward before I could roll the sleeves back down.

I felt like someone had kicked me in the gut. What happened? Where were the marks?

An excellent question, Tor. We will have to be careful.

Chapter Seven

I WAS SO STUNNED THAT I wasn't paying attention as we neared the Jadefire House of Marvels.

Remember. Watch and wait.

Oh, I was watching alright. I watched as we found a backdoor on the lower level and Apeq whispered something to a 'servant' who was leaning casually against the wall beside the door. The servant was twice as wide as I was and taller, too. I watched as Apeq whispered something to Zyla and she laughed. What made a laugh sound like music? Could I make music that sounded as good as that laugh? That would be a neat trick.

Focus.

I was watching when Apeq ran a considering glance over me before motioning me and his servant to lift Bataar and follow him inside.

Oh, I was watching, alright. I was watching everything.

The Jadefire House of Marvels was even bigger on the inside than it seemed to be on the outside. The entire place was built around a central spiral staircase with so many ledges and nooks and small rooms that you could spend all day looking for something you had lost. Upon entry, I finally realized what the place was.

Apeq was a dealer in curios.

He seemed to have no guiding principle in what he chose to sell.

There were odd looking masks of metal or wood, statues ranging from the size of my smallest finger to one at the center of the spiral staircase that rose almost to the top of the second level, mirrors and instruments and rods of various lengths, rings of metal, rings of stone, rings of wood, displayed on shelves or in cases or hanging on walls, things that looked like weapons but glowed strangely. And that was just a list of things I could put a name to.

There were devices or ornaments or weapons there that I found impossible to name or even properly describe. All of them called to me, as if my curiosity was lit aflame simply be being near them. I felt a warmth in my chest as I entered the room that never really left.

I reached toward the first statue in reach and Apeq slapped my hand away from it. "No touching the merchandise! What am I supposed to do? Sell it with fingerprints on it?"

I turned my attention back to Bataar. It was odd that there were no customers or staff in sight, just wall upon wall of interesting things.

My eyes were huge from the moment we walked in the door to the moment we reached a back room and Apeq directed us to lay Bataar down.

"I'm afraid I couldn't move all the overstock out," he said, feigning sheepishness at the splendor that spilled over into even a backroom with a cot. Even the bed frame around Bataar's cot seemed to be valuable. The tangled metal that formed the four-post bed twisted in ways that boggled the mind. "But I did find a healer."

I froze, bracing myself for one of the oak-leafed goons I'd met before. My hand hovered near the axe. I was still rattled by the inspection outside and now this unexpected place was giving me the jitters.

Whatever is happening there, you should know that something is happening here, too.

Apeq ushered a middle-aged woman in a simple dress and apron into the room and I slumped with relief. There were no oakleaves on her attire.

Remember the building we hovered under? The one where we overheard the people speaking of not using the ropes to pull up supplies?

How could I forget?

The woman examined Bataar under our watchful eyes, laying a hand across his forehead and inspecting his leg where the bolt had hit him. She bandaged the wound there, but she couldn't stop shaking her head.

There have been people coming and going from that building all day. It's strange. They're of every status in this society and foreigners, too.

I felt a pull at her words, as if I should be there investigating instead of here, but I knew better. Bataar needed us.

"This wound cannot be healed by natural means," the woman said.

Told you.

"Do you know another way?" Apeq asked. I hated how wise and sensible he sounded and hated even worse how much Zyla smiled when he spoke.

The woman frowned. "I don't deal in magical arts, Ex-" He held up a hand and she paused, smiling. "Honored Apeq. If one of your marvels did this, you'll need to consult the Oak Order. My work is done with herbs."

"Can you give him any herbs to help?" Zyla asked, her voice thick with concern.

"They will only delay the inevitable, but yes, they may delay it by a few hours," the woman said. "Give me some space to do my work."

We left her to it, squeezing into the corridor beyond and following Apeq down a winding staircase lined with bookshelves. Books of every size and binding imaginable filled the shelves and were stacked or wedged on top of the orderly stacks so that there wasn't an inch of space not filled with books. I couldn't keep my eyes from widening. I'd never seen so many books in my life.

"I have a place for your sister here, Zyla," Apeq said, ushering us below. "Madame Rosen can see her after she is done with Bataar." He seemed to notice me suddenly. "We don't need you for this, boy. Go and find the kitchens. You look like you haven't eaten in a month."

I flushed, but it was hard to be angry at anyone who was offering me free food.

Besides, we have to think about this warehouse. Something odd is going on in there.

Well, I told you we should have investigated.

I feel ... drawn to it. It calls to me.

Ha! So, she criticized me for being drawn by danger and she was no better. This house of marvels was impossible to navigate between the narrow corridors and winding staircases.

Before I could finish the thought, the narrow corridor I was traveling opened to a huge room, three stories tall. The ceiling was shaped like a half of a sphere and painted with golden constellations over a blue cloud background. Someone had embellished it with white intersecting lines and notations. Beneath the ceiling, rose a large bronze contraption of spinning gears and wide concentric bands. Round spheres ticked slowly along ratcheting paths and the entire thing made a whirring sound that was oddly comforting.

There were chairs along the walls with small tables. The tables were useless as tables since every inch of them were covered with scrawled papers and books of notes. Around the room were tall, wide windows with those strange panes of glass that warped the world outside. They let light in, but the figures beyond were blurry as if I was looking through deep water.

I tried to inspect the central contraption, reaching toward the nearest sphere when a hand on my arm stopped me. I whirled and almost bumped into a man with a tray. He wore Apeq's livery.

"Who are you?" he asked, his eyes narrowing. There was a strange gleam in them.

"I work for Apeq," I said.

"You most certainly do not, boy. I am Vern Redgers and I run the staff. Here," he shoved the tray at me. "Eat something and try not to disturb the device." He looked around with a frown. "In fact, don't touch anything in this room."

I took the tray and sat at one of the overloaded tables. The tea was hot, the toast buttery, and a fruit I'd never seen made my mouth water with its tart smell and deep red coloring. I didn't wait for someone to come and snatch it all away. I started eating immediately. If the tray was for someone else and they noticed the mistake they would be back for it, but by then I would have had my fill.

When I had eaten far more than I could hold, I took three of the eggs off the tray to juggle. I needed to think. Juggling helped with that.

We had a problem – Bataar.

He was a wanted man and if he died there would be questions. Worse, I had a feeling that Zyla would never forgive me if I didn't find a way to make him well. Apeq was doing his best, but his best wasn't good enough to heal Bataar.

I juggled the eggs round and round and thought about the problem.

What healed magic? More magic.

And who had magic around here? Magikas – which were a definite 'no.' Those Oak Order guys. I shuddered at the memory of their 'healing house.' No, thank you.

So where else did you get magic from?

Remember those guys with the magic items? Like that spider you had. Maybe one of them could heal a person.

But how would I know which one and how would I find a place where magical items were stored?

I hate to say this, I really do...

Spit it out. No need to be shy when you frequently read my mind.

Wouldn't those Magikas sneaking into the city have more magical items?

They would.

And we know where they are sneaking in ...

I nearly dropped an egg.

Saboraak! You surprise me. I thought you didn't want me going in there.

That was when I thought it was a needless risk. Helping Bataar is different.

I changed the simple circle I was juggling into a more complicated back-cross and I let my thoughts drift on it. It was a risk and I was no hero – but I was willing to take a gamble when I needed to. And I actually didn't want Bataar to die. Mostly for Zyla, but also because I was beginning to feel just a little responsible for him. After all, if I hadn't tried to grab that spider I might have run to Saboraak quicker and maybe we would have launched into the air before he was hit.

The thought of that responsibility made me shudder and one of the boiled eggs flew out of my hand, hitting a table full of papers and knocking them over. I grabbed the other eggs hurriedly, left them on the tray and rushed over to hide what I'd done.

Bits of egg were scattered over the fallen papers and an open book was smeared with egg where it sat on the table. I gathered up the cooked yolk from the book, my face flushing at the waste of good food.

As I cleaned the book, a sketched image caught my eye. It was like a cross-bar with wings suspended from a chain. Beside it, someone had scrawled the words, 'increased luck, heightened fortitude.' Below that was a sketch of a fan with a strange bird etched on it. Beside that were the words, 'creates an impenetrable box.'

Wait. Was this book a list of items of magic? The next entry made my blood freeze. A bracelet of metal feathers was drawn and beside it were the words, 'heals magical wounds, lost.'

Hurriedly, I brushed the egg off the book and flipped through it. There must be a hundred entries here. I looked around and listened carefully.

There was no one around.

Good.

I stripped off my cloak, turned the coat with Apeq's sigil on it inside out so that the sigil was hidden and then put my clothing back on, shoving the book in the back of my pants where it was hidden by both jacket and cloak.

With this book, I could find a healing object. I knew where to look and I could compare anything I found to the rest of the notations.

But there are guards everywhere looking for you.

There were guards everywhere looking for a man with marked arms and mine were bare.

I found a catch on one of the paned glass windows and eased it open on stiff hinges. Time to go save Bataar.

I think you should wait for Apeq and Zyla.

If I did that, they'd send me to a corner somewhere to eat eggs while they had all the fun.

I thought you weren't a hero.

I wasn't. But couldn't a regular guy find a magic item, save the life of a friend, and count on his dragon for help?

Sounds pretty heroic to me.

Don't drag me into this hero nonsense.

Chapter Eight

IT TOOK MOST OF THE rest of the day to maneuver through the packed streets and roadblocks to find the warehouse. The task was even harder since I had only seen it from below. Fortunately, Saboraak was guiding me.

So close! I can see you every now and then when you pop into view between the buildings.

The walkway I was on now was narrower than many of the others, only allowing the traffic to be two people wide. We were nearing a very large red building with four different peaked roofs at various heights. In front of it, a large sign depicting a glowing gem hung over the walkway. It read *Bright Redemption.*

I think that's the place.

Really? It was hard to tell from here ...

Try it.

I thought that you disapproved of me doing this alone?

Well, now that we are here ...

There was a shadowed nook between the Bright Redemption and the next building. I snuck into that space to gather myself.

"Boo."

I jumped, my heart leaping into my throat before a hand slammed over my mouth.

"Shh!" In the darkness, Zyla's golden eyes seemed to almost glow.

"Zyla?" I gasped. "How are you here?"

Her expression was wry as she pulled me deeper into the shadow. I couldn't help the stab of enjoyment I felt at our close quarters. She could pull me into a shadow any time.

Focus.

"You left egg everywhere at Apeq's house," she scolded, her fists on her hips to emphasize her point. My eyes trailed down to them and she sighed. "Eyes up, Tor. You aren't the only one with half a brain! Apeq and I already knew we were going to need magical items to help Bataar. We came into the observatory to look for you and found that mess you made. Seriously, do you need to be house trained?"

Well, that just took the cake! Here I was risking myself to help someone else and she was scolding me?

"If you could just learn to talk to us and stop running off on your own, Tor Winespring. I swear, you are going to be the death of me! I was so worried about you that I had to leave everyone with Apeq and chase after you!"

"Worried about me?" Why did I like the sound of that?

"Of course, I was worried about you! You don't know what you're doing!" she hissed. "You don't know who these people are. You should have left this to Apeq!"

Apeq? The sound of his name on her lips made my teeth clench. *Apeq*, was it?

"Was it Apeq who rescued you out of that camp?" I asked. "Was it Apeq who took your sister along, too, when the dragon didn't even have room for her? Apeq who found the arch and flew us through? Apeq who risked his life looking for a healer for Bataar? I don't remember Apeq doing those things!"

"Are you so self-centered, Tor Winespring, that you expect a thank you for every single thing you do? You can't just do good things for the sake of doing good?"

She kept using my full name like it was some kind of weapon.

"You can't show a hint of gratitude?" I countered. I just couldn't stop thinking about her practically throwing herself at Apeq with all those sultry-eyed smiles.

"If you hate helping so much, what are you doing here?" Her expression sharpened, like she thought she was scoring a point.

"Well, I can't leave these things to you. You'd waste the day away smiling at Apeq instead of *doing* anything to help. Someone had to get up off their comfortable backside and find a solution."

She smirked. "You have a comfortable backside?"

"Don't twist my words, woman!" I felt the blood rushing to my cheeks. Why did girls always manage to make a fellow look like a fool? "If you want my help – and trust me, you need my help! – then stop pestering me and join in. Maybe you don't realize this, but this building has magical artifacts in it – like the kind that might heal Bataar."

She rolled her eyes, but her smile seemed genuinely amused. "Yes, I can read signs, Tor."

"Signs?"

"Bright Redemption? Apeq told me that it buys and sells ancient items and that some might have some magical power to them."

"Oh."

So, Apeq had known where to look, too. My face felt even hotter. Just when I thought I'd gotten ahead of him, it turned out he was ahead of me.

"Don't scowl, Tor. He's helping us! We should be grateful, not truculent."

I wasn't ... whatever that was. I was here to help a friend. She might make me feel knee high, but I could still help. I took a step toward the daylight, but I was pulled back by my cloak. There was amusement in Zyla's eyes combined with ... what? A softness of some kind.

Could it be compassion? It's foreign to you, but she might know what it is.

"Tor?" she said in that husky voice. My breath caught in my throat.

"Yes?"

"Let me do the talking, okay?"

"Why? I'm good at talking." I flashed her my charming grin, though it wobbled a bit under her intense gaze.

"Because I need you to watch my back. Apeq warned me about this place. He said he was worried that there might be some sort of ... deception going on. Things aren't precisely what they seem."

I wasn't going to promise not to talk. That wasn't my style.

"I'll watch out," I agreed, turning.

"And Tor?"

I turned back again.

She took a deep breath, like it was hard to say the next words. "I am thankful."

Women were the most confusing creatures on the planet. They were even worse than dragons.

I heard that.

Chapter Nine

THE INSIDE OF THE BUILDING was not at all what I expected. For such a huge building, the anteroom was tiny. A long counter ran across the small room and four women in maroon livery, with silver embroidery on the fronts of their jackets and multiple necklaces and bracelets of every style and metal and gemstone I could imagine, stood behind the counter.

A pair of braziers filled with glowing embers warmed the room and people lined up for a chance to speak to the women behind the counters. Some held items in their arms that they clearly hoped to sell. Others had empty hands, likely here to buy.

I stood nervously in line with Zyla. She kept her face in a bright open expression, but her lips were pressed firmly together, a sign that she was nervous, too. With no open shelves and nothing on display, it was going to be much harder to find what we needed. We couldn't just sift through items looking for something that matched what was in the book.

It was my job to watch. I watched and listened carefully to the people bargaining.

"It's here or nowhere," the woman behind the counter told the man in front of us. "If you want any price for your item, it will be the price we offer."

"I'm certain it has value, lady," he said, his voice gaining a shrillness with his desperation. "I think it may be magical."

"You know such items are rare," the woman said with a dry look.

"Yes! Rare! It should fetch a good price!"

They continued to barter, but I already knew he would lose. There was a spark in her eye like a silver coin. Maybe I was just seeing things.

I was watching an older woman ghosting behind the women at the counter. She whispered a word in one woman's ear while slipping something under her part of the counter, raised an eyebrow at another who jumped as if she had seen a ghost and proceeded to drive the hardest bargain yet.

The older woman must run this place. I wished I could hear her voice. I had a feeling that I might recognize it as the voice from below.

She had eagle sharp eyes and they drifted often to me, and to my arms. I scratched my forearm whenever she looked, needing to remind myself that they were covered by my sleeves. Not that it mattered, the signs were gone.

I felt like I saw sparks of silver in her eyes, too. I was seeing silver everywhere. I needed to stop thinking about it and maybe I'd stop seeing it in the eyes of every person I encountered.

The room gave nothing else away. There was no décor. Nothing on display. A harsh room full of harsh bargains.

Our turn was next, and I watched the woman with the hard eyes as we stepped forward. She was watching me just as intently, her dark eyes narrowing over her hawkish nose. A face that tolerated no nonsense.

"We're looking for an item," Zyla said confidently.

"What sort-" the woman behind the counter began, but she stopped, ducking her head respectfully when the hawk-nosed woman came to the counter. That really was a swirl of silver in her eyes, wasn't it?

It was. A sense of foreboding flooded over me, immersing me in a sudden almost panicked fear. Was Saboraak safe?

Safe and fine. The attendants here do not bring fresh straw often, though. I don't like living in dirty quarters.

I think this woman is like the men with the silver in their eyes!

Have her eyes suddenly popped and let silver leak on the floor?

No.

Call me when they do. Until then, let's take a moment to remember the squalor I am living in.

We'll get out and fly soon – hopefully sooner than later. I'd just help Zyla get the item and make sure that Bataar was okay and then Saboraak and I would fly away from this place. Maybe if we went to Ko'Loska there would be some kind of instructions for us. Here, it just felt like I was getting into more and more trouble.

In all the excitement with Bataar, I hadn't even remembered to ask Apeq if Hubric had left instructions for us. If he was our true contact, he would have those, wouldn't he?

The woman looked past Zyla to me and I barely suppressed a flinch at the swirl of silver in her eyes when she said, "Buying or selling?"

"Buying," Zyla said confidently, stepping between us to get the woman's attention again. "Your name, please?"

The woman flicked a fingertip and as if she had shot an arrow into a crowded room, the atmosphere of the place changed. Along the counter the woman began to wrap up their business, suggesting their customers leave immediately. Protests were quashed with urgent whispers.

"I am Karema Lo'Torlan, Keeper of the Bright Redemption," the woman replied. Her smile did not touch her eyes.

My hand drifted to my axe and I licked my lips as I watched the last customers being hustled out the door. Was this a trap? I put a hand on Zyla's shoulder – a warning. She brushed it off, leaning forward as if she could intimidate this Karema Lo'Torlan.

"You are here for an item of healing for your friend."

Zyla stiffened and I sucked in a breath. They knew who we were and why we were here. I could already envision Magikas pouring into this place.

Someone is here! They are entering my cote.

Saboraak sounded worried, but it was probably just an attendant freshening her straw.

"Healing items are extremely rare and valuable." Karema smiled.

I was trying to keep my eye on the serving women. They had us surrounded in a loose circle. Skies and stars! I'd allowed us to get trapped in here! I should have watched this place before assuming it was safe to enter. This was all my fault.

I can't get a good look at them. There's more than one ...

"I require a great payment." I didn't like Karema's smile at all.

"Whatever it takes," Zyla said.

Good.

A show of confidence in a sticky situation was a good power move. No need to let them see you sweat – even if we had nothing of value to trade for this item. Maybe we could 'borrow' it later if we knew it was here.

"I want something equally rare and valuable," Karema said.

"What do you want?" Zyla's head was held high, her tone bold.

"You booked a dragon cote for a purple dragon – though there is a gold in there right now. A girl with two dragons should have one to spare, yes?"

My eyes popped open at her words. No way! Saboraak wasn't for sale!

Skies and stars, they're here for me!

Saboraak? Saboraak, get out of there!

There was a gleam in Karema's eyes that had nothing to do with the silver swirls. Were those her people in Saboraak's cote?

Her smile widened to a toothy grin. "The dragon for the item. Or no deal."

Chapter Ten

SABORAAK? MY HEART was pounding and my breathing ragged. I really liked that old lizard. She'd better be okay. Why was she so quiet?

Karema pulled a bracelet of metal feathers out of her pocket and it was all I could do to keep my features from betraying me. That was the exact item we needed for Bataar! In the book, it had said it was lost.

"I have what you need here," Karema said, showing the bracelet to Zyla. When Zyla reached for it she pulled it away. "We don't let customers handle merchandise until we receive payment. This is not a charity."

"So, you need the dragon first?" Zyla asked. Her confident front was beginning to waver. I saw her hands fidgeting with the hem of her short coat.

"It's your lucky day today," Karema said. I had a feeling that if Karema thought something was lucky for me then the opposite was probably true. "We already have a deposit. You can take the item with you – but to get your deposit back, you must bring us payment. You have two days. If we don't receive payment by then, we will keep the deposit."

Saboraak? They wouldn't have taken her as a deposit, would they? If they took her, I'd tear them limb from limb. I'd pour that silver swirl in Karema's eyes on the ground myself. I'd –

I had no idea you were so attached to me already. I am touched. Though you will not need to become a barbarian on my account. I'm safe.

I breathed a sigh of relief. It had been a false alarm.

Not exactly. I had to flee the city.

What?!

"What sort of deposit do you have?" Zyla asked warily.

"Do you mean, what sort have we *taken*?"

Zyla was so still as she watched Karema that I thought she might be magically frozen in place. Karema's expression took on a deadly look.

"Bring out the deposit."

From behind her, a pair of armed men came out of a single door. They were holding Zin by her upper arms She was wearing a simple grey dress – a gift of Apeq's most likely. Her eyes were blank, as if she wasn't able to even see us here. But I noticed a small bulge in her dress pocket. She still had the book I'd lent her! Perhaps she was not as distant as we sometimes thought. My eyes narrowed as I tried to catch her gaze. Could she give us a sign? Any sign at all? There was nothing.

The thought of her a captive once again filled me with an unfamiliar coldness that had nothing to do with the temperature in the room. This couldn't be allowed to happen. I would not allow it.

I will fly back and give myself up for Zin.

No. There would be a third way.

I don't see another alternative. How many armed people are around you?

The jewelry on the attendants here suddenly took on a new meaning. Was it magical? Should I consider that to be a weapon? If I did, then we were surrounded by seven armed guards.

I will come to you.

Stay away! I was at the bottom of this mess. I'd brought them all here and I'd decided to come to this place. Skies and stars! A man sure could get himself in trouble just by trying to do the right thing. But since I'd made the mess, I'd be the one to clean it up.

Like you did with the egg?

Forget about the egg.

"Do you understand?" Karema asked, a sinister note in her voice.

Zyla lunged forward, but I caught her around the waist at the same moment that energy crackled around the twin bracelets Karema wore. I was right about the jewelry. The thought was not comforting. If anything could be a weapon, everything could be one.

"Let go of me!" Zyla yelled. I liked her fighting spirit. I'd probably do the same thing if I didn't realize what was going on here. We'd been suckered. We'd been suckered and trapped on every level and only idiots doubled down when they'd been suckered.

I bit my lip, anger at my foolishness flooding me.

"I'll take that bracelet now," I said through clenched teeth. At least we should get what we came for. Apeq would be expecting us to arrive home with it. Wouldn't he?

After all, we wouldn't be in this situation if he hadn't betrayed us. How else would they have Zin?

Chapter Eleven

THE CITY SMELLED OF spices and snow. It was strange how often that thought whirled into my mind with the others. We made our way back to Bataar's side through the dusk and slowly falling snow. My thoughts were a whirl.

I'd been suckered. I wasn't used to that. Usually, I pulled the cons around here, but now that I looked back it all seemed so obvious. Apeq with his bright coat and charming ways had distracted us all from what he was really doing. He wasn't after Zyla's heart – as I'd feared – he was after Saboraak. I should have remembered that she was more valuable than all of us put together.

I don't endorse that thought.

I should have realized that he was making me jealous on purpose, getting us away from our dragon on purpose, separating us at his home on purpose.

Worse, I was beginning to realize that I wouldn't be able to wiggle out of this like I usually did. When my mom died – so very long ago – her last words to me were, 'take care of yourself.' I took those to heart. I'd taken care of myself when I left her frozen in the streets before the city watch could snatch me up. I'd taken care of myself all those years in Vanika. You can't trust anyone else when you're living one risk to the next, but that was okay. After all, they were just trying to take care of themselves, too. That was only fair. And it made solving problems easy. As long as the solution meant you'd live to see another day, then you went with that.

But things were more complicated now. I had Saboraak. And surprisingly, I thought that maybe taking care of her might *be* taking care of myself. I wasn't sure I would survive without her anymore.

In fairness, you should know that Hubric made the bonding when we said our vows of commitment to each other.

What is the bonding?

It's a ... thing ... between dragons and humans. A sort of magic, perhaps. And not an entirely fair thing. But it does mean that your survival depends on mine.

How?

If either of us dies, the other dies, too. You would die within weeks of my death.

And no one told me? I felt the equivalent of a mental shrug.

Just don't die and it will be fine.

I didn't know if I felt betrayed or not and I didn't have time to sort that out. It was just one more complication in what was becoming a very complicated life.

Because Saboraak wasn't the only change. I felt very responsible for the girl back there who had wanted to read my book, and to the one who was stalking angrily by my side muttering under her breath. I even felt responsible for the man lying in a bed in a betrayer's house. And responsibility was certainly not my thing.

I was a free spirit, beholden to no man. I lived and died on my own efforts. I didn't ask anyone else to save me and I didn't go saving anyone else.

Except now I had four people to save.

Technically, I don't need saving.

Okay, three people to save.

There is a kind of freedom that comes from duty. A kind of freeing of the spirit that only loosens when you stop clutching your own interests so tightly.

That sounded like something you would tell children to con them.

Keep on caring for people and you may find it is true.

Or I might end up a broken man, betrayed, controlled by others, and left to die of starvation in a ditch somewhere.

Stop caring about others and that is exactly where you will end up.

I wasn't sure I believed her, wasn't sure I dared to live so exposed, but I didn't have time to think about that right now. I couldn't betray these people in this moment, so I needed a plan to save them all. Something that conned the con man. Something that took me from being a mark to finding a mark. Something really good.

Chapter Twelve

I WAS STILL BROODING on it when we reached the Jadefire House of Marvels. I only noticed that Zyla was shaking when we reached the door.

"Zyla?" I asked, reaching toward her.

She stepped back, her arms curling around her body protectively. "We left her."

"Only for tonight. We will get her back tomorrow."

Was she crying? Her hands twisted around the feather bracelet as her hot tears fell in the cold snow.

The snow was a blanket – so thick it shielded us from the people of the city even though we stood right on one of the boardwalks. I took a step toward her and into the shelter of the building and after a moment Zyla stepped into the shelter with me.

"We need the bracelet for Bataar," I reminded her. "We'll take care of that and then ..." I scrubbed my hand through my hair as my mind raced. I hated that downfallen expression on her face. There had to be a way to cure it. "And then I'll go in there and get her myself."

"You'll go in through dozens of guardians and magical items?" Zyla asked, her mouth twisting ruefully. Tears spilled slowly from the corners of her eyes.

"What? You don't think I can?"

She sighed. "No one can, Tor. Your confidence won't help. It will just mean you disappoint me."

"Look at me," I said, waiting for her golden eyes to meet mine. "I won't disappoint you."

She nodded but I could tell she was just pacifying me.

"I promise, Zyla."

Her broken smile broke my heart.

I was gentle with my next words. "Now, how are we going to sneak Bataar out of this place?"

"Sneak him out?" She sounded surprised.

"Well, we can't trust Apeq. He's clearly involved in your sister's capture."

"He can't be," she argued, wiping her eyes as her expression turned muley. "He's our contact here! We can trust him."

"If he's our contact, why hasn't he given us further instructions?"

"He was about to when you disappeared!"

"But – "

"Don't." Her expression hardened. "I have enough going on without dealing with your jealousy. You want me to trust you about Zin? Then trust me about Apeq."

I opened my mouth to tell an easy lie and froze. There was something about Zyla that made it impossible for me to lie to her. Instead,

I took a step back, shaking my head.

"Let's go get this bracelet to Bataar," I said instead.

At least we could agree on that.

Once Bataar was healed, all I needed to do was save Zin and then Saboraak and I could be free to leave this complicated city. I just needed to make sure Apeq didn't twist the knife in deeper than he already had before I could make those things happen.

The Jadefire House of Marvels was dark despite the occasional braziers warming the place and lanterns hung through the halls. Oddly, none of the staff seemed to be on duty – not even guarding the door, and there was not a customer to be seen.

"I don't know how they keep the braziers so full of embers," I told Zyla as we meandered through the labyrinth hallways. Everything seemed spookier there at night. The masks seemed to hide actual faces. The sculptures seemed alive in the flickering light. Any one of them might hold magic within. I almost thought I could hear faraway chanting. A trick of the imagination, no doubt.

"Coal," Zyla said. "They mine it here in the mountains. Why do you think they have a city in such a strange place? It's for the coal."

I didn't even know what that was.

A tasty snack. I ate the extra in the corner of my cote. I'm almost drooling thinking about it.

So, it was food?

It's rock – I think.

Rocks that burned? Impossible. But I didn't have time to think further on it. As we neared Bataar's room, Apeq stepped from the shadows as if he had been waiting for us.

"Zyla! I'm so pleased you've returned unharmed – and with the boy. I have sad news. Your sister is missing. She slipped away just after you left to find the boy."

Boy, was it? And did he really think either of us would believe that Zin left on her own? I knew her well enough to know she'd rather be curled up with one of the books in this House of Marvels than venture anywhere on her own. I pushed past him, unable to stomach his lies.

Behind me, I heard Zyla apologizing for me. "He's overwrought. We both are. Someone took Zin! They are holding her for collateral!"

"Collateral? This is serious, Zyla! Tell me how I can help."

I ignored him. I heard the sound of lies in his voice. I never should have believed he was safe to trust.

There was no lantern lit in Bataar's room, but moonlight flooded through the glass panes creating a watery-light effect through the room. I scanned the room quickly, but it was small, and no one could hide here. Something on the bed caught my attention and I took a step toward Bataar.

Bataar's sleeve had pushed up as he lay unconscious, and in the moonlight, a silver design wound around his forearm. A design I had never seen before.

Frowning, I pulled my own sleeve up and gasped when the design on my own arms lit the skin. Guiltily, I shoved my sleeve back down and hurried to Bataar, tucking his sleeve over the pattern. No one needed to know this about us. No one needed to know we both had ...

Ko. That's what they called it. Ko. Apparently, they are only revealed by moonlight.

I swallowed nervously, but I had no time to ponder it before Zyla and Apeq entered the room, holding up a bright lantern.

"Leave it to me," Apeq was saying. "I will speak to the authorities and we will find a legal way to settle this."

It sounded harmless enough – if you weren't watching for the deceit gleaming in his eye.

"Thank you, Apeq," Zyla said and I hated that her smile was so genuine. She believed him when she hadn't believed me. And he was playing her as a mark. I clenched my jaw until the muscles hurt. "Let's help Bataar."

Zyla slipped the feather bracelet over his wrist and we waited.

"It will take time," Apeq said. "Magical healing can take days. Don't expect miracles."

I watched him, looking for any twitch in his expression that might give him away. How did he know so much about items imbued with magical power? Or was this just another con? I knew he was in league with those people at the Bright Redemption and I knew he was working against us. Would they really heal Bataar, or was this just another move in a game I still hadn't solved?

We move tonight, Saboraak. You and I. You're the only one I can trust.

A wise choice. I'm afraid that everyone else feels – complicated – at the moment.

Which was just another way of saying that they were lying. And whether they were lying just to me or to themselves, too, I couldn't work with liars. Not on this. Not when I was about to put everything on the line.

Chapter Thirteen

BY THE TIME I REACHED Saboraak at the edge of the city, it was nearly morning. It had taken time to sneak out of the House of Marvels without being caught. More time to navigate through the icy walkways and staircases with only the moonlight to guide me, warming myself by street braziers as I went. Men and women in white livery filled the streets at night, trimming lantern wicks, filling braziers, hauling packages on their backs, and chipping ice from staircases. I realized that they must work for the ruling families of the city. Black embroidery on their chests always displayed one of four different sigils, an oaken wreath, a single flame, a soaring eagle and a swirl of smoke.

I was conscious of their eyes on me and found myself tugging my sleeves down more than I needed to. I didn't dare let them see the Ko on either arm. By the time I reached the far side of the city, I was growing anxious to find Saboraak.

I've been hiding under a warehouse here. I snuck back into the city when the guards weren't looking.

I thought Zyla said that sneaking past them was impossible?

Maybe I'm better at this spy stuff than you might think.

Speaking of which, I should probably tell her what I was planning.

I believe I have gleaned most of it from your thoughts. You want us to con the con men, yes?

I did.

You want to arrive at the Bright Redemption at first light, riding me like a charger strutting across the battlefield at dawn. I will be golden, of course.

Well, my thoughts hadn't been quite so fairytale-esque.

Then you will exchange me for Zin.

I flinched, anticipating her anger at that part.

A sensible idea. When the switch is complete, you simply return Zin to safety and sneak back to release me. I will morph into a different color and shape and who will be the wiser?

It seemed like a great idea. Which was why I was nervous about it. Was I missing something? I'd missed all the cues that something was wrong when I brought Apeq into our lives.

I will be fine. I'm a dragon, remember? A few tiny pawn shop owners in a human-built house will not stop me if I choose to leave. I will flame the place to ash – leaving time, of course, for their escape.

Of course. I had the only dragon in history who was nervous about killing humans. She was probably worried about those yudazgoats, too. I felt embarrassment through our mental link.

Actually, I found them very tasty. You didn't expect me to eat the food in the dragon cote, did you? It was disgusting.

How so?

It was already dead!

Yeah, we tended to prefer our meat dead. Funny, that.

Mock me all you like, I think it's boorish.

I ducked in behind the warehouse she'd described. There was a variance in the rock here that left a large gap behind part of the building. Ah! There she was. I couldn't help the affectionate pat at her muzzle, though I pulled my hand back quickly when she tried to return it and drooled on my sleeve.

Well, we were *just talking about food ...*

Time to mount up and fly to the Bright Redemption. Wait. No saddle? Again?

I can't very well saddle myself.

I shuddered. Riding a dragon bareback made me feel my mortality a little too intensely.

There was nothing for it but to take the gamble.

I climbed awkwardly onto her back and gripped with my knees. She needed a leather strap necklace. Something to wear all the time so I at least had something to hold in moments like this.

If you get me a necklace, could I at least request a gemstone pendant?

She could ask for anything she wanted as long as she realized I was broke. Okay, enough chatter. Let's fly!

We flew over the sleeping city together. Saboraak was good about adjusting her glide to keep me on her back as we flew past the layered buildings and tiered streets, all frosted with white snow like Sata Day cakes.

I just wished I knew why Hubric sent us to this country. Who were we supposed to be watching and what were they supposed to be doing? We seemed like a bad choice for this job. Saboraak wasn't meant to be cooped up in a dragon cote and I wasn't meant to be trying to keep two girls safe.

I'm okay with it, Tor. I want those girls safe, too. And I'm curious about Bataar. How do you think he got those marks?

Maybe he found a door in the wilderness and put his hands on the symbols just like I did.

How many of those doors do you think there are?

Maybe it was the same one.

I doubt that.

We were almost at the Bright Redemption and the sun was just coming up over the horizon. I could count on my fingers the number of hours I'd slept since I met Zin, but I was going to make sure she didn't lose any more sleep by being held prisoner.

Okay. Focus. When we get there, you will do the talking.

She was a joker after all! I liked that.

Smoke hovered over the boardwalk as we landed, a tiny localized cloud from the braziers and the morning sun. I slid off Saboraak's back as soon as her feet alighted on the walkway. It was a tight fit. These walkways were never meant for dragons. I scrambled around her to lead the way to the door, hoping she'd fit through it.

Maybe if they take me down below, I can find out if they really are smuggling people through this building.

Now who was being irresponsibly adventurous?

You might be rubbing off on me. Don't tell anyone.

Just follow the plan.

I was starting to get nervous. I didn't like the way my breath hitched in my throat and my thoughts scattered like leaves in the wind. Hold it together, Tor! Hold it together.

It was time to take the gamble.

Chapter Fourteen

IT WAS A TIGHT SQUEEZE for Saboraak to push through the door while I held it open. This building wasn't made for dragons. Once she was in, I followed, circling her to come to rest beside her snout. She placed it delicately on the counter.

"I knew you'd eventually see the light," Karema Lo'Torlan said, coming through the sliding door to the backroom.

She moved lightning fast – much faster than I expected a middle-aged woman to move. She was nose-to-nose with me before I could gasp, her eyes narrowing as they squinted into mine. There was a glimmer of silver in them, swirling like milk in tea.

I took a step back, but she reached beneath the counter and pulled at something and with a *snick* the long counter began to slide, grinding like rock on rock as it withdrew into one of the walls. Karema smiled with satisfaction and then stepped forward to fill my vision again.

I gave her my best cheeky grin – middle-aged women loved it – and tried to ignore the stab of fear down my spine.

"I see all sorts of things," I said, lifting an eyebrow suggestively. Let her guess what that meant. It was important to keep an opponent on their toes, always guessing what you were really saying. "I'd like to see Zin."

"Of course, you would." She stepped back, and I swallowed.

While we were talking, people had crept into the room, forming a circle around the edges. A big man just behind Karema shoved Zin at me before I could even get a good look at him. She stumbled into my arms with a squeak and I tottered backward, trying to stabilize us both. She shoved something into my trouser pocket so fast that I doubt anyone would have seen her move and then, when we had caught our balance, she looked up at me with huge eyes – eyes that were actually looking at me – not faraway like they usually were. There was a plea in them.

"The girl may go," Karema said, her words like iron. "You, must stay."

Wait. What?

"That wasn't the deal," I said.

"The deal was for the dragon," Karema said coolly. "But we are not fools. We know how this works. Without you, the dragon is useless to us. So – you come with the dragon. Tell your friend to go quietly. No need for her to get hurt, hmmm?"

I swallowed.

"Go, Zin," I whispered. I hoped she could find her way to Zyla. Or that Zyla would find her. I hoped she would be okay. It felt like letting a child leave unsupervised. She was too innocent for a city – too vulnerable.

Someone behind us opened a door.

"Don't even think about it, Tor," Karema said smoothly. "Any move from you and we will snatch her back. And yes, we know your name."

My smile twisted into something darker. Of course, she knew my name. Apeq told her. I had no doubts about that. Especially now.

I watched Zin walk out the wide doors and tried to keep from clenching my fists. Now what, Saboraak? Should I jump on your back and we can flame our way out of here?

You know I hate to kill people.

Even if they were trying to kill us?

I shall make an exception in this case.

I shifted toward her, about to mount when there was a low laugh. The big man – the one I hadn't had time to look properly at – was laughing. He looked familiar, though I couldn't place his face at first. His head had a scarf wound around it veiling his face and he wore a short black coat and gray breeches. Had I seen him before? When he spoke, all doubt faded away.

"You are clever for a street urchin," Shabren the Violet said. He looked different outside his violet robes, but his voice remained the same. I would have known it anywhere. It haunted my dreams. "That's what you were before Hubric recruited you, isn't it? I heard word from the men I stationed at his mountain retreat that the two of you were together. So now I know why you robbed me of those girls. But, no matter. I do not need them. I do not even need the Kav'ai who was with them – not with you here."

"Let me guess," I said smugly. "You're looking for fashion advice. Purple never was your color, but that scarf isn't doing much for you, either."

"Always the joker. You really think you can talk yourself out of this? Tell him what to expect, Karema."

Behind me, the door slammed shut. Zin was free. I didn't hesitate. I pulled my dagger free from my belt and launched myself toward Shabren. The man was lightning fast, but it wasn't his wild dodge that sent me flying, it was something powerful slamming me from behind like the fist of a giant.

I slammed into the doorframe behind Shabren and dropped to the ground, my whole body shaking and convulsing. I couldn't stop it, couldn't control it, couldn't even form words from behind my chattering teeth.

"Don't kill him! We need him alive to manage the dragon."

I wanted Saboraak to run. I wanted her to flame them all, but she wasn't doing any of that. Docile, she waited as one of the side walls slid open to reveal a staircase. Like a pet dog, she followed Karema's gentle urgings.

"Come along, dragon. Follow Karema."

She followed.

"Take him below and lock him up. He won't be able to move again today." Shabren's voice seemed far away.

I was still shaking uncontrollably when rough hands lifted me up and carried me after her. I couldn't control my head and neck and when we took a turn at the bottom of the staircase and I lost sight of Saboraak. I felt a tear leaking from the corner of my eye.

Trust me, she said as my consciousness faded away.

My last thought was that it had been a mistake to trust anyone – even myself.

Chapter Fifteen

I SHOULD HAVE KNOWN that there would be a trap there for me. I should have known that people like that didn't make deals. They took what they wanted one way or another. They only let people go when they had no value. Fortunately, they hadn't thought Zin was valuable and they didn't think Zyla was. Maybe, they'd even let go of the idea of needing Bataar. If I was lucky, all my friends had escaped unharmed except for Saboraak.

When I woke, cursing and grumbling, I found myself in a huge room, twice as tall as it was wide – and it was wide. The room was divided into two parts with a wall of bars down the middle and a barred door to enter or exit between them. On the other side of the bars lay Saboraak. She was lying right up against them as if worried about me.

I've been very worried.

On her side of the room, there was also the trapdoor we'd hidden under just a day ago and a large arched door that looked identical to the one we'd flown through to get to Ko'Koren.

On my side of the bars, there were shelves and shelves of items. Some of them had small paper tags tied to them. Shelves soared toward the ceiling, shelf upon shelf, so high that ladders stretched up between them, rolling on small wheels to span the shelves.

Apparently, I was an artifact just like the rest. Available for trade ... or study. Perhaps I would end up a shriveled skeleton on one of those shelves with a small paper tag attached to me.

Don't be so dramatic.

We've been kidnapped and imprisoned and you think I'm being dramatic?

No one has tried to kill us yet.

Then what was their plan?

Saboraak looked sheepish. What did she know?

Shabren is from the Dominion, so he knows about our bond.

And?

He knows that if you die, I will be useless.

They were keeping me alive to use Saboraak. They'd said as much. What did they want her for?

That has yet to be determined.

Did that mean they didn't know what they wanted her for, or that she didn't know?

I don't know. I've been trying to read their thoughts, but I can only read what's being thought in the moment and trust me, it is not a pleasant experience. Karema is an ambitious woman – driven and hungry. But Shabren – there is something rotten inside him – something that affects everything he is near. I don't like going near his thoughts.

Well, I didn't like being caged. We all had to make sacrifices.

It's not simply that it's unpleasant, Tor. Thoughts are infectious. And I am particularly vulnerable.

How was that true?

I am compassionate.

I thought she was always saying that a lack of compassion was my weakness.

I am. But a lot of compassion is also a weakness. I can see things from many perspectives, feel things from a thousand different narratives. It leaves me open to ... altered viewpoints. Ideas not filtered through logic or objective truth. It leaves me ... weak to the narratives of others if they are strong enough.

You mean he could change your mind?

An apt summary.

That was ridiculous.

I fear for my integrity.

There was no way I'd let her become infected by someone's erroneous view of the world. I'd just set her straight. No one could fool *me* that way.

It's true. Your imperviousness to the opinions of others lends you an armor in this that I simply do not possess.

Could she get me out of here? Nothing would be a problem if we weren't here to deal with it.

I could flame my way free, but that would still leave you trapped. I can't rip your bars apart with my mouth and I fear that were I to try to flame you loose, I may inadvertently kill you.

We were in quite a pickle.

It was long hours before we saw anyone and when we did, it was one of the jewelry-bedecked counter women. She seemed surprised to see me awake but she left food and water for me and water for Saboraak. She didn't say anything, not even when I gave her my most charming grin and offered to play cards with her, but I did see a silver swirl in her eye as she left. Either my imagination was playing tricks on me, or all the people at the Bright Redemption had that same swirl in their eyes.

The hours dragged. I went from fearful to bored and frustrated.

This was all Hubric's fault. After all, he sent us here without proper guidance. If we had clear instructions, we wouldn't have trusted the wrong people and ended up in this mess. If I ever saw him again, I'd want some answers.

Eventually, I remembered the book Zin had jammed in my pocket and brought it out. If nothing else, it would help with the boredom.

I flipped through to the pages with the cramped hand. Those ones interested me the most. Anyone who took time to write something down when they were clearly under a lot of stress must have something important to say.

I flipped too far in the book, to the last few blank pages and a folded page fell out. I picked it up, unfolding it. The writing here was nothing like the flowing letters of the Ibrenicus prophecies or even the scrawled commentary. It looked more like a spider had walked across the page, sliding in the ink. It said

Headstrong Bull,
Three there stand but four there be,
One the shape of gnarled tree,
Wait for moon before you go,
Fail and you will never know.
H

Cryptic.

Headstrong Bull – that's funny. It's almost as if it were written to you.

Tor meant bull in the tongue of the ancients. That's what Ephretti told me. I didn't really like that. Bulls were not known for their sneakiness or intelligence.

Why not?

Because they were big and ungainly.

So are dragons. No one would make the mistake of thinking us unintelligent.

You'd be surprised. People can make some pretty stupid mistakes.

It could be a note to me. After all, Hubric had given me the book and "H" could easily be him. I repeated the little poem to myself a few times. It rhymed nicely, and it stuck in your head. Could it be possible that I'd been blaming Hubric this whole time for leaving me without direction when he'd left me a note?

I think so, yes.

Could it be that this note would take us right to whatever we were meant to find?

Maybe.

But why write it in a riddle?

Aren't you a spy?

And spies were clandestine. They snuck in shadows and passed coded messages to hidden allies. They had hideouts and cool items to help and amazing allies.

Ahem.

And the best of the best in fighting power.

That's me.

And ingenious mastermind plans.

That would have been nice an hour ago.

If I could just puzzle out this riddle, then I could find out what Hubric wanted.

I hate to burst your bubble, but it probably isn't a bunch of cool stuff. If this riddle leads to something, it's probably just better instructions. He wouldn't want to leave them directly in the book. That might be too obvious. Too easy to slip into the wrong hands.

I pondered the note as the day passed, pulling systematically at each door and trying the hinges as I thought. I investigated the items on the lower shelves with an equally systematic approach, comparing them, by light of the brazier, to the scrawled pictures in the book I'd stolen. None of them matched, though they were endlessly intriguing. I couldn't even tell what half of them were.

Three there stand but four there be.

What three? What four?

I pondered it as day faded to night and our captors came down to feed us, refill the coal in the braziers and shove a blanket through the bars for me.

"Don't mess with the items on the shelves or Karema will be angry," was all the woman in jewelry said as she left.

The stuff they give dragons to eat in this place is disgusting. Can I have your coal?

I needed that fire to survive the night.

You can sleep pressed up against me.

With metal bars between us?

It will be fun.

I pondered it as Saboraak ate the coals from her own brazier, complete with the fire rushing through them.

Pondered it as I stared at the doorway on her side of the bars. It seemed to sing to me, a song only I could hear. It was as if it was trying to pull me through the bars toward it. Trust me, doorway, I wanted out of here without any extra pull. What was a doorway like that doing here? Could they be moving people through it like we flew through the other doorway? Perhaps that was what they were discussing when Saboraak and I had been hiding under the floor.

Maybe Saboraak should see if she could go through that metal doorway. She could probably escape that way.

And leave you alone to freeze in the night? I don't think so.

I'd be happier if I knew she was free and safe. And she could fly, so where could that doorway take her that she wouldn't survive?

Underwater? The heart of a volcano? So high up the air is too thin for me? I don't think so! I'm happy to stay here.

Maybe it would spit her out where we started, and she could go for help.

I am not willing to risk it.

Come on, Saboraak!

I won't budge on this, so you might as well stop asking.

I kept watching the doorway and wishing I could push through the bars to test it myself. I pondered threes and fours as I stared at it until I eventually grew tired and gave in to sleep. I cuddled as close to Saboraak as I could. She was warmer than I would be on my own.

See?

And I dreamed of fours and threes and strange doorways until my eyes popped open.

Chapter Sixteen

"TOR?" THE WHISPER HISSED through the echoing room. I shivered awake. The side of my body pressed along Saboraak was warm, but the air was frosty, and the remaining brazier had burned down to ash.

I didn't recognize the voice in the dark. I scrambled to my feet, letting the blanket fall to the floor. Who was that?

A lantern was shoved up through the trapdoor and a figure scrambled up. I didn't think anyone could get up there without the help of a dragon. You would have to climb that huge cable to do it at all. In the light of the lantern, I saw Bataar straightening.

"Bataar?" It couldn't be him. Only yesterday I thought he might not survive.

"It's me, alright," he said, a grumbling tone in his voice. "You should be glad Zyla likes you so much that she sent me after you. Do you know how hard it was to climb that cable with a lantern in my teeth? Do you know?"

"I have no idea," I said drily. "Here I was, just relaxing in the comforts of captivity with no respect for all your hard work."

"I don't know why those girls like you, Tor. You aren't the charming guy you think you are." Bataar strode over to the door of my prison.

"Are they okay? Zyla and Zin?"

"They're with Apeq. They'll be fine. He gave them dresses and he was taking them to a dramatic performance this evening."

Dresses? Dramatic performances? While Saboraak and I rotted here? That was beyond cold! I clearly didn't need to worry myself about the two of them.

Bataar jiggled the handle on the barred door.

"Don't bother trying to pick the lock," I said. "I already did. It's unpickable."

"Just because you can't do a thing doesn't mean it can be done," Bataar said airily.

"I'm glad to see that your recent illness hasn't damaged your sharp tongue," I replied, but I was actually pleased that he was okay. And I was pleased he was here. At least someone had come to our rescue.

I saw the feather bracelet glint on his wrist. If he was still wearing it, then maybe he wasn't all the way well. I felt a nervous pang. Maybe he shouldn't be here trying to rescue me. It could hurt him.

Bataar stopped fiddling with the handle and lifted the lantern to look around the cavernous room. I heard a low whistle as he caught sight of the door.

"Don't touch it," I warned. "It could take you anywhere."

But he had those Ko on his arms, right? Which means he must have seen one of these before.

"This shouldn't be here," Bataar said, anger in his tone. "Look! They chipped it out of the rock! They affixed the slab right here in the floor. It's blasphemy!"

"It's certainly dangerous. Only a fool would want to touch one of those doors twice."

Bataar lifted the lantern as if he was trying to get a good look at me to see if I was joking. All it did was show his own face, curiosity painting every feature.

"You know about the Doors of Heaven?"

"I know you have a silver swirl on your arm that came from these doors," I countered. Ha! Beat that, Bataar.

His face paled suddenly, horror filling his eyes. He hurried back to me, grabbing the front of my coat through the bars and whispering.

"Who have you told?"

"Relax, man. I haven't told anyone. I saw them last night before I snuck out to get Saboraak and come to pay the price for the little bracelet you're wearing."

He flushed, glancing at Saboraak who was snuffling quietly in her sleep, her drool scoring the stone floor like acid.

"If you tell anyone ... you won't tell, will you?" His eyes were so wide I thought they might fall out of his head. He looked more desperate than I'd ever seen him.

"Of course, I won't," I agreed.

He ran a hand over his face.

"Look, Tor. You're my Secret Bearer now." He said 'Secret Bearer' in a way that made it almost possible to hear the capital letters. I'd never been anything so formal sounding in my life. He continued, "If I'd known ... I had no idea you would bring me to this city. I can't be here. I don't dare be here. I was trying to flee to the Dominion when I met you and I still need to go there. I can't stay in Ko'Torenth."

"Well, here's a thought. Break me out of here and I'll help you leave."

He nodded briskly. "And the doorway?"

"We could go through it. The girls are fine here without us. Dramatic performances and dresses and all."

Bataar's brows squeezed together. "We must not enter this doorway under any circumstances. It is taboo to speak of it."

"Well, then why are you asking about it?"

"It should not be here."

"We can't take it with us," I said calmly. "It's literally built into the floor."

They'd laid the rock the door was attached to in the floor when they carved this huge room from the rock. Only one wall and a piece of floor that held the trap door were made from wood. No surprises there. It was why the building looked small from the outside when it was massive.

He nodded as if I'd said something profound. Maybe the illness had messed with his mind.

"Why don't you try looking for a key to my lock?" I suggested. "Then we can leave doorways and psycho Magikas and all this craziness behind, what do you say?"

He nodded as if I'd given him sage advice and pulled a burlap sack out from his belt, handing it to me. "Gather your things."

I didn't really have things. But my captors did. I eyed the shelves, chewing my lower lip. They'd stolen me, so it stood to reason that stealing from them wouldn't be wrong. It would only be fair. But what to take? I had no idea which items were magical. The ones I'd looked at hadn't been in the book.

I'd searched the lower shelves. So, my best bet at finding something magical would be to take it from the higher shelves. And the more the better, so small things. Jewelry. Tiny statues. This kind of thing.

I climbed the shelves to where I hadn't searched yet and began to stuff handfuls of small items into the sack until it was so full that I could hardly tie the top.

"Tor?" Bataar whispered through the darkness. And then there was a loud squeak as the door to my prison was opened.

I leapt from the shelves to the ground. If there were guards posted, they would have heard that! I rushed out the door, but already I heard feet rushing toward us. I double checked that both books were secure in my pockets as I ran.

Saboraak! Wake up! Wake up!

Her snoring increased.

I rushed over to her, my burlap sack clinking as I ran.

"Saboraak, wake up!" I pushed at her, trying to wake her. "Come on! Come on!"

Bataar, always a pragmatist was already scrambling up her back. "How do you ride her with no saddle?"

"With difficulty!"

I said. I scanned the room looking for anything that might protect us against the guards when they came but the room was mostly empty. There were a few empty crates to one side of the room and looped ropes. I grabbed one of the ropes in case that would do any good and threw it to Bataar who caught it one-handed, his other hand still holding the flickering lantern.

Was that my axe hanging on the wall? I rushed to it at the same time that Saboraak woke with a jaw-breaking yawn. She shook herself, and Bataar yelped, the lantern flying out of his hand and smashing against the wall. Darkness flooded the room as my hand closed around the axe handle.

What now? I couldn't see anything in this dark. There was a shout from the other side of the door and I settled into a defensive squat, my mouth dry and hands shaking. I was no hero. This wasn't what I'd been made for at all.

Steady now. Who is this on my back?

Bataar. Get ready!

The door opened with a crash and light flooded back into the room. I spun, threw the sack to Bataar, and then gripped the axe in both hands ready to fight. My breath was already too fast, and my eyes blinked too rapidly, like they'd forgotten how to operate properly on their own.

Karema stepped through the door, jewelry on her arms and around her neck catching the light of her lantern and refracting it.

"What do you think you're going to do, hack your way through us like a country lad through a forest?" Karema asked.

My breath caught in my throat as my mind raced to try to decide on my next move.

What was she doing awake at this time of night? I'd expected Shabren. He seemed more like a stay-up-all-night-and-torture-people kind of guy.

She lifted a hand and a powerful but invisible force hit my hand. The axe flew out of it, clanging as it hit the bars in my former prison.

Steady!

Behind me, heat flashed through the air, so hot that I felt the hairs on my neck singe. If she'd burned off all my hair, she'd have some explaining to do. What was she trying to scorch back there? Not the doorway?

A new hairstyle could only be an improvement.

Bataar yelled something I didn't understand. I swung my head to see him leap off of Saboraak and rush toward the doorway. It was brightly lit along the edges as if someone was shining a bright blue light – brighter than any sun – from behind the door.

"They're coming through!" he said, reaching toward the doorframe.

Karema twisted her hand toward him and I leapt in front of it. If we had enemies coming through that door at our backs, then Karema and her gang were my problem.

A second powerful force knocked me backward. Lantern light gleamed off Karema's bracelet as I sailed through the air, hitting the ground and sliding across it.

The bracelet! All that jewelry they wore was full of magic!

Knowing didn't help me. I was climbing to my feet and trying to recover my axe, when Bataar rolled up his sleeves and grabbed the doorframe with both palms. Light flashed up his arms – silver and sun-bright along the lines of his silver tattoos – the Ko. The light faded from the edges of the door and Karema screamed.

I leapt just in time to block a second blow from her magic rings – a blow that felt less like a punch and more like a gale-force wind – and then I was flying through the air and hitting the stone floor with a thud.

I saw quick glimpses of Bataar rushing back to Saboraak and flinging a rope around her neck, of Saboraak flaming the guards who burst out from behind Karema. Her flame narrowly missed scorching me.

I was still skidding across the stone from Karema's last blast. The wind hadn't let up.

Grab something!

There was nothing to grab.

I slid past the doorway – dim now – too far away to grab it. That force must be pushing me across the ground! Why did the air behind me feel so cold?

I blew a hole through the wall while you and Bataar were distracting Karema so we could escape.

Now she tells me!

Frigid air bit at me as I clawed at the floor trying to stop my careening. The magic gale pushed only me, but it pushed with a force I couldn't fight. In front of me, Karema's eyes widened with horror and then there was no more floor underneath me.

I plunged through the empty air.

Chapter Seventeen

STEADY!

I was falling, falling, the air rushing around me. My heart was in my throat. My eyes streamed with water. Where was Saboraak? She was my only hope!

But above me, I saw flames and bits of wall flying outward and no dragon emerging from those flames. Seconds felt like hours as I fell. In the darkness, the bright flames burst like flowers in the night. At least I would die watching a spectacle.

Steady!

My heart was racing as if it was trying to get every beat possible in before I smashed on the ground below. My mind rushed, trying to see and think every thought before time ran out. My gaze scanned across the three faintly glowing peaks of the three parts of Ko'Koren.

What was that strange outcropping to the side of the last mountain? It looked just a little like a gnarled tree.

From the bright flames above, a sudden boom shook the air and a dragon burst out through the wall, debris and flame and ash scattering in the air around her. She dove toward me.

A very nice effort, Saboraak.

But she would be too late. The city was growing too distant. I was falling too fast.

At least no one could say I'd lived a boring life.

I looked one last time at the bright moon and then I closed my eyes. I didn't want to see this last part. I wanted the last thing I saw to be the moon. It felt good to know it would still be there long after today.

Long after I was gone.

Unbidden, the riddle came to mind:

Three there stand but four there be,

One the shape of gnarled tree,

Wait for moon before you go,

Fail and you will never know.

Wait. Had I just solved it?

I felt something tighten around my ankle and then my spine shivered like the crack of a whip and I was buoyed upward, dangling by one foot.

I told you to stay steady. I had to make sure Bataar was fastened tight before I took the dive.

I dared a look through squinted eyes.

Saboraak gripped my ankle between her teeth, her wings flapping hard as she gained height. On her back, a shaken Bataar clutched the gunny sack and the rope slung around her neck and stared at me with wide eyes.

Yeah, welcome to my world, Bataar. It only gets weirder from here.

I'm afraid he cannot hear your thoughts.

Really? How surprising.

Oh. You have once again resorted to sarcasm. Can I assume that means you were afraid when you were falling?

Afraid? Was she kidding? Anyone would be afraid if they were falling to their death!

I did solve the puzzle. Which was handy since we couldn't exactly go back to Eski now that we'd set one of the local businesses on fire.

Where to, Tor?

We're going to that fourth peak – the small one that hardly seemed like a peak at all but instead looked like a gnarled tree when the moon was behind it. And quickly, if you don't mind. I'm getting lightheaded dangling like this.

I love adventuring with you!

You love this? Falling through the night, bursting out of flaming warehouses, constant danger, never enough to eat or sleep?

Precisely!

I'd bonded a mad-dragon. Did dragons go insane?

I'm not insane. I'm just beginning to find the fun in life you always seem to find.

Well, if this is fun for you, Saboraak, then stick around. I have a lot more where that came from.

I'm counting on it.

The gnarled peak was growing slowly closer and I couldn't help but feel excitement. Maybe there would be instructions there from Hubric – or even just a place to sleep for a full night. Hope blossomed within me.

I'm counting on you.

I didn't dare let her down.

Dragon Chameleon: Mist of Power

Chapter One

MY FOOT HURT. I WASN'T saying that Saboraak had pierced the skin or broken it or anything, only that it hurt like crazy. And my head hurt, too. I wasn't meant to be dragged through the air upside down. That was hero stuff and I was no hero.

You could have fooled me.

I was still holding the axe. I couldn't have said why. It made more sense to just drop it, but my frozen fingers couldn't relax if I tried.

Above me, Bataar was riding like a king on Saboraak's back. Tor? Oh, don't worry. We'll just scoop him up like a fish and drag him to wherever we are going.

Don't be so dramatic, Tor.

And we were in trouble. We were being hunted now. Powerful people wanted us dead or wanted to use us. Neither Bataar or I could show our faces at night – just in case someone demanded to see our arms. We had no safe house, no money, and nothing of value except the items I snatched from the basement of the magical pawnshop. My whole life dangled from a thread just like my body dangled from a foot.

Maybe you should be acting at the theatrical performance Zyla is watching. Histrionics would suit you.

Don't remind me. She's with that stuffy Apeq. He betrayed us. I know he did. And now he's charmed Zyla and Zin into his pocket.

Forget him and focus. We're nearly at the peak that looks like a gnarled tree. What should we be looking for?

I didn't have an answer to that. I'd only figured out the first part of the riddle so far.

Three there stand but four there be,
One the shape of gnarled tree,
Wait for moon before you go,
Fail and you will never know.

We found the fourth peak. Which meant that the next clue must be about the moon – somehow.

The three mountain peaks ascending from a single base, Eski, Balde, and Ziu were lit up by smoking braziers and hanging lanterns, but their lights were small from here. The gnarled peak was just out from the edge of the middle peak, Balde – out on its own tiny peak like an island in the air, almost hidden by the perpetual mists that rose from the base of the mountain. The moon hid behind the jagged rock of that peak, but there were no lights, no ladders, no walkways, no signs of people at all.

Let's fly closer.

Saboraak – my dragon partner and dare I say, friend? – drew so close to the peak that she almost scraped her wing tips on the rock as we flew

If I'm not your friend after saving your life three times, then I'm not sure what else I could do to earn that title. You're a hard boy to please, Tor.

Wait. What did I see glimmering in the moonlight? Was that the symbol of the Lightbringers, a rising sun over a hill? It was scrawled as if written by hand in silver on the side of a rock. The marking was so small that you had to be nearly on top of it to see it.

Saboraak flew closer and I tried to twist to get a better view.

Stop squirming!

Why was it so faint?

I think it's an ink that only can be seen in the moonlight.

Did everyone have that stuff? Don't even get me started on doorways that tattoo it to your arm ...

There! Behind the symbol, a rock jutted out and behind the rock was a dark shadow.

You want me to try to squirm into that shadow with you in my mouth?

She was already landing like a bird of prey on the lip of it, ducking her great head and slipping inside the rock.

"I've been meaning to ask you," Bataar said from above. "Where are we going, exactly?"

"I'm following a hunch," I said through gritted teeth. My head bumped against the rock below. "Oww!"

Sorry. It's dark in here and I can't flame for light with your foot in my mouth.

We all have our trials to bear. I wished I could roll my eyes mentally.

There was the sound of flint striking and then a flickering flame above us.

"I always keep a flint and candle stub on me," Bataar said.

I bet that when he was a kid the grownups were always pointing to him saying, 'You should be more like Bataar,' to other kids. I was never friends with kids like that.

It was hard to be too bitter when his candle lit the cavern with weak light. It was big in here. Bataar lit a lantern on the wall and I gasped as the light grew stronger.

Saboraak dropped me.

"Ow!"

I crashed to the ground, barely shielding my head with my arms before I landed. My legs and back hurt from the drop.

You were only an inch above the ground. Don't be a hatchling.

You should know, Saboraak, that humans are not built with permanent armor. You could have snapped my neck!

So easily? You are delicate things ...

But I didn't have time to chastise her more. I checked my leg for gashes and was relieved to find that her teeth hadn't broken the skin.

I leapt to my feet. Time to explore. I'd fuss about the bruises on my legs later.

Or you could thank me for saving your life ...

In one corner there was a fireplace – venting through a tunnel to the outside, I guessed – with wood set in the hearth and stacked in an alcove to the side. Bataar was already dismounting with his gaze set on the fireplace.

A pair of cots were near the fire and a wide rug with a small table and chairs of various types were set between them. Bookshelves lined one wall and a set of shelves with supplies lined the other wall. I set about exploring immediately with one of the lanterns while Bataar lit a fire.

This main room was the size of three dragons, mostly empty, and smelling of acid – a sure sign that Saboraak was not the first dragon to occupy this area. Tack hung on the wall beside the entrance – dragon saddles, bridles, and saddlebags. I almost pumped a fist in excitement.

Small rooms led off from the main room through jagged doorways with no doors. One led to a room with water flowing slowly down the rock, another to a room with a stone-carved lavatory, another to a dry storeroom. There were barrels and casks sealed within. I grabbed a crowbar and cracked a small cask open. It smelled of cider. Tasted like cider, too. My eyes grew big as I looked around the storeroom. If all of this was food, we could live here for months!

I snatched up a slip of paper lying on the shelf beside the cider and read it in the lantern light.

Tor,

I'm assuming you found the food first and this note. There is coin at the back of the shelf. Please use it sparingly. It may be hard to get more to you.

There are doves on the upper floor. Use them wisely to send messages through my network. If we have been separated, please send a report immediately.

If we were separated, then no doubt the note I gave you brought you here. You may have no idea of how vital your role here is.

Gather as much intelligence as you can on the Doors of Heaven.

If a man arrives in the city with Ko on his arms, this will begin a disruption in Ko'Torenth society that will ripple throughout the world. Send word to me immediately if this happens, but at all costs, avoid the succession war that is bound to follow.

Avoid the Exalted, except to gather information on them. I think specifically of an Exalted by the name of Apeq A'kona of the House of Flame. I do not know what he is planning, only that he seems to be entangling half the city in his scheme.

We are most keen to find out a few things. Watch for these:

First, are the Magikas fleeing the Dominion allying themselves with Ko'Torenth?

Second, has Ko'Torenth found a solution to the problem of magic disappearing from the world?

Third, does Ko'Torenth plan to continue their covert operations against the Dominion?

A succession war would certainly delay all of these outcomes. While that would be beneficial to the Dominion, I caution you in the strongest words: Do not start a succession war. Do not search for a Door of Heaven. If you find one, do not touch it. Avoid entangling yourself in the affairs of Ko'Torenth or becoming known to any of the Exalted.

I will return to you soon.

Hubric.

Oops. Too bad I didn't find that note sooner. I would have at least pretended to try not to break all of his rules if I'd known what they were.

I looked up from the letter to find Bataar in the doorway. He leaned one shoulder against the wall, arms crossed over his chest.

"How long have you been a spy?" he asked.

Chapter Two

MY MOUTH FELL OPEN. I shut it with a click and then grabbed the cask of cider and shoved it at him to cover my pause.

"Here, take this out by the fire. I'll bring something to eat."

He rolled his eyes, but he took the cask and I opened a sack on the bottom shelf, grabbed a handful of white potatoes from it and followed him to the common room, shoving the potatoes on the hearth close to the fire.

"That's it?" he asked.

"I'm not a lord's chef. Just be glad there's food."

"There's enough food and supplies here to keep us stocked for months," Bataar said. He was looking healthier. His clothing was loose, but his drawn face was warm with color again. The bracelet must have worked well. "I found another sleeping room and a room filled with clothing – all sizes and types. You're a spy."

I ran a hand through my hair. I still didn't know if I could trust Bataar. I never had known that. He saved my life last night – but he could have his own motives for doing that.

I sat on the hearth, warming my back by the blazing fire. He stood opposite, arms crossed and a scowl painting his face.

"I don't know who you are," I said. "I don't know if you can be trusted. The only thing I know for sure about you is that you have those marks on your arms. And you knew what that door was. You shut it when people were trying to come through, didn't you?"

I didn't like sitting when he was standing, but the fire felt warm at my back. And I wasn't going to stand up just to make a point. What did I have to prove?

Don't stand. It will increase the tension of the confrontation. Take a sip of that cider instead.

I swallowed and reached for the cask of cider. There were no cups nearby. I sipped cider right from the cask as Bataar's frown deepened.

"What do you want to know?" Bataar asked.

"Who are you?" I took another sip.

"That's complicated."

"Where are you from?"

His mouth hardened. "Kav'ai."

"I know nothing about Kav'ai."

He shrugged. "We are desert nomads. Ko'Torenth claims the land we wander on. We say they are only settlers there. We are the land's true inhabitants. Now that their magic is running out, they want ours."

"Does that have something to do with your arms?"

"What if it does? Are you a Magika, that you would regulate magic?"

I shook my head. Talking to Bataar was like walking without shoes in the winter. His arrogance could freeze a puddle in midsummer.

"Why are they hunting anyone with those marks?" Maybe if I kept my tone friendly he'd at least try to be helpful.

"I don't know. I was unconscious when you brought me to this city. I know they are ... picky ... about who they allow to wear them, but how they would know that anyone has them ... ?" He shook his head. "Who would be fool enough to show them off?"

I felt my face flushing. I had shown them.

"What were you doing in Shabren the Violet's camp?"

"I was fleeing Ko'Torenth – looking for safety in the Dominion – when he scooped me up as a captive. He didn't know who I was, but they didn't want anyone to go south and tell the people there about the Magika camp."

I poked the potatoes, turning them so the heat of the fire would bake them evenly. Maybe there was salt back in that storeroom.

"Why would you flee Ko'Torenth?" I asked.

He looked away for the first time, gaze running across the wall and then the ceiling as if he were trying to avoid answering at all."

"Why would you flee Kav'ai?"

Eventually, he spoke, his voice hoarse and thin. "There are prophecies about me. I don't want to end up like that. I *won't* end up like that."

I cleared my throat. "Maybe you won't. Prophecies are just words. They have no power."

He laughed, a dry, mirthless laugh. "Words have ultimate power, street boy. They will drive me mad."

I almost rolled my eyes. Saboraak always complained that I was too dramatic. She should listen to this guy.

He makes a strong point.

Really? This guy?

"Now, do you trust me?" Bataar asked.

"I'm not a boy, I'm a man." I was – technically. Nineteen was a man, right? I was probably nineteen. Maybe twenty. Okay, maybe eighteen. I wasn't really sure. I was some age in there, but definitely a man.

"As you say." He shook his head like he just didn't care.

"What do you want?" I asked him. If I knew what he wanted, I'd know if I could trust him.

"I want to escape my destiny. I want to get rid of these Ko."

Get rid of them? That seemed impossible.

"Are you allied with any of the Exalted here?"

He flopped down on one of the cots, throwing a forearm over his face. "No."

"Do you plan to sell me out to earn their favor?"

"No." His voice was muffled by his arm.

"And Zyla and Zin?"

"What about them?" His words were hard.

"Will you betray them?"

"No." His answer was fast.

"Are you going to mess with that doorway?"

He spat to the side of the cot so violently that I flinched. "If I never see another doorway, I'll die happy."

I sighed and poked the potatoes. I had his word – for all the good it did me. Words were nothing. Ephemeral as spider web.

"Are you a spy, Tor?"

"I am," I said. "And now that we have that out on the table, you are going to tell me everything you know about the Doors of Heaven, the Ko and the Exalted families here."

"Can we at least eat those potatoes first?"

"Sure."

After all, maybe we'd both be in a better mood with full bellies. The potatoes, it turned out, were surprisingly good.

Chapter Three

YOU CAN'T SPY FROM inside an isolated cave. That was the first thing that occurred to me as I drifted off in the cot beside the fire. Saboraak had crawled over to place her muzzle along the side of the cot as I fell asleep. Oddly, it felt nice to have her acid-smelling breath beside me. No one snored like a dragon, but even that was comforting. When I woke in the night with wispy memories of friends I hadn't seen since they died, of fire ravaging my city, of falling through the air – well, a dragon snore is a very solid thing.

We were going to have to leave the hideout to discover things. And we were going to have to gather information. It had taken me hours to decide if I would really trust Bataar last night. He had napped in the cot while I finished cooking the potatoes and investigating the other rooms.

Read his mind for me, I urged Saboraak. Tell me if I can trust him.

It's harder than you might think. Sometimes you just have to take a gamble with people, Tor.

I liked gambles, but not where people were concerned. It was too hard to cut your losses if things went bad.

When we were eating the baked potatoes I eventually said, "Do you still want to go to the Dominion?"

Bataar sighed. "What's it to you?"

"I'm still worried I can't trust you."

"But?"

"But I have to trust someone. I'm worried about Zyla and Zin and I have a ... task ... to accomplish."

"Are you saying that if you can trust me then you'll let me help with the task?" His eyes had a surprising light in them.

That's hope.

"Sure," I agreed with a shrug. I didn't really want help, but I didn't really want to be stabbed in the back either, and having him nearby meant I could keep an eye on him.

Bataar surprised me, rolling up his sleeve to show me the bare skin underneath. "Follow me."

He led me to the door and showed me the skin again, standing out with the silver-bright tattoo his arms had when I looked before. I noticed – now that I could see the whole thing – that it was a stylized bird soaring over mountains. The Ko.

"I received these Ko at the Door of Heaven in Ashadana of Kav'ai. By these marks I swear, you can trust me."

I scratched my own arm awkwardly. There was no way I was going to show mine.

"Okay, so I'll trust you. But why do you want to work with me?"

"You're spying for the Dominion, right? My people are threatened by Ko'Torenth, too. Maybe if I help you, I won't need to fulfill any moldy old prophecies. We can overthrow this place with just human actions. No magic. Just ingenuity."

I put my hands up. "Whoa! No one said anything about overthrowing anything!"

"Don't be naïve. Your Dominar wouldn't have sent spies if she wasn't planning on moving on Ko'Torenth. If she attacks, they'll forget about the Kav'ai, and I won't have to be the Ko Bearer. I can just be Bataar Bayanen – son of Mynaar, son of Lataar, Chief of the Stone Basin Kav'ai and my people can continue their traditions in peace."

"What are your traditions?"

"Like I'd tell you!"

I shook my head trying not to sigh. "You can keep your secrets, Bataar, so long as you tell them to me if it turns out I need to know them."

I needed to know everything. I hated that he wouldn't tell me, but he would slip up eventually and his secrets would all come tumbling out. I just needed patience.

People never really kept secrets. Secrets were like mice. You could box one up, but it was always looking to get out and the second it saw an opportunity it would be squeezing through whatever crack it found and scrambling all through the house.

Bataar's secrets were no different. They wanted to get out and show themselves to old Tor. I just needed to be patient and let them do the work.

"Deal," Bataar said. His first mistake. I always turned deals to my advantage.

But we went to sleep in peace and the next morning we were both more cheerful as I cooked breakfast over the fire. I'd washed and then found a fresh set of clothes that I rather liked. They were certainly grander than anything I'd worn before. I was almost certain that the white shirt was made of real Baojang silk and the close-fitting leather trousers, knee-high boots, bracers, and leather vest were well made and durable with just enough buckles and trim to make them fashionable. My clothes were fine enough to pass for nobility or a well-to-do merchant, but plain enough that they wouldn't look strange on a craftsman or traveling bard. I even found a new fur-lined cloak to wear when I went out. The clothing alone made the trip to this cave worth it.

For my part, I think I will shift to a new pattern, Saboraak said in my mind. *I have never liked Gold.*

To be honest, it didn't really suit her.

Over on her side of the room, she morphed from Gold to Black – it really didn't matter which color she chose. The war had dispersed dragons in every direction as they fled wholesale defeat at the hands of Ifrits and Dusk Covenant that any color of dragon may have ended up here. The frill around her head disappeared and large horns sprouted from her head and chin.

I grinned wickedly at Bataar's shriek of fear.

"It's a demon!" he yelled, leaping onto his cot.

"It's Saboraak," I said calmly, scooping porridge into bowls and handing him one.

"He – "

"She," I corrected.

"She just changed her shape and color!"

"She does that." I took a bite of porridge, keeping my face straight. I was enjoying this.

"This is the same dragon that saved us before from the tents of Shabren?"

"You didn't know that?"

"I thought this was a different dragon!"

I laughed.

"Do they all do that?" Bataar asked.

"You mean the other dragons?"

"Yes!" He got down off the cot gracelessly. I liked that. Bataar was always so smug about his good looks and flowing graceful movements that it was nice to see him thrown off his game. He was dressed like me in clothing found in the back room, but instead of a leather vest and bracers, he wore a fine red brocade coat that made him look even nobler than I did.

"They're all male out there. Only the females can shift color and shape – and now that you know that you are *my* Secret Bearer. So, don't tell anyone."

He snorted. "Secret Bearer is a sacred title. You can't just swear someone to secrecy with it."

"Okay, let's put it this way," I said, taking a bite of porridge. "Keep the secret or Saboraak will make you regret it."

She hissed dramatically, baring her teeth.

You know I won't hurt him.

He didn't know that, though. Bataar looked pale as his gaze danced from Saboraak's snarl to my stern gaze.

"Of course, her secret is safe with me. She makes the perfect spy, though, doesn't she? No one can tell which dragon she is at any time. If you got to know which dragons are in the cotes, she could impersonate any of them. Especially if one had a rider who looked anything like you."

Now that was an idea with potential. I mulled on it as we finished our breakfast and prepared for the day. This time, I packed little items like a pocket knife and a flint and steel in a small belt pouch. Some of Hubric's gold made its way into the pouch, too. Things on this mountain were unpredictable, and I didn't want to be caught out again.

My last trip was up a winding staircase to where doves were housed in a small dovecote. It was open so they could come and go. Was that normal? Hopefully, the dove I chose would actually take the message to Hubric and not just fly off. I carefully attached the handwritten scrap of paper I'd prepared to the leg of one healthy-looking dove.

It read: *In Ko'Koren. Ko revealed. Door of Heaven found. Magikas gathering. Collecting more information. T.*

It would have to do for now.

Chapter Four

IN EVERY CITY THERE are entertainers. They can sit on any street corner and juggle or play an instrument or perform an act and no one pays them much attention except to throw a few coins in their hat if they find the act to their liking.

Before heading out, I had reluctantly changed my cloak from the warmth of the lush black one to a threadbare cloak at the back of the room. There were clothes here for every purpose and the items that went with them and a little rummaging had found an appropriate cap and juggling balls. Perfect.

It had been even harder to leave Saboraak behind for the day. I was worried she would be bored.

Since I met you, I have sustained many injuries and seen little sleep. I need time to regain my strength and that means a deep dragon sleep. Don't get into trouble. I won't be able to hear you when you call.

With that, she had gone silent, eyes closing and breath slowing. Well, that was one problem sorted out. Our next problem had been finding the way back to the city without being seen, but we were lucky enough there, too. One of the corridors leading off from the room was a long cavern that eventually ended in the wine cellar of a boarded-up building in Balde.

Bataar and I had argued the whole way up the corridor about how we would go about spying, but eventually, I had won. He would traverse the cities to make his way to Eski, check to see that the girls were okay, and return undiscovered. It would also be nice to know if the Door of Heavens had been damaged in our escape, but I wasn't sure if he could find that out without discovery.

"You're insane," was his only response to that. "The girls, yes. I will check on them. The door can go back where it came from."

"And where is that?" I had asked, but he shut his lips tightly, compressing them into a firm line.

I had an equally challenging job, though Bataar had claimed it was the easier one. I worked my way up through Balde to the upper levels, juggling on boardwalk corners and crossways near to inns or important houses. I was trying to collect whatever information I could. Even here in Balde there were house guards checking for Ko, but they didn't trouble me. It was daylight. As long as I didn't stay out beyond dark, I was safe enough.

I heard scraps of conversation as I went.

"They say the Exalted of House Tanagers have welcomed the Magikas from the Dominion," one woman said as she passed me. I strained my ears as she paused nearby with a well-dressed friend. "The other Exalted won't want them to have an advantage, so everyone will want to bring these Magikas into our lives here."

"You should think about offering them a cheaper price at your inn, then," the other woman said. "Succession war or not, people still need places to stay. And of course, your inn is the best, the home of the Kav'ai artifacts."

Sometimes it was hard to remember that these people treasured lying, and then other times it was plain as the nose on your face.

"Hush, Sash!" the other woman sounded horrified but she looked pleased with the flattery. "No one has spoken of a war ... yet."

They looked around furtively before hurrying away, but I shivered and almost dropped a ball. If every Exalted house in the city welcomed the Magikas, they could establish a powerful base here – maybe powerful enough to attack the Dominion again. I hoped that part was a lie, too, but I was worried there was truth to it.

I traveled up another level, still listening as I took a place beside a fancy house with stylized bird banners. Guards were stationed at every entrance, their glances trailing any passersby, but I began my juggling, hat placed at my feet, and they ignored me after that.

"Exalted House Ye'Kut is throwing a Midnight Masque!" a young noblewoman said excitedly as she passed me. Her golden dress swirled in the gusts of snow, peaking out from under her thick snow-fox pelt cloak. I was so distracted by her big eyes and pretty smile that I almost dropped a juggling ball. She laughed, tossing a coin into my hat and her companion, almost equally pretty pulled her past me.

"It's a pity that parties have to be masked. It feels like such a shame to cover our faces! And I barely have time to have a new mask made! The one I had before was in the old style and it just isn't fit to be worn. The Masque is tomorrow night!"

Their chime-like voices were caught by the wind after that and blew away, but my mind was racing. A masked event thrown by the Exalted. What better place for a spy than that? I could almost bet that there was a mask in the items back in Hubric's hideout.

The wind was growing colder and the stares of the guards were starting to unnerve me. Time to pack up and move on.

I was just about to retrieve my hat when a familiar laugh caught my ear. I froze, gaze whipping up to see Apeq and Zyla strolling arm in arm toward the house with the Bird banners.

"You are most kind Apeq – " the rest of Zyla's words were caught by the wind, but as she passed her gaze caught mine and her eyes widened. She saw me! She gave a quick shake of the head as she passed, as if she was warning me not to try to talk to her.

I gathered my cap up, my heart racing. She was with Apeq – who I now knew was one of the Exalted and who I was almost completely certain had betrayed us just last night. And she was smiling and laughing as if she was completely safe. Blood rushed to my head and it took all my self-control not to rush in and snatch her away from him.

As they drew up to the door of the great house she glanced over her shoulder, caught my eye again and gave me a fierce warning look. Whatever she was up to, she didn't want me interfering with her.

My breath caught in my throat.

Apeq said something and her musical reply drifted to me over the wind.

"A Masque? How delightful!"

That settled it. Bataar and I were going to that Masque.

Chapter Five

"ARE YOU SURE SHE'D want us to be there? If she was scowling at you, she might want us to leave her alone," Bataar protested as I shoved a mask in his hands.

Like I was going to let Zyla run this whole show. She kept thinking I was incompetent, but hadn't I been the one who had saved her sister from the Bright Redemption? Hadn't I been the one who saved her out of that tent? I could handle spying just fine without having my hand held all the time. I couldn't wait to see the look of admiration in her pretty eyes when she realized how I'd managed what she couldn't.

I shrugged a fancy brocade coat on – similar to Bataar's but blue instead of red.

"It doesn't suit you," he said as I buttoned the front. My tiger's eye pendant slipped out of my shirt, catching the lantern light and I tucked it hastily back into my shirt. Bataar froze. "I've seen that on you before, haven't I?"

"The coat? I took it from the back." Why were the buttons so small? It was like they weren't even designed for men's hands.

"No, the pendant. That's heartstone."

"We call it a tiger's eye," I muttered, fumbling with a particularly tricky button. I wasn't made for noble clothes. Give me a proper manly coat any day of the week over this peacock-bright thing.

"It's not a tiger's eye," Bataar argued. "They're similar, but a heartstone – they have magical properties. Like the Doors of Heaven. They are made from the same mineral – the rock that forms from the souls of our ancestors."

"Because that's not at all weird," I muttered. Oh great, now the buttons were crooked. Frustrated, I pulled the coat apart and began to button it again – this time from the bottom.

"Do you know what this means?" His voice was high pitched in his excitement.

Couldn't he just leave me alone to dress in peace?

"I bet you a silver coin that you're going to tell me."

I buckled on the wide belt Zyla gave me when we flew into the city. It didn't really match the rest, but it felt ungrateful not to wear it. After all, she gave it to me. Other than the pendant that Bataar was so obsessed with, no one had really given me much. I still felt bad about losing that cloak from Hubric.

"Have you had any extra protection against magical attacks?" Bataar asked, his eyes still alight.

"No," I said gruffly, but I froze. Because I had been protected, hadn't I? When that magical lightning hit Bataar he had been so ill he needed extra healing, but when it hit me it only left a small burn.

"I knew it," Bataar said triumphantly, reading my expression and not my words.

I scowled. I hated that he always knew everything. Why couldn't I know something he didn't for a change?

"And are you drawn to the doorways? Drawn almost inexorably to them?"

"In Ex what?"

"Are you drawn to them in a way that you can hardly fight? Like, they pull you?"

I clenched my jaw. They did pull me. He didn't need to know that.

Bataar's jaw clenched, too and he reached toward my neck. "That's mine, by right."

"Whoa!" I threw my hands up, taking a quick step back. I shoved the pendant into my coat. Out of sight, out of mind.

"This was a gift from a friend. It's not whatever you think it is. It's just a gift, okay? So, you can keep your hands to yourself."

Bataar stayed back, but his eyes narrowed, and he seemed poised to jump again. Boy, was he touchy.

"All heartstone belongs to my people," he said, his slight accent stronger as if to prove the point. "And so anything made of it belongs to us. That means the Doors of Heaven and that means your pendant."

"I don't see you banging down the door of the Bright Redemption demanding the doorway back," I protested.

"Don't think I won't! Any of the Exalted here would go crazy if they knew that place held a Door of Heaven! They consider them sacred just as we do and have tried to take them from us."

"Why do they want them so badly?" Instant travel was nice, but it hadn't worked out so well for the Magikas on the flying carpet. They'd plunged to their deaths and that could happen to anyone.

"The Code of Ko'Torenth states that whoever bears the Ko of a House is the rightful ruler of that house. It's an idea that came from when they were our brothers, but no one has worn the Ko in a century or more."

I was adjusting this ridiculous facemask when I paused. "Wait. Are you saying that by right you should rule whichever Exalted family has that eagle symbol?"

He flushed. "The Exalted House Tanagers. And I'm not sure if it's an eagle or a tanager."

"And I bet the Exalted house Tanagers wouldn't like that much."

"Why do you think I was running to the Dominon?"

Well, now things were making sense. Bataar was slated for greatness – or instant death. And he was fighting that destiny as much as I liked to fight my own.

"Why would they just show up on your arms after a century?"

"The Doors choose their master. It cannot be forced."

I swallowed. I didn't like where this was going. After all, one of these Exalted houses would probably like to kill the guy with the smoke on his arms as much as the House Tanagers would want to kill Bataar.

He continued, "Every year the children who have come of age from the houses of the Exalted line up beside the one door they have access to. It is a grisly journey up a steep cliff with ropes and picks. They each try to master the door and they each fail. They have failed for a century."

I knew that door. I'd flown through it myself. But why would this Door of Heaven refuse the brave, noble, mountain-climbers? They were hero material if there ever was such a thing. And why would they choose me? I was nothing but a kid with a bit of luck and a dragon friend.

"I shut the Door of Heaven in the lower level of the Bright Redemption," Bataar was saying. "But anyone with the Ko can open it again. Just because I haven't heard of anyone else having them, doesn't mean they don't have Ko. There are three other symbols that might be out there, and anyone at all might bear those symbols on their bodies. The prophecies are clear:

Four to rule and four to reign,
From four the power of mist came,
From four it will come again,
But who and what and where and when?"

"Well," I said, grabbing the cloak and wrapping it around me. "That doesn't sound very threatening. It just sounds like a silly riddle for kids. Put on your mask and let's go. We have enemies to spy on."

"There's more," Bataar said as he tied on his full-face mask. His voice grew muffled as he put it on.

"*Woe to those who gain the marks,*
Feel the power of depths it sparks,
Destruction raining down on man,
On every house and every clan."

"Oh yeah, that's specific," I said. "I can see why you're worried. Oooooh! Destruction! Ooooh! Nameless threats. Get back to me when there's something real to worry about."

The quiet from behind his mask was scathing as I shoved him in front of me down the passageway back to Balde.

I didn't believe that nonsense. It was only meant to scare children. But I couldn't help the sense of foreboding that filled me. Two of us were marked. What if there were two more out there, destruction following us all?

Chapter Six

PARTIES WERE A LOT of fun. It was all I could do to keep myself from picking easy pockets as I went. Women wore bracelets so loose that the clasp could be pinched off and the whole thing pocketed in a single motion. The men had fancy fasteners on belt pouches that were more decorative than solid. My fingers itched at the thought of slipping them loose.

Whenever I found a crowd of people, a quick sleight of hand trick – a pulled feather from behind an ear or a flower presented to a lady with the flick of a wrist – was enough to dispel curious glances. There were other entertainers here – also masked, and I blended in with them effortlessly.

I'd lost track of Bataar within minutes of arriving and we weren't supposed to be together, anyway. The more ground we covered, the more likely we would stumble across some useful information. Plus, he claimed I embarrassed him.

"I can almost smell the foreign drifting off you," he said. "Your accent is as thick as a rug. Try not to speak if you can help it."

I hadn't spoken since arriving, schooling myself to disciplined watching and silent entertaining instead.

The Masque, to my utter surprise, was not indoors. For such a frozen landscape, these people sure liked to do things outside. Instead, extra braziers were lit along the boardwalks with something added to the flames that made them blaze blue and green instead of orange. Green and blue lanterns were hung in strings along railings and over rooftops and where the boardwalks joined or crossed. Hot ciders and mulled wines were served in pewter mugs.

Ladies in fur dresses, their masks a riot of color over the monochrome furs, and men in stark white or black masks laughed or chatted together in knots, drifting apart and reforming as the party progressed. Guards in house colors were dotted through the crowd, and to my surprise, some of them wore masks and drank cider, too.

There had been a stopping point on the spiral stairs when I reached this level and no one without a mask was allowed in. No one in shabby clothing was let in, either. Even the servants with the cider wore crisp, clean clothing.

I'd never been in a place like this or to a party like this in my life. Living on the streets was rarely clean and never orderly. Could get used to this, though. The hot cider alone was worth the trouble.

I looked out over the city from my vantage on the boardwalk, turning to watch the moon rise over the horizon, it's silver beams gilding the harsh lines and jagged planes of the mountain city of Ko'Koren. Puffs of smoke and mist rose up from the heat spots around the city, swirling in silvery patterns between the buildings and around the tangle of stairways and boardwalks and soaring bridges.

I felt an exhilaration just looking over the scene that dwarfed my own personal goals. This place never ceased to stun me. Tiny flakes of snow – barely a sprinkle – began to fall like a silent army invading. I breathed in long and slow, enjoying the cold air as it hit my lungs. As I exhaled, I heard a voice.

I turned my head slightly to listen better, still pretending to admire the beauty below.

"... just think on it, Ye'kut. House Gamni can aid you. Together we could keep House A'kona from seizing power. They are too strong. Do you see that little gem Apeq shepherds around? They say she is a dignitary from another land. I heard whispers of Baojang."

"The women of Baojang are fearsome warriors. Your agents may not be feeding you solid information, Ganmi. House Ye'kut would never make such a mistake."

Had I stumbled upon a conversation between two Exalted Houses just by pausing here for a moment? I glanced toward them to see a man in a brilliant orange brocade coat and white mask – his figure heavy like a once-strong man weighed down by age and another in an emerald green brocade, lithe and short with a black mask. Best to keep my eyes on the city below. Maybe they wouldn't notice me here.

"If you want to see House Gamni at work, Ye'kut, then keep an eye out. We'll strip A'kona of his gem before you can blink."

There was a loud laugh and I was pushed against the railing as a group of young men and women shoved past me. For a few moments, I could hear nothing but their idle chatter and laughter. One of the women's skirts rustled as she squeezed past me, her laugh as piercing as a hunting bird's cry. And then they were gone and when I turned around, the walkway was empty.

Bread and butter! I'd lost them.

I scrubbed a hand through my hair, smiling absently at a man who walked by, his gaze piercing through his black mask. I froze when a swirl of silver met my eye. This time, it couldn't possibly be my imagination. There was something strange going on with those silver-swirling eyes. And what was worse was that the silver didn't seem to always be there. Sometimes it was, sometimes it wasn't, and sometimes it burst into a fury of dust and destruction that still haunted my nightmares.

I needed some of that cider. This spying business was stressful work.

I ambled to the nearest barrel where a crisp servant ladled piping hot cider into mugs. I reached out to take a mug from the serving man and froze. Vern Redgers – the serving man from Apeq A'kona's Jadefire House of Marvels smiled a sly smile at me as he handed me the mug. Silver swirled in his pupils and the cider sloshed in my shaking hand, burning my hand and wrist.

I hissed, shoving the mug of cider back at him and fleeing into the crowd. It was long minutes of dodging and weaving through people before I remembered I was wearing a mask. I stopped, suddenly, face to face with another silver-pupilled face. This time, a golden mask hid his face, but I would recognize the way the man stood anywhere.

Apeq A'kona.

And on his arm, just as the men had said, was Zyla – her buoyant curls barely tamed by the thick red mask-ribbon that held them back and her mask worked with feathers and bright stones to look like the jade-colored fire outside Apeq's House of Marvels.

I stuttered an apology and slipped back into the crowd, ducking into the first shadow between two buildings that I could find and leaning deep into the darkness of the shadow, my heart pounding like a drum.

Perhaps, Bataar had been right. Perhaps, I was a poor choice for a spy.

I let my eyes close and took in deep, steadying breaths for what felt like minutes until I could still my racing heart.

"Boo."

The whisper made me jump, banging my head against the low hanging eaves of the roof above me.

Chapter Seven

ZYLA SQUEEZED INTO the tiny space with me. There was barely room for two. I could feel her every breath.

"Tor?" she whispered, her whisper so quiet I could barely hear it.

"Zyla?"

"What are you doing here?"

"I could ask you the same thing!" I hissed.

"I thought they'd killed you!"

Oh. I hadn't thought that she might think that. Her breath was coming awful quickly, and it was getting warm with the two of us squeezed in this tiny enclosure. I leaned just a little bit forward as I composed my thoughts and my mask clinked against hers.

"It's tight in here," she said in a strangled voice.

"We need to stop meeting like this." It sounded like a foolish comment while I was still saying it. I could almost feel her eyes rolling. "What are you doing with Apeq?"

"Surviving!" She hissed. "You and Bataar disappeared and no one told me anything!"

"How is Zin?"

"She's a captive, in case you haven't noticed. Just like me."

"A captive who takes trips to theatrical productions and masked balls?"

"Yes!"

I pulled off my mask, not sure what else to do in my surprise. I couldn't talk through these stupid things.

"I thought you didn't believe me about Apeq! I thought you trusted him."

"I was wrong, okay?" Her voice was muffled by the mask.

"What?"

She fumbled with the ribbons for her own mask, letting it slip free and then looking up at me, her huge eyes reflecting the blue and green lights from outside our hiding place.

"I was wrong." Now her voice was clear and husky.

"How did you slip away?" I whispered.

"He was distracted by the Exalted of House Tanagers, but I don't have long."

"And then?" I breathed. I could feel her breath on my skin.

"And then I have to go back with him. Zin is at his mercy."

I hadn't thought of that. Her sister was a hostage.

"If you're going to be a spy, Tor, you need to learn to see with those bright eyes of yours." It sounded like she was scolding me, but her expression as soft.

"Look," I said, glancing around. "Bataar and I are on to a few things –"

"He's with you?"

"Yes. We found doves and money. We can communicate with Hubric. We can set you free, too. Okay?"

"No!" Her answer came too quickly. Had I misjudged? Did she want to stay with Apeq after all? "Apeq is up to something. I can do more spying from within."

Now she was just confusing me. I thought she said she was a captive?

"But Zin – "

"Will be fine until it's time to leave. Just don't step on my toes or reveal who I am by getting too close. We have to pretend to be strangers, Tor."

She was so brave. And so crazy. So full of fire and power and intensity. I wanted to reach out and pull her against me. It was all I could do to suppress the urge.

There wasn't room in this crevice to even nod my head, so I said, "If you say so."

"I do." She pulled her shoulders back to show her determination and I swallowed hard. "Leave it to me until then."

I could tell she was about to leave.

"Zyla?"

"Yes?"

"Have you noticed silver in Apeq's eyes?"

She hesitated as if she had expected me to say something else. Eventually, she said, "Yes. Is there anything else?"

My hand flexed and unflexed, longing to do or say more, but I had no idea what that might be, so I just said. "Don't die."

After all, it's what Saboraak would have said to me.

She nodded curtly, tied her mask back on and slipped into the night. I had a terrible feeling that I'd done something wrong. That, somehow, I'd disappointed her.

Women. They were worse than dragons. Even worse than color-changing girl dragons.

I heard that.

Chapter Eight

I FUMBLED WITH MY MASK strap, trying to tie it back on. Who invented these stupid things? Who thought that covering half your face was a good idea at a party, anyway?

A body moved, blocking the way out of the crevice and I hunched further into the darkness. I didn't want to answer questions about what I was doing in here.

How is the spying going?

I'd learned almost nothing of value except that Zyla was in more trouble than I thought and there were people with silver swirling in their eyes everywhere. What was causing that? It was a mystery just begging to be solved.

The figure that had been blocking the exit pushed, suddenly, into the crevice and I had to back up further into it to keep from being discovered. The buildings were separate all the way to the rock wall, but it was so narrow as the crevice went back that there was only room for me to stand stretched as tall as I could and sucking in my breath to fit in the tiny space. I could barely breathe. My heart was racing. If the newcomer reached back to where I was, he could touch me. It was hard to believe that he couldn't hear me breathing.

A second figure squeezed into the crevice and the two of them put their heads together to whisper. Ha! This was a popular place to share secrets.

"The Midnight Artificers have made big promises, Apeq. But so far I've seen nothing." The whisper sounded like it came from a man who was not used to being quiet. Even his whisper boomed.

"You will tonight. We have everything in hand."

Apeq! I didn't trust that man. The more I heard and saw of him, the more sure I was that he was planning something.

"The explosion at your warehouse suggests otherwise. People say it knocked a wall out."

"The Bright Redemption had a small problem with a shipment. That is all. We will have it repaired in short order."

I knew he was involved with that place!

"You promised us a force that could sweep across the Dominion, Apeq. Instead, we have a succession war brewing. That boy heir is nowhere to be found. My men combed Kav'ai looking for him. And the man who ruined Festival has yet to be found. He wore Ko on his arms!"

"And he jumped from a height so great he would need wings to break that fall!" Apeq said harshly. "He's dead."

"My spies tell me that they saw a dragon catch him."

"All the Dominion Dragon Riders are contained. None of them may leave or go anywhere near their dragons."

"And how long can we maintain that? Their government will notice!"

"Your cold feet are a problem, Mandrill," Apeq snarled. "Are you so gutless that you can't make a minor move without panicking?"

"My father is not convinced it is the right option."

"Leave your father to me."

"The Dominion is strong. They resisted our attack and we had Ifrits!"

Apeq laughed. "Our Ifrits weakened them. The Dominion is a shell of what they once were with a girl Dominar leading them. All we need is a strong force and we will sweep them off the earth and gain their dragons for ourselves."

"And Baojang? The Rock Eaters?"

"They're licking their wounds. The Dominion cracked their teeth. If we play this right, they will fall to us, too."

"Your ambitions are too strong, Apeq. We don't have the population for such a sprawling campaign. Ko'Torenth hasn't taken land from anyone for three generations."

"Then it's time we did."

"And you certainly won't gain the support of the other Exalted Houses at this rate. We are divided. No one can agree on one leader."

"By the end of tonight, that won't be a problem. Now, rejoin the party. I've wasted enough time here."

They left and I waited long moments before wriggling out of the inky-black shadow. This was bad – worse than I thought. Ko'Torenth really was planning to take over the Dominion. Hubric needed to know this. He needed to know all of it.

It's why he sent us here. He knew they were planning something.

But he couldn't have believed it was this bad or he wouldn't have sent just me and you!

And Zyla.

He should have sent full Dragon Riders!

Maybe we were all he had.

Maybe I should go find those Dragon Riders held by Apeq and tell them what is going on.

It sounded like they were prisoners.

Then its time for a prison break!

You don't even know where he is holding them.

But I could find out.

I was still gathering my breath and wondering how I would find them when distant screams began.

Chapter Nine

I SCRAMBLED OUT OF the crevice in the rock and the cold hit me in an icy blast. I hadn't realized how warm I was out of the wind.

Around me, people in masks and fancy dress were standing on tiptoe, craning their necks. A second burst of screams ripped through the air, from a level higher and to my left, I thought, but it was hard to tell in the icy air.

I have a bad feeling about this. I'm coming.

She would blow my cover.

Better to be discovered than to be dead.

She had a point. But I didn't know what to do. I fumbled at my belt. I'd left the axe behind. It was too bulky to bring with me. My belt knife was there, but six inches of steel wouldn't do much if there was a good reason for those screams. Maybe it was just one of those silver-eyed guys dying horribly. They did that from time to time.

I could hope for that, couldn't I?

There was another scream, ripping through the air and then the people around me began to shuffle away from the sound, moving slowly, as if unsure of themselves. But despite their careful movements and cautious – almost nonchalant – surge to the ladders and stairs, there was an acid feel of fear in the air. It twanged through my own nerves, freezing me to the core.

I pressed against the tide of bodies. There were people here that I cared about – Zyla, certainly, and even Bataar wasn't a bad sort. If they were in danger, they would need my help.

I tried to ignore the voice in my head asking me how I would help them if they were in trouble. After all, I was no warrior. I had no weapon beyond a belt knife, and I was as dependent as they were on Saboraak for any real help.

I will not let you down!

Dragons.

If I knew where the Dragon Riders were being held, this kind of distraction would be perfect to free them. Or free their dragons.

The crowd pushing past me was growing quicker and a little more frantic as the ladders and stairs leading down from here filled with pushing bodies and those behind them had to wait a turn. Masks hid faces, but fear filled the eyes of the masked as they pressed forward.

What a stupid idea – to put a half of a city of people into masks and fancy clothing and jam them all into one area. It was like a disaster planned to happen!

Pretty girls in bright fur dresses and cloaks and decorated masks breathed heavily as they passed, elderly people were pressed against rails or walls, not strong enough to keep up with the mass of bodies. I pressed against the tide, diving into spaces and dodging bodies like a salmon swimming upstream.

The screams were growing in intensity from single shrieks to the horrified shouts of many voices. Whatever was happening was on a massive scale.

There was a cry from above me and then, from the walkway above, a body plummeted past, smacking against the railing a level below. I leaned over my own rail to look down. A man sprawled faceup on the railing, bent the wrong way, his back clearly broken by the fall.

I swallowed hard as gasps and faint cries rose around me. A panic in a vertical city with nothing but narrow passages to follow was a terrible thing.

Beside me, a fight broke out as a group of men tried to press their way into a nearby window and were repelled by armed servants. There were screams as one of them fell, a gash across his belly and then the crowd pushed past them, forcing the servants back and flooding into the house.

Not everyone would fit in these houses. I scanned the boardwalks and the houses pressed against them. People were flooding into every house I could see, but still, there were people rushing down the boardwalk like water loosed from a dam long after the houses were full. I gritted my teeth, waded through the crowd, and grabbed a spear from the hand of the fallen man. I tried not to look too closely at him, not even when I wrenched the spear from his still-strong grip. I was no healer. I couldn't fix a belly wound. And he wouldn't need this spear anymore.

Callous.

I'm not callous! I just don't want to hurt! Don't you see?

I pushed against the crowd, teeth gritted, eyes narrowed, pushed toward danger and not away. There was no chance I would find Zyla in this. No chance, and yet I couldn't not try.

If I didn't force myself to be strong in the face of hurt and pain, I would crumble. I'd built these walls for a reason. But could I help it if she had put a crack in them? Could I help it if the thought of her in trouble spurred me to run faster? Could I help it if caring for her made me suddenly aware that everyone around me was precious to someone? At the end of that road lay madness. I'd seen people go that way before. If you cared too much, the pain of the world would sweep you away until you were nothing but a hollow shell.

I tripped on a fallen body and leaned hard on the shaft of the spear for support. I didn't dare look down. I didn't want to see what I had tripped on.

Screams ripped through the air one over another until there was no chance of hearing anything else.

I didn't even look anymore when a shape dropped past, falling to his death over the railing. I didn't dare look. There were too many just like it as the minutes dragged out. Too many fading screams. Too many gasps of collective horror. It was enough to fill my nightmares for the rest of my life.

The stairway nearby was blocked, but with the screams coming from above, I needed another way up. Every ladder or stairway in sight was choked with people trying to flee downward. From the sounds above, the fighting was a level or maybe even two levels above me.

How far could Zyla have traveled after our conversation? It had only been a few minutes. Maybe Saboraak could hear her mind?

Not a chance.

Maybe I could fly up a level on Saboraak's back.

I ... ummm ... got involved here.

Involved? I thought she said she was coming to help me!

I thought you said there were dragons in the cotes whose riders were captured. Dragons who are as much prisoners as their riders are.

Uh oh.

And then you mentioned that now might be the perfect time – when there was a distraction – to save them and it occurred to me that I might be the only one who could *save them.*

From what? Three square meals a day and a warm place to sleep? There's nothing holding them there!

Something holds them! Some kind of magic binds them in place.

Then it would take some kind of magic to release them!

There was this thing shaped like a whip in the hideout.

Are you flaming kidding me, Saboraak? I've got my hands full with a mass panic situation and people falling to their deaths all around me and you are in the middle of a prison break?

You aren't the only hero out there, Tor.

Skies and Stars preserve me from heroes! And from dragons with their own agendas. Was that sheepishness I was feeling from her? It had better be!

I heard a scream from above that sounded terribly familiar. Zyla!

Well, there was no other way to do this. I'd have to scale the side of a building and see if I could find my friends and get them out of here – or even stop whatever was causing this madness in the first place. I had a feeling it had something to do with Apeq and these Midnight Artificers.

Maybe, if Saboraak was done her side quest by then, she'd be able to help a guy out.

Don't be so cranky. You'd do the same thing if you were me.

I rolled my eyes, shoved the spear through my belt, and began to climb up the rock-work on the side of the nearest building. Maybe I could reach that low roof and then jump from there to the boardwalk just above. Or maybe I could scale the roof tiles to get high enough.

Time to gamble with my life. Again.

Don't be so dramatic.

Chapter Ten

STONEWORK IS NOT EASY to climb at the best of times – though I'd climbed it a lot living in the streets of Vanika. It's amazing how few people bother to put bars over upper windows.

I tried to ignore what was going on around me and concentrate on spreading my weight evenly over the holds in the little ridges between the stones. I only had to get as far as the roof and then I could climb up on the tiles there.

This whip thing is horrible. It binds them in place! No one told me that humans did this! Why would anyone be so cruel?

I don't know. Why would anyone kidnap Zin? Why would they stab a man in the belly for trying to climb in a window? Why did people do any of the awful things they did?

Dragons don't do this.

Don't get on your high horse. I bet dragons do bad things, too.

What's a high horse?

When people ride a high horse, they get to look down on other people.

What about when they ride a dragon?

I guess you get to look down on everyone.

I think I like that.

There! The edge of the roof. I reached up, struggling to make the climb with the spear still stuck in my belt. I might need that for later. I didn't want to show up weaponless. The way the screams were intensifying, whatever was up there was something you'd want to face with a weapon.

Almost there ... just a few more to go ...

What were we going to do with all those dragons? We'd have to shelter them, and that hideout was not big enough. Plus, it was bound to draw attention if dragons swooped in and out of that small crevice.

Leave that to me.

I was going to have to. I had enough on my plate as it was.

I scrambled onto the roof tiles, fighting the wind and slippery ice. If we stayed in this city long, I'd need gloves. My fingers were cherry red and felt like pins and needles were piercing them from the cold. I'd deal with them later. By the time I was balanced on the roof, huffing and puffing and clinging with those frozen fingers, the screams had grown even closer. I scrambled up the roof tiles, thanking the stars and skies that I had chosen a roof with a shallow incline instead of one of the steep ones.

As I climbed, drawing level with the boardwalk and then springing past it, the scene beside me unfolded. People ran along the boardwalk, screaming, or were pressed by the mob until they were pushed up and over the rails, their cries falling from earshot as they careened to the levels below. In some places, knots of guards formed trying to defend them, only to be scattered as easily as the civilians.

It was easy to see why they fled. Two massive creatures pursued them. They were nearly the size of a dragon, but they had no wings or tails, only wide, snapping jaws and glowing eyes. They moved swiftly, but with an odd gait, almost as if they were worked by pulleys and ropes rather than by muscle and bone.

Wait. I wasn't seeing things. These creatures – if that's what they were – seemed to be made things. They were not fueled by human intelligence or animal instinct. Their movements were too perfect, too exact – like how one would expect a horse to move but not how they actually do move. Their faces were wrought of metal and porcelain and looked like wolves caught mid-snarl, but no wolf would move as they did.

I gulped and forced back a sudden icy chill in the back of my thighs. Who cared what sort of thing was bent on killing you? Stopping it was more important than identifying it. And yet the dead-stare of those glowing eyes hollowed my belly and left my knees wobbling.

With everyone masked, it was impossible to tell who was who in the fleeing crowd, but out of the corner of my eye I caught a glimpse of a red coat and a white mask. Was that? Yes. Bataar dangled from a railing, his feet kicking in the air as he tried to get enough momentum to pull himself back up. The edge of his tattoos shone in the light of the rising moon. If it hadn't been for the chaos around us, that alone would seal his capture.

He was four houses down from me, and though the crowd was moving in his direction, I wasn't sure how I could cross such a torrent of people to get to him before he lost his grip.

Saboraak! We could use a friend with wings right about now!

Almost done ...

Hurry! Bataar needs you!

So, do these prisoners!

I gritted my teeth. I needed to jump into that crowd and sprint to where he was. I was trying to plot angles and the best landing place but everything kept shifting. The – mechanical wolves? What did you call them?

Golems are made things powered by magic.

The golems – good word! – were almost upon my building. There was no place to leap in front of them before they surged past. I'd have to wait for them to pass and hope that Bataar could hold on.

We come.

The golem nearest me turned and I almost could see him mechanically snuffling toward my roof. I couldn't save Bataar if this thing seized me. Beside him, the other one pushed forward, snagging a fleeing Ko'Torenth noble from the crowd with his massive teeth and breaking him in half with one snap of his jaws. A dog would have shaken the broken prey. A wolf may have dropped it to examine it or at least taste what he had worked so hard to kill. The golem flung the husk of the man over the rail in a single, efficient motion.

I swallowed, backing up from the one near me. It was like he knew I was there, like this fake snuffling was him sniffing me out.

I wasn't ready to be broken in metal jaws by a creature who wouldn't even enjoy killing me.

Would it help if he enjoyed it?

Yes! At least there would be some point to it all!

Humans are confusing.

And dragons are never there when you need them!

The golem wolf snapped at me, missing by inches. I scrambled backward, slipping, barely catching myself and almost being caught by his ripping jaws a second time. I couldn't stay on this low roof.

And then suddenly the dragons were there. They flew straight up, their bellies toward me, as they gained height.

I see him!

I watched as Bataar's grip finally gave out and he fell, flailing toward the level below.

Saboraak whipped out of formation, lightning-fast. She spun like a fish in water, darted down and under my falling friend, cushioning his fall and then leveling off to stabilize him.

She wouldn't be able to transport me, too. I could see that she was already struggling to keep Bataar in the saddle, already struggling to get the other dragons to turn around and follow her. None of them was Purple. None of them would be able to speak to a human mind.

Everyone froze, watching the dragons – even the wolf golems. I didn't dare freeze. This distraction would only last a moment. I scanned the world around me, eyes rushing over the fleeing humans, the snapping golems, the creaking walkways straining under the new weight, the houses in flames where the golems had passed, crunching and shredding lanterns and braziers so carelessly that fire had spread through the howling night.

There was an answer here somewhere.

And then I saw it. Looking down from a window five buildings down the walkway from where I was, Shabren the Violet stood in a wide window, his hands raised and bright light glowing all around him. I didn't know how I knew that he was directing the wolf golems, but I did know it.

He had to be stopped.

Chapter Eleven

THERE WAS NO TIME TO think about odds or wonder if I was making the right choice. I had mere seconds before the dragons would be gone and with them, my distraction.

I scrambled backward three steps and then ran toward the edge of the roof, leaping at the last moment to clear the edge, over the wolf golem's snapping jaws, past its broad head and landing cleanly on its back.

The landing hurt, sending shooting pains up my spine and through my hips. It was all I could do to hold on to the slick metal, quickly flipping around and grabbing the molded saddle – a part of its back. Whoever had invented these things had made them to be ridden. That much was obvious. But I was willing to bet that they'd never expected someone in the crowd to take advantage of that.

That was my specialty – doing the unexpected. Surprise was a friend to everyone.

Remember, you can be just as easily surprised as they can.

Did she think I was playing around? Did she think I didn't know what a dangerous situation I was in?

Do *you know? You are riding a golem with no way to stop and no way to get off of it. If you try to do either, it will bite you clean in half!*

I shivered. I hadn't even thought of getting off of it. The creature was already loping forward again. There had to be a way to disable it. What is made by man can be destroyed by man.

Fools rush in where dragons fear to tread. There was a pause as I examined the golem and then she sent another thought. *But maybe we need a few fools. If everyone lived safe lives there wouldn't be any heroes.*

I was no hero. She would learn that eventually. She was the one who just saved Bataar.

I examined the golem. There was nothing up here except for a smooth surface with the molded saddle. I could stay on, but I couldn't disable it. There was no switch or lever, no gear or cog.

The wolf-golem bucked and wove, forgetting the people in front of us in its desperate attempt to get me off its back. I held on to the pommel of the saddle, clenched my teeth, and rode for my life.

After all, I'd ridden a dragon, and she flew in a lot more directions than this thing could run.

I also wasn't trying to buck you off.

A point. A fair point. I dodged a sign hanging by a chain and then a flapping oak leaf banner. The boardwalk hadn't been designed for racing down it on the back of a metal golem. If Shabren had weapons like these, why had he fled the Dominion? Why hadn't he brought them there?

Maybe he found them here. Maybe he is still planning to bring them to the Dominion. Didn't Apeq tell the other man to watch for his sign tonight?

This wasn't a sign. It was a massacre.

It can be two things at once.

We were coming to the end of the boardwalk. I could see it far in the distance. When we did, things would get interesting.

Maybe I could leap off of this thing and land on Saboraak. Where was she?

Settling Bataar and the dragons. I need a safe place for them. You're on your own until I return.

On my own? She was going to leave me to sort this out for myself?

You're a tough guy. You'll be fine.

The golem jerked under me, jostling me sharply to the side. My shoulder hit the wall beside us with a smack and I nearly lost my grip.

I was not going to be fine!

The second golem surged ahead of us and out of the corner of my eye, I noticed the shoal of people maneuvering around a statue ahead. It plunged up from the masses like an island in the sea. Two figures clung to it like survivors of a shipwreck. One of them looked at me with big golden eyes, her mouth in the perfect shape of an "o." Her mask hung around her neck, the ribbon torn and frayed. Zyla!

The wolf golem ahead of us raced toward her. If he got there first, what would he do? Already, he was tearing the people ahead of him apart, flinging bodies in either direction as easily as he scattered masks and loose clothing. Some smacked against houses or rock walls with sickly thuds while others shrieked as they soared over the railing to fall to the rocks below.

My heart was in my throat, thudding as loudly as Saboraak's snores. If anything happened to her ...

I reached behind me, grabbed the spear from my belt – thank the Skies and Stars it was still there! I was no hero, but even a plain street-lad could see a possibility here.

I whipped my golem in the flank with the spear. If we could just get ahead of the other one ...

The spear couldn't hurt him, but it must have enraged him. He burst forward, metal muscles squealing in his haste. I gripped the pommel as we lunged forward, nearly falling off his saddle before I righted myself. I shifted the spear to my other hand, pulled a leg up to wrap around the saddle pommel. I was as ready as I could be.

This would need to be timed perfectly. I tried to breathe, forgetting in my haste whether it was in or out and then gasping from choosing the wrong one. Come on, Tor! Pull it together!

Here we go ...

She covered her eyes with a hand at the same moment that I leaned out and snatched her from the air with my free arm. All I saw was a look of horror in the other person's face as I pulled her from the statue island. Apeq. He had been there with her. He couldn't have been behind this. Not when he was in danger, too. Could he?

The memory of Shabren with lit hands filled my mind, but I had no time to puzzle out anything more. We were careening toward the end of the boardwalk where both the walk and the buildings beside it ended in solid mountain rock. I needed to stop this creature.

The other golem surged past us, something brightly colored and limp in its mouth. I tried not to look too hard at what it was. He sped ahead, whipping the last survivors out of the way with swiping metal paws and then dashing vertically up the rock.

My head suddenly felt light. I couldn't hold on to the pommel hard enough to keep us both in the saddle if this golem did that. Zyla was scrambling to find a seat behind me, her arms wrapping uncomfortably around my neck. I tried to ignore the choking sensation as I readied my spear one last time.

It was a long shot. But better a long shot than nothing, right?

And we couldn't jump. There'd be no way to control our landing if we did. We'd be as likely to smack walls or fall to our deaths as anyone else.

Shaking Zyla off my neck, I leaned as far forward as I could, aimed, and jammed the spear in the golem's glowing eye.

There was a howling whistle and a gust of steam whuffed up from the golem's mouth as his front legs collapsed under him.

I lost my grip on the spear and rocketed forward over the slick metal of his wide head, falling to the ground and bouncing from the force of my landing. Oof! Pain made me hiss as something hard and heavy landed on top of me.

"What were you thinking!" That low, velvet voice made me want to melt into it at the same moment that I wanted nothing more than to get her agonizing elbow out of my belly.

"Ngh!"

At least she was alive. At least we were both alive.

I risked a look up to the golem, but the light was out of his eyes and he was frozen mid-stride, only his front legs collapsing, the back ones still stiff and solid. In his place at the end of the boardwalk, it looked as if someone had poorly chosen the site of a new statue.

I barely managed a breath out in relief before my vision was filled with Zyla.

"Look at me! Look at me, street scum!"

Her eyes were alight with fury, dancing with irritation, and yet somehow that made her prettier. I looked into them, just looking at the color, at the flash, treasuring the fact that they were still alive to be angry.

"We could have both been killed! *You* would have killed us both with your fog-brained foolery!"

I pushed myself up to a seated position. Everything hurt. My back, my arms, my head. The screams had stopped but shouts and cries continued. Who could even guess how many were dead or injured in the insanity of the golems? How many dead would need burial? Did they bury people here? How many people still dangled from railings or lay injured in crumpled heaps?

"I didn't want to see you hurt," I said stupidly. "I thought it would rip you to pieces."

I flinched at the thought. Too many images of others being shredded or flung to their deaths were trying to flood my mind.

"So you rode it? And you pulled me up there with you?" Her curls shook with her fury, but she looked like she was on the verge of tears. "When I find out where your brains went and what Hubric replaced them with, I will stuff you both into jars and keep you in my pantry for the rest of your lives!"

My eyes felt dry from growing so wide. You saved a girl's life and this was what she did! I would never understand women. They were as crazy as dragons!

"Do you hear me, Tor Winespring? Do you?"

I nodded.

She seemed to sag, looking up at the golem with glassy eyes. She turned back to me and leaned in so close that I thought she was about to yell at me again, but instead, she leaned all the way down and kissed me so thoroughly that I almost forgot I was aching all over.

My arms wrapped around her instinctively, but almost as soon as they did, she pulled away leaving them suddenly feeling emptier than they ever had been before.

"Stop being a hero. I don't want you to die." She sounded so serious that I almost smiled, but at her frown, I shifted the smile to match her seriousness. At least we could agree on that.

"I don't want you to die, either."

She gave herself a shake, stood up and straightened her party dress. It was torn and smudged in a dozen places, but she seemed satisfied with simply rearranging it before she spoke.

"I need to find Apeq. His plots won't stand still just because half the nobility of Ko'Koren are dead or wounded."

I gaped. "Don't you think you should come with me."

"Don't go thinking that just because I kissed you, you have the right to arrange my life, Tor Winespring."

I held up my hands defensively. "Of course not."

She nodded firmly. "He still has Zin. And I still have a job to do."

And then she was gone before I could catch my breath, a flurry of determination and energy.

One thing was certain. I would never understand girls.

I can help you now if you want. Things are settled here.

Or dragons.

Chapter Twelve

FOR THE NEXT THREE days, the city was in mourning. Everyone wore white from head to toe and Bataar and I squabbled over the only white cloak in the storeroom.

"I'm going to sneak around Apeq's Jadefire House of Marvels and see if I can get a glimpse of Zin or Zyla," he said when he snatched it from my hands.

"You would be more use helping me look for the Dragon Riders. They're somewhere in this city and the one place we know they aren't is at the House of Marvels. I think they might be with those Oak Leafed Order guys." I argued, but my argument was half-hearted. I was worried about the girls, too. And I couldn't stop thinking about that kiss. What made Zyla do that? It definitely wasn't something I said.

Bataar smacked my shoulder good-naturedly. "If I see an opening, I'll steal Zin away. You're sure she doesn't want to be there, right?"

I nodded, scowling slightly. If I knew Bataar, he'd also try to steal Zyla away from Apeq ... and from me.

He'd taken his fall from the railing during what people were calling "the madness" in stride. He refused to talk about it, but I knew he was as haunted by that night as I was. He tossed and turned at night and spent any time we weren't searching the city sitting by the hideout entrance looking out over the mountains and the mist and muttering about things I didn't understand. But he also helped me and Saboraak find a place for the dragons around the side of the mountain range, tucked away in a place inaccessible to humans.

"Watch out for patrols," I told him. "Your face is clearly Kav'ai and they're looking for anyone who stands out."

"Are you sure you saw Shabren the Violet up in a window during the fighting?"

I'd told him everything – not that he believed me.

"Are you going to make me tell you the whole story again?" I asked, irritably.

I was in a bad temper. I wanted a closer look at the golem I'd disabled, but I'd had to flee almost as soon as Zyla left the scene. Guards had rushed in from every direction and they hadn't left the statue-like creature since the moment it froze on the boardwalk. There was a rotating patrol there and when I tried to sneak close to it, they'd grabbed me and demanded that I show my arms. Fortunately, that had been in the daylight.

Worse, no one knew where the second golem went, and everyone feared it would return. There was a curfew now and patrols everywhere. Long parchments with names scrawled in a list were posted at every crossroad and square. Lists of names of the dead. More were added every day as their names were discovered.

They didn't bury their dead here, or even use funeral pyres. They stored them in big caves. When Bataar told me that, I barely slept the whole night afterward. I still got the creeps just thinking about it.

"It's just strange that no one has mentioned him," Bataar said. "With half the nobility dead and the city gripped with fear, you'd think that someone would have noticed a foreign Magika at the heart of it all."

"Does Ko'Torenth have Magikas?" I looked up from the food I was stuffing into a pouch.

"The Order of the Oaks. They used to be very powerful, but rumor has it that they are losing their magic."

"I'm going to look there for the Dragon Riders," I had said.

That had been yesterday.

After a day spent freezing in the cold, I hadn't managed to find anything out about Shabren or the Order. I sat all day in front of one house with Oaken leaves or another, juggling and doing tricks for coins and watching, watching, watching. No one going in or out looked suspicious. No one came in through the windows but only the doors. And there was no sign of Shabren's hulking form anywhere.

Discouraged and bone-cold, I returned to our hideout to find Bataar just as gloomy, sitting in front of the fire.

"Anything?" I mumbled, as I levered the top off a small barrel. It was packed with dried and salted meat. Maybe I could make a soup or something.

Bataar shoved half a loaf of bread in my hands. "I bought food. We can't eat only meat."

Meat was fine. "I meant, did you find anything?"

"I heard an interesting piece of news," he said, a brooding look in his eyes. "With so many nobles dead, the ones still living are looking to Apeq A'kona for leadership. He'll be giving a public speech on the uppermost level tomorrow."

I felt a chill go through me. If Apeq had loosed those golems, then perhaps he had done it for just this reason – to seize full control of the city.

"Delegates from the other cities of Ko'Torenth will be attending," Bataar said.

"Any sign of the girls?"

He shook his head. "But something is happening in that Jadefire House of Marvels. I've seen that butler of Apeq's bringing people in secretly through the back door. There's something odd about them."

"Let me guess. They have silver swirls in their eyes." The bread really was good. It went well with the salted meat.

Bataar's eyes narrowed. "How did you know?"

"Just a hunch. They are the same people who were hunting you, aren't they? Because of those Ko."

Bataar hunched low. "If Apeq A'Kona seizes control of Ko'Torenth, then maybe they won't be hunting me anymore."

"Or maybe it will only make them want you more, Bataar." He was a fool. He couldn't run away from those marks and every time he tried, he just ran into more trouble.

Then you are a fool, too. You also have the marks.

Well, I wasn't running from them. I just didn't care.

Maybe you should use them.

To do what?

To challenge Apeq.

I almost spat my bread out in my surprise. My dragon wanted me – a street boy turned Dragon Rider – to try to seize the power over another nation? Ha! She could think again. I was going to rescue the girls and those Dragon Riders and then I was going to fly south and find Hubric and that would be the end of it. The spying life was a bad fit for me. Anyone could see that.

"One of us should go listen to his speech tomorrow," Bataar said looking at me significantly.

"And one of us should sneak into his Jadefire House of Marvels while he is making it and rescue Zin," I said, adding my own significant look to the conversation.

I was done eating and there was finally time to do something I'd been waiting for. Carefully, I pulled out the burlap bag of items we'd taken from the warehouse at the Bright Redemption, laying them out along the ground in a row. I took the little book I'd borrowed from Apeq and began to flip through it, looking to see if any items matched while Bataar babbled in the background.

"A delegation of Kav'ai have arrived in the city – Oosquer riders. At least a dozen."

"Mmmm hmm." I scanned the pages as quickly as I could, checking each item as I went. That bracelet with two separate bands and tiny chains connecting them, that looked a bit like the picture, but it was missing the engraved wings along the bracelet. No match. What had it been for? Some sort of speed enhancement. That would be fun.

I kept scanning.

"And if they see me, they will know it is me." Bataar was still babbling, a mile a minute. I was only picking out the highlights as I scanned the book.

What about this strange clasp? You could put it on a cloak or a belt. It was shaped like a mountain. It was in the pile! I picked it up, turning it around in my hands. It was supposed to make eyes slip over you, not quite seeing what was there. That was my kind of magical item!

"And with the oosquer there, they will be a sight to see!"

"What do oosquer look like?" I asked idly.

There was a flap of wings as Saboraak returned from checking on the other dragons. She settled in her area and began to drink the water I'd put out for her.

"... the size of a dragon, but pale and with skittish movements. Their skin hangs from them like leather bags and their feet are heavy and they have no tails. We cover them in heavy saddles and hanging cloths to keep the sun off their skin, so you barely see anything of an oosquer beyond the eyes and snout."

I looked up at that. "So, you could easily disguise a dragon as one. You would just cover them in cloths and a heavy saddle, right?"

"And chains. They are decorated with heavy chains."

Sounds terribly frumpy. I hope you don't plan on decorating me that way.

I stood up, a sudden idea bringing a smile to my face. "Bataar, you're a genius! You, too, Saboraak!"

The skeptical looks they both threw my way only made me grin wider.

"I know exactly what we're going to do!"

Chapter Thirteen

I WAS THE ONLY ONE not complaining.

I did not *sign up to let other people ride me!*

Saboraak had been protesting for the last hour and she'd complained whenever I woke up in the night, too.

It wasn't the first time she'd let other people ride her.

Always with you, too. You *are my human, not Bataar.*

But she'd saved him when he was hanging from the railing.

You're throwing my compassion in my face!

Ha! Well, that was what she got for being so compassionate all the time.

She flamed irritably against the cave wall, leaving the rock black and singed. Bataar leapt back from where he was fussing with her cloth coverings.

"She's not going to do that again, is she?"

"You'll be fine," I assured him. "You have the mountain thing?"

Bataar fiddled with the clasp that was holding his cloak in place. The cloak was a dark grey and strapped oddly around him with wide belts and smaller leather straps in the way of his people. The scarf wound around his face ought to have been enough protection, but the carved mountain clasp that made eyes slide over you was added protection.

"I don't believe that it's going to help, Tor. That book can't be trusted. It belonged to Apeq."

I would have liked to keep it for myself. In my eyes, my mission was more dangerous, but Bataar was a ball of nerves and he needed all the help he could get. Besides, I hated putting Saboraak in danger.

I would rather go with you.

But she wouldn't squeeze through the door of the Jadefire House of Marvels. I needed to get in and out of there unseen.

I could burn it down.

Yes, let's set the whole city on fire. That would be helpful.

Do you think so?

It's called sarcasm, Saboraak. You should give it a try.

I might. It sounds like fun.

"Just remember the plan," I told him. "You and Saboraak will join the Kav'ai delegation as they arrive. You'll blend right in. Hopefully, with the disguises and the pin, they'll never even notice you. You'll listen to his speech, watch for Shabren, collect information, and try to make contact with the Kav'ai. We could use any allies we can find. Meanwhile, I'll be rescuing Zin and seeing if I can find out what's happening over at that House of Marvels. Easy Peasy, Bacon Greasy."

"Tell me that isn't something your people say." Bataar rolled his eyes at me.

I scowled. "Just do your job and I'll do mine and remember, Saboraak is not a toy or a pet. She's a valuable member of our team. Bring her back safely."

He rolled his eyes again. "I know, Tor."

I'm not a child, Tor. I can handle myself, Saboraak chimed in.

No one appreciated my concern. Fine. Then I wouldn't bother being concerned.

Oh, I love your concern.

You have a funny way of showing it.

You're right. Sarcasm is lots of fun.

I cleared my throat irritably and made my voice stern. I didn't dare let these two get out of hand. They needed me to remind them of common sense.

"Just don't die. Get out of there safe and with what we need. Understood?"

Bataar's face became serious. "Same to you, Tor."

We clasped hands reluctantly, neither of us wanting to be seen wishing the other one well.

You're worse than females battling over the same male. I don't know what it is with you two.

And Saboraak had better take care of herself or I'd ... I'd

You'd what?

I'd swear off dragons for good!

Her mental laughter echoed in my mind as Bataar found his place in her saddle and they snuck out the crevice in the rock.

I sighed, checked my pockets one last time – I wasn't leaving the hideout this time without all the basics and a good handful of gold – and then shook myself and straightened my shoulders.

I'd spent a little time reading those scrawled prophecies of Savette's last night from the little book that Hubric gave me. One of them kept ringing in my ears and if I didn't figure it out, it was going to drive me mad.

Toss the dice, and hear them roll,
Depths and shadows take their toll,
And under deception lies a sting,
A bell which rung can not unring,
A mist of power growing strong,
And arm that will stretch wide and long,
And swallow up the hope just bought,
Cloud the dawn of light we wrought,
And sink peace in her grave.
Unless you gamble brave.
And taste midnight on your tongue,
Feel the rush and fly the run,
And sound the warning cry.

It was all nonsense of course. Just scribbles. But why did they haunt my dreams and echo in my brain as if they had something to do with me?

Chapter Fourteen

THE JADEFIRE HOUSE of Marvels was quiet. I had already surreptitiously tried the front door – which was locked – and now I was watching from the side of the boardwalk where I had set up my juggling act. No one looked at street performers – not really. If they felt like leaving a coin, they didn't want to look in case they felt bad that they weren't leaving enough. If they didn't leave a coin, then they felt shame. Either way, begging and street performing were two great ways to suddenly turn invisible.

Vern Redgers was not invisible. He stood by the service door on the lower level of the House of Marvels like a too-old, too-weak guard. But people didn't guard things unless they thought they could defend them. And it worried me that I could see that swirl of silver in his eyes even from here.

It worried me even more that when he thought no one was looking, he twisted a heavy metal rod in his hand – about as long as his arm and as thick as his thumb. It looked like silver light swirled around the rod, too.

There was something about those swirls. They were connected somehow. Interesting. Everyone we had met so far with those swirls in their eyes had items with trapped magic inside them – the men at the house in the mountains, Apeq and his marvels, the Bright Redemption. Was there a connection there?

We've joined the Kav'ai delegation.

Saboraak sounded nervous through our connection. Hopefully, she'd be okay. She was smart, but Bataar could be unpredictable.

So far, our clasp is working. They hardly notice we are here. Their eyes glaze over when they look at me.

She was actually passing for an oosquer. I had worried about that, even after she changed color to a dull grey and streamlined her shape to the most boring one available, even stunting the size of her wings and tucking them in tight. A dragon was a dragon no matter how many blankets you threw over her back.

I'm glad you think so. I would hate to be mistaken for one of these. They smell terrible!

Just keep your eyes peeled, Saboraak. We need to know what is going on up there and if there is anyone from Kav'ai that we can trust.

I will not fail you.

I grunted. I hoped I could say the same thing to her. If I was going to get into the Jadefire House of Marvels, I was going to need to distract Redgers. And how would I do that when the man cared about nothing except for guarding his master's possessions?

I grinned as the answer came to me.

People who were single-minded were easy to trick. I still had that book of his master's. The one that showed magical items. I'd probably regret this, but I'd deal with that when I came to it.

A man in craftsman's attire walked by close to where I was. He would be passing Redgers in a moment. I stumbled, dropping a ball and crashing into him.

"Watch it!"

"My apologies," I muttered.

Perfect. He passed me, and my gaze followed him, doublechecking that I'd planted the book in his boot top correctly. It was a little too obvious but it would do. He was still shaking out his cloak and muttering when he passed Redgers' eagle eyes.

"Is that your book, sir?" Redgers demanded, turning his back to the door.

That was my cue. I leapt up, abandoning my juggling balls and the wooden bowl of coins and sprinting toward the door.

"It's in my boot, isn't it?" The man sounded uncertain but irritated. I knew the type. He'd never admit that book wasn't his. Perfect. Ko'Torenth lying was going to extend the distraction.

"It's in my master's handwriting," Redgers said, his voice so loud now that the whole boardwalk could hear him.

I slipped in behind his turned back, eased the door open and shut it gently behind me. I was going to miss that book later. But for now, it had served its purpose.

Onward!

Are you in the House of Marvels yet? Saboraak's anxiety was increasing.

What's wrong?

The people here smell of fear and violence. I do not like this gathering.

Was it a mob?

On the outside, they are dressed in the finest white of mourning. On the inside, they breathe fire and blood.

Just keep it together for the speech. Do any of the Kav'ai look promising?

Bataar keeps looking at an older man as if he knows him.

That could be good or bad. But I couldn't afford to wait and find out. I needed to get moving before Redgers or someone else caught me.

The light was dim in the House of Marvels and my heart pounded as lantern light threw strange shadows on the walls. As I passed a tall vase filled with carved spears, I snatched one up. Better to be armed than not armed.

A tingle shot up my arm the moment I touched the spear. Was this thing magical, too? It seemed to vibrate in my hand. And I just gave away the book that probably had the answer to that in it. Smooth move, Tor.

I started for the rooms tucked down below. Perhaps Zin would be in her room. She was the kind of girl who kept to herself.

Surprisingly, there were no servants in the halls, but I heard the sound of a door closing above. Was Redgers back inside? Would I turn a corner to find him looking at me with those swirling eyes? I shivered.

Every mask and vase cast a shadow and I peered at every shadow with a pounding pulse. A creeping sensation started in the soles of my feet and slowly worked its way upward until my whole body was gooseflesh – nervous, anticipating, jumping at every shadow.

Skies and Stars! If a magician had a house, this would be the one. I could imagine looking in a mirror here and turning around to find myself in a new world or putting on one of those masks only to find I could never take it off.

Here was Bataar's old room. Empty, of course. The bed was made and pushed to the side. Come to think of it, I didn't know where Zyla and Zin might have their rooms. I hadn't seen them in the brief time I'd been here.

Time to explore. I turned down a winding corridor. There was a squeak behind me and I spun, spear held out like I thought I would actually use it.

Zin threw her hands over her mouth, her eyes big. I sagged in relief. I'd found her. Good.

There was a creak in the floor behind me.

"Now how did you get in here, little mouse?"

Redgers wasn't guarding the door anymore. He was right behind me.

Chapter Fifteen

I FROZE.

Apeq is starting his speech. Zyla is with him, but she has a strange look in her eye.

"Redgers," I said casually, while I tried to tell Zin to run with just my eyes.

"Don't turn around," Redgers said. "Don't even twitch."

"Or what? You'll dust the spunk out of me? You'll deliver sandwiches laced with disappointment."

I could feel the ice coming off him even though I couldn't see his face. Good. Get him all riled up and maybe he would make a mistake. Zin still wasn't moving. It was like she didn't realize how much trouble we were in.

"Oh, trust me, mouse. I will do far more than that." His tone was dangerous. "You've run all through this building without realizing how powerful the things were that you rushed right by. You passed a mask that would make you invisible and a sword that would cut to the core of truth. A rug that flies. And you were too fool to notice any of them. All you grabbed was an ordinary spear. A desert hunting spear for killing coneys and lizards. Fool."

"Let's play a little game, Redgers." I didn't like that he thought I was worthless. I didn't like that he thought he was in charge here.

This is getting intense. Saboraak sounded nervous. She was never nervous. *I think these people are listening to him. The crowd feels ... intense. Like they are falling in love. Especially the leaders from other Ko'Torenth cities.*

With Apeq? Really? I didn't see it.

With the idea of making him their king.

Uh oh. I needed to get Zin out of here. She was more vulnerable than ever if Apeq was gaining power – and so was Zyla.

"I don't play games," Redgers said.

"Well, no I suppose not," I said, turning slightly. "You can't call it playing if you always lose, right?"

He grimaced. "What's the game? And stop moving."

How could I convince Zin to run? She just stood there with her hands over her mouth staring at me.

I considered my words carefully. "What if you let the girl go and then we'll square off man to man. You choose something off the walls to fight me with and I'll choose something off the walls to defend me with and we'll see who wins and who dies."

"Ha! I almost want to watch that. You wouldn't stand a chance. I know what each of these things does. I was there when they were wrought. I was part of the making of them."

"I don't believe you," I said.

Zin's eyes were glued to me as if she was fascinated by me – but that was ridiculous. I jutted my chin forward, trying to point without my hands, to encourage her to run down the passageway instead of staring at me. She needed to go. She needed to be safe.

"You don't believe me?" His voice was low. "I don't need to prove anything to you. Who are you to even ask?"

His words were low and threatening and they stirred something within me that crawled in my belly like a gnawing worm. I knew that tone. I'd heard that before. When I'd been no more than twelve, I'd run with a gang of boys my age and one day we grabbed a soft leather purse that wasn't ours to grab and a Castelan's guard came looking for us with four of his friends. He'd grabbed Sannin by the scruff of his skinny neck and dangled him up so high I could see the holes in his boots.

"You aren't even worth killing," he'd said when he stabbed my friend in his belly. "Not even worth the time to finish you off."

He'd been gone with the purse leaving us there on the street frozen in horror at our suffering friend. I clamped down on the memory before I had to relive what came next.

Better to leave with only the lesson I learned – if people think you are nothing, they think taking from you doesn't count – even if the thing they are taking is your life.

I needed to think of a way to make him think we were something.

And I needed to do it before he killed me with whatever magical weapon he was holding. If only Zin would run! If only she wouldn't just stand there.

"I'm the guy who knows you have silver swirls in your eyes," I said, gambling. He couldn't call that bluff. Not without revealing something too big to share. "I'm the guy who knows what happens when they become too strong to resist."

"Say that again," he hissed.

"Let the girl go, and we'll talk." I pitched my voice low.

There was a long pause and then I felt something cold and hard press against the base of my skull.

"I don't think so. I have plans for her. And after this little talk, I have plans for you, too. But first, I'm going to prove you wrong. I'm going to show you how I know what every item in this building does, and I'm going to let you see your future."

Chapter Sixteen

"MARCH AND STAY SILENT. You too, girl, or he gets it." Redgers pushed me forward and I walked carefully in front of him through the darkened halls. I didn't know what he had pressed against my head, but I wasn't in a position to find out. If I turned and tried to use the spear and that thing was magical, he could destroy both Zin and me in a moment. I needed to wait for the right opportunity.

Uh oh. This is bad.

What was bad? Saboraak?

Zin was moving now, shaken out of whatever had frozen her. Her mumbling was too quiet to pick out words, but her whispering raced faster and faster as we were pushed forward.

"The thing about magical items," Redgers said, "is that you don't control what they will do when you make them. It takes study to find their true capacities. But you can guess. The raw materials give hints of what they might be – and the more powerful the raw material, the more powerful the item."

Interesting, but hardly important when someone was threatening you. Zin's muttering grew louder. I could almost make out a word here and there. "Prophecy" was one of them and "sacrifice." Two of my least favorite words.

What was going on with Saboraak? It wasn't like her to stop communicating. Why hadn't she answered my question?

"For instance," Redgers continued. Maybe he just loved listening to his own voice. "The item I have pressed against your skull is an interesting one. The first of its kind – though I hope to have nine more soon. When I unleash the magic within it, white-hot fire blasts from the end that is currently pressed to your head."

I swallowed but whatever was in my throat wouldn't budge.

"Curious, don't you think?" Redgers asked.

"Do you have one that shuts people up? I could use that right about now."

When you were scared witless there were only two alternatives. Panic, or pretend you were braver than you were. I'd never seen any point in panicking.

You should be panicking now! I am!

Saboraak? Saboraak, why are you panicking?

I hated that she didn't answer me. What was going on up there?

Bataar couldn't handle Apeq's speech.

Well, the guy *was* a windbag.

"If I had a device for quieting people, I would use it on the girl," Redgers said.

At the same moment, Zin's chanting grew loud enough to hear the words. I recognized them from the little handwritten book I carried.

"Into the belly of the stone,
Death below but not alone.
Rising to challenge the flame,
Not for might and not for fame,
Twin of heart, twin of mind,
Only together a future find,
Bird and Smoke,
Flame and Oak,
Cast the lot and wait.
Cast the lot and hope.
Cast the lot and die."

Pleasant stuff, Zin. Just keep on chanting that.

He stood up in the middle of Apeq's speech and challenged him for the right to lead Ko'Torenth. He says he's marked by the prophecies. That this is his destiny. They must meet for judgment on the ko'tor'kaen *in two days time.*

I leave him alone for a few hours and he starts a political war. As if we didn't have enough to deal with. I rolled my eyes but ended up clenching them in pain when the rod in Redgers' hand hit the back of my neck.

Things are ... dicey ... here.

Just get out alive, Saboraak. I sent you guys to find out news for Hubric, not *create* news!

You don't need to remind me.

Just get out fast.

That may prove ... difficult.

Saboraak? Saboraak?

I'll be out of contact for a while. I need to focus. I don't want to flame anyone innocent.

Oh, Skies and Stars! They were in a battle up there and I was stuck down here being held captive by a servant. I needed to find a way to change my luck and get Zin away safely. What was I waiting for anyway? If Redgers was going to use that thing he would have done it already instead of marching us down an endless spiral staircase.

"Here we are," he said, as Zin opened a door and stepped inside.

I'd wait to make my move until he was walking through the door.

I'd wait until ...

Skies and Stars!

The blood drained from my face so fast that I saw stars blinking across my vision. Horror made my knees wobble like jelly.

No.

Not this.

No.

Chapter Seventeen

ZIN WAS SHAKING SO hard I thought she might fall, like a tree in a windstorm. Her hands were both clasped over her mouth again, as if she were holding back a thousand screams.

I swallowed hard. My own limbs felt shaky and my belly was roiling like the storm had shut itself inside me and was going to try to come out any time now.

It wasn't enough reaction.

Not to what we were seeing.

We stood on a wide rock shelf overlooking a cavern. The shelf stood over a platform built right beneath it that was as big as all of the Jadefire House of Marvels, but the cavern was even larger. Faint purple light glowed from the depths of it, but from the door, I was not close enough to the edge of the shelf to look down at whatever was glowing.

I didn't need to.

What I could see was bad enough.

Five men and four women were hanging from the stalactite roof. Their feet were manacled to the rock above and their clothing – black leather with a thousand buckles and straps, faint writing scrawled on all of it – was torn and dirty. They weren't wearing their usual colored scarves, but I could still identify them by those leathers.

Dominion Dragon Riders. The very ones whose dragons Saboraak had freed. They hung limply, their skin wrinkled and shrunken like old apples.

That alone would turn my bowels to water, but what I saw was worse.

Chanting rose up from the mouths of hooded people clustered under them on the platform in a ring. Their hands linked around a table and on that table were nine rods – just like the one that Redgers was pressing against my skull.

From each of the limp Dragon Riders, a line of silver flowed into one of the rods and as that line pulsed and wavered, little swirls of silver fell from it, settling onto the people in the ring. Their eyes swirled with silver. The same silver I'd seen in staring eyes throughout Ko'Torenth.

"Welcome to the home of the Midnight Artificers," Redgers said in a low, proud voice. "The items we make are truly amazing."

The items.

The magical items that lined the halls and shelves of the Jadefire House of Marvels. The magical bracelet worn by Bataar to heal him. The magical clasp he wore to help stay unnoticed.

Oh, Skies and Stars, no!

My hands felt dirty from having touched them. My eyes were dirty from having looked at them.

"Remember when I mentioned raw material?" Redgers asked, his tone smug now. "This is what I meant. The raw material we use is – "

"Souls," I said in horror.

"Yes." I could hear the satisfied smile in his voice. "When the magic began to run out from the wells of the earth, we set our minds to finding a new way. Kav'ai proves difficult to bend. The Dominion holds back their greatest source of magic – for now. But there is a magic in a person. The magic of their soul. And that magic can be tapped and extracted and affixed to an item. What sort of soul a person had determines what sort of item you can fashion."

"That's why you've been keeping Zin here." That suddenly made sense. She was unique – precious. They must see that.

"She's a puzzle that one. Strong. But what sort of item can we fashion from her? We have yet to decide. You, though, will be easy. You're a Dragon Rider like these others. You'll make Dragon Flames to use against our enemies."

Ice filled me and this time when I tried to swallow, I retched instead.

"Exactly," Redgers said.

I wiped my mouth with the back of my sleeve, trying to force the nausea aside. I felt feverish, my head spinning like a juggled ball.

"And the men with the silver eyes? The ones like you who are consumed by their own demons in the streets?"

"An apt description. Tor. I like that. Consumed by their own demons. Hmmm. We should test that theory. There is a build up, yes. And yes, you can see it in the eyes, but that's one of the dangers of this business. We're hoping we can find ways to mitigate the effects now that we've been joined by Dominion Magikas."

As he said those words, one of the figures below looked up, his hood falling from his head and his face clear in the silver light. He looked familiar. A face surfaced in my memory. Cormaz. One of Shabren the Violet's Magika associates. He smiled wickedly.

"I'm afraid you'll need to remain here now, Zin," Redgers said. "We can't keep you in the main house when there is a chance you could tell someone about this."

Beside me, Zin began to keen, a quiet, high-pitched, chilling sound like a wounded rabbit.

We'd been above this place all along. Zin and Zyla had been living here. I'd juggled hardboiled eggs and strolled through the house like nothing was happening and all that time this had been beneath us. Horror, torture, death.

Right beneath our feet.

I moved so quickly that I surprised myself, spinning and stabbing with the spear while I ducked to avoid the rod. Something hot washed over my left cheek and ear, searing my vision with bright light and blinding me, but I felt resistance against the point of the spear. I pushed forward, leaning all my weight against that point. I felt something give, and then I fell forward.

Zin's keening was louder and over it, shouts bubbled up from below. I blinked back purple afterimages, fighting to clear my vision.

A little help here! Saboraak called.

Ha! Same to you, old girl.

My vision was clearing, though ghosts still danced across it.

Skies and Stars!

Redgers lay beneath me, blood bubbling from his lips. I'd hit him with the spear, alright. It had gone right through his chest. I snatched up the rod from his hand. No need to let him blast me with it again. My face and ear felt strange. Tingly but numb.

Footsteps echoed behind me. Someone was running up the steps. We had moments. Just moments. Think, Tor! Think!

I scrambled to my feet, locating Zin in the afterimages still clouding my vision. I grabbed her by her upper arm as gently as I could and guided her toward the door.

"Hurry!" I said.

"Into the belly of the stone, Death below but not alone," she whispered.

"We're in the belly, alright. Let's hope it digests slowly."

The first hooded figure was cresting the top of the stairs. I pointed the rod at him, feeling sick at my own actions. It wasn't right to use an object made from a person. People weren't resources to be used and harnessed. Desperation trumped conscience.

Fire, you flaming –

The rod fired just like a dragon, white-blue flame licking out of the end of it in a terrible blast. It struck the man in the chest, flinging him backward through the air like a doll thrown by a toddler. He struck the figure behind him, knocking them both backward. No time to watch them fall.

I maneuvered Zin past Redgers, ignoring his spasms.

"Take the book." I pulled it from my pocket and shoved it in her hand. "Close the door behind you. Get out of this house. Don't stop to take anything with you. Climb up through the levels and look for Saboraak. She'll bring you to safety."

Don't make promises I can't fulfill!

There was no one else. If Saboraak failed, then that was it. There was no lock on the door to this cavern. Not on the house side at any rate. I'd seen that when Zin opened it the first time. We couldn't both flee – not and survive. She'd have to go on her own and I would have to hold them off for as long as I could so she could escape.

Your death will help nothing!

Great. I wouldn't even get that right? Someone should have told me that the odds were stacked so badly against me!

Seriously, Tor! This is no joke! You must flee.

I pushed Zin through the door and slammed it behind her, spinning to put my back to the door.

I'd always been good at long odds, though. People liked an underdog. Time to show these swirly-eyed maniacs why that was.

Chapter Eighteen

I DIDN'T LIKE RAISING that metal rod. Not now that I knew what it was – who had died to provide it. My hand trembled as I thrust it forward. I willed it still. I could buy Zin minutes to escape if I was strong – if I didn't let them kill me in their first try.

Maybe they'd want to take me alive. Maybe they'd want to suck my soul out just like they had to all those other Dragon Riders. Would it hurt? Would I remain conscious but stuck in an object forever? Fear made my head buzz, painted my thoughts a jagged purple, made me feverish so that sweat sprang up between my shoulder blades and dripped down my temples.

It felt like minutes had passed, but it had only been seconds. Redgers still gurgled unpleasantly between my feet. The Midnight Artificers were still scrambling for weapons. Nine of them had already claimed the half-made rods.

I trembled as I watched them raise the rods in firm, sure hands. Nine to one.

I'd seen worse odds.

Maybe at least Saboraak would survive this. Maybe she could find Hubric afterward and give him her report. Maybe she could bring Zin to him. I was glad Zin was free. She was so wounded, so bruised, so helpless. There was something about her that made me flinch at the thought of harm coming to her. I wasn't the self-sacrificial type. I wouldn't play the hero for anyone, but she needed saving and what kind of man wouldn't step up to do that? Right? Even someone like me knew that. Even street scum had enough honor to know that he couldn't walk away from her without scarring his soul. If I'd left her to her fate and run, I'd never sleep again – not really. Never enjoy a hot drink on a cold morning. Never share a kiss with a pretty girl – certainly not Zyla! Not with a free conscience, anyway.

And if a man's conscience wasn't free, then he wasn't free either.

You monologue when you're under stress.

So, what? It was my prerogative to tell my own story – even if it was only being told to myself.

It's a villain trait.

We're all villains in someone's story, Saboraak.

My enemies' feet were on the steps now. I heard their harsh breathing as they ran.

"We all fire at once!" Cormaz was shouting in his booming voice.

At least death would be fast.

Maybe in Cormaz's story, I was the villain. Maybe in the next few minutes, I'd be confirming that.

There was a squeak behind me, as if the door was opening. I didn't dare look back. If there was an enemy there, too, I'd just have to live with it – or die with it more likely.

I raised my arm. Time to use the rod. I had seconds before they'd be on my level. Time to kill as many as I could.

But all I could think about were the people dying yesterday, fleeing in panic and being shredded by golems or falling over the railing into the vast space below. I'd tried so hard not to look, but their faces were seared into my mind forever.

All I could see before me were the hollow husks of the Dragon Riders. I drew in a long breath and dropped the rod. I wasn't going to win, anyway. Why desecrate the soul of a Dragon Rider if I was going to die anyway?

Salute, Tor. Salute, Dominion's Son. Honor to you.

Saboraak's praise was unexpected. I felt warm with her thoughts. Who would have thought that anyone ever would associate honor with Tor Winespring?

I let my mouth form my best cocky grin and raised my hands in a "can you blame a guy for trying stance."

I'd go out as myself.

I watched in slow motion as nine rods were aimed at my chest. Cormaz's exaggerated nod set off a burst of triumphant expressions. Their grips went white on the rods.

A figure pushed past me, small and lithe and faster than light. She leapt between me and the white blasts.

No, Zin! No!

The fire of the rods smacked her right in the chest as my mouth dropped open in horror, slammed her into me with the force of the wind behind it. I wrapped my arms around her, protective in the only way I knew how as we flew backward against the door like two juggling balls thrown against a wall.

Shock filled me as the fires rebounded off of Zin, zipping backward twice as fast and fanning out as they rebounded, searing through the Midnight Artificers. My arms – where they were wrapped around Zin – stung like they'd been splashed with hot water.

No one had time to scream. The only sound was the howling of the wind behind the fire, the sizzling of human flesh, the puff of evaporating hooded cloaks.

I was frozen in shock. I couldn't move even if I knew which way to go.

The rods clattered to the ground. The white light from the rods and the white lines from the hanging Dragon Riders extinguished like a pinched candle. The only light left was the faint, pulsing purple from below and the crack of light pouring through the door.

Zin collapsed on the ground in front of me, slipping through my numb grip, and a sound like tearing fabric ripped through the air.

Chapter Nineteen

YOU LIVE? Saboraak's thoughts pierced my shock.

I did. I could barely believe it myself.

We flee.

You and Bataar?

Yes.

Thank goodness she was okay. She was okay, right? Her silence worried me.

I didn't have time to dwell on it, though. If I didn't get Zin out of here fast, someone would find us here and string us up like those poor Dragon Riders.

She was in a puddle at my feet, her white dress fanned out around her and sobs shaking her apart.

"Zin?"

I reached for her but froze. What should I do? I was afraid that touching her would make it worse. And she wasn't responding to my words. I thought that she might be looking at the Dragon Riders hanging in front of us.

"Zin?"

I squatted down beside her, trying to get her attention. Her sobs were gasping, shuddering, ugly things, and emotion whipsawed through her eyes, fear, anger, desperation, insensate numbness, back to fear.

If I waited for her to be whole, I'd be waiting forever. If I waited too long, they'd steal her soul.

I bit my lip and ran a hand through my hair. What did you do for broken people?

Gently, not sure if I was even doing the right thing, I wrapped her in my arms. She gasped, turning to cling to me like a child. She was light, like she'd been created out of parchment, a parchment bird folded into shape. I held her like I'd hold a bird, careful not to break her. Afraid to move too fast or even at all.

We sat like that for long breaths. I counted them. Counting and worrying. Worrying we'd be found. Worrying that if I moved there would be nothing left of Zin to find at all.

I could probably carry her. But people would notice a villainous rogue carrying a pretty girl away. They'd notice. and they would remember, and they would tell whoever Apeq sent looking for us.

Perhaps, if I wrapped her in burlap sacking or a sheet so she looked like a sack of some kind of goods. Perhaps then she would go undiscovered.

We breathed five more breaths together as I thought it through. We'd take the bedding from the rooms above. I'd wrap her gently. How far could I carry her? Could I carry her far enough? I needed to get her to the secret tunnels that would lead us to the hideout. It would be the only safe place for her.

I stood carefully, never letting go of her. She clung to me like a child as I stood, weighed no more than a child as I carried her past the bodies and up the stairs, out of the horrors of this deep cavern to the light above. Her sobs turned to silent tears as I wrapped her first in warm blankets and then in covering sheets and tied a curtain rope around them like a package. She turned her head into my chest, soaking my shirt with her tears as I stumbled out the door to the cold world outside.

No one noticed as I slunk down the street toward our hideout. Would I make it there? Would my legs stay strong that long?

Whatever you do, don't go back to the hideout. Promise me, Tor.

Saboraak?

Saboraak?

There was no reply.

We were on our own. I stood, staring around me at the city as the snow came down heavy and wet and wondered what to do next.

Continue Tor's story in:

Dragon Chameleon: Episodes 5-8

Dragon Chameleon: Episodes 9-12

To the intrepid reader:

DEAR READER,

You've made it this far in your journey with me and my stories. Thank you for caring about stories and the characters that leap from the page.

They say that real book lovers just can't say goodbye to the stories they love, and I'm sure that's true for you, too. I'd like to invite you to download another story in the Dragon School and Dragon Chameleon world. By downloading it, you'll be added to my newsletter, so you won't have to take any extra steps to be alerted to new releases.

You can find the link to the story on my website at *www.sarahklwilson.com*.

I am – wholeheartedly – yours in fiction,

Sarah

Behind the Scenes:

USA TODAY BESTSELLING author, Sarah K. L. Wilson loves spinning a yarn and if it paints a magical new world, twists something old into something reborn, or makes your heart pound with excitement ... all the better! Sarah hails from the rocky Canadian Shield in Northern Ontario -

learning patience and tenacity from the long months of icy cold - where she lives with her husband and two small boys. You might find her building fires in her woodstove and wishing she had a dragon handy to light them for her

Sarah would like to thank **Harold Trammel** and **Eugenia Kollia** for their incredible work in beta reading and proofreading this book. Without their big hearts and passion for stories, this book would not be the same.

www.sarahklwilson.com[1]

DISCORD[2] | AMAZON[3] | FACEBOOK MESSENGER[4]| NEWSLETTER[5]

1. *http://www.sarahklwilson.com*
2. https://discord.gg/gUy82R7
3. https://www.amazon.com/Sarah-K-L-Wilson/e/B0064MSJRE/
4. https://m.me/sarahklwilson?ref=w3907539
5. https://dl.bookfunnel.com/csw4phr87p

www.ingramcontent.com/pod-product-compliance
Lightning Source LLC
Chambersburg PA
CBHW060808310726
48980CB00002B/273
9780987850249